Into the Twilight

Sela Channing

PublishAmerica
Baltimore

First printing

ISBN: 1-4137-3385-9
PUBLISHED BY PUBLISHAMERICA, LLLP
www.publishamerica.com
Baltimore

Printed in the United States of America

DEDICATION

To Sunny,
My Wonderful Sister And Mentor.

CHAPTER I

The weather had taken an unseasonably cold turn, with the wind whipping and gusting furiously, encouraging us to close ranks and pull our coat collars up for warmth. It was as if fate was angry with the preceding events which led us here today, to the premature graveside service for one of our own, Juliet.

Although the air was frigid, it was a gloriously beautiful, Pennsylvania autumn, a palette filled with shades and tints of oranges, reds and yellows. You wouldn't think grief could survive but for moments in this breathtaking beauty, but you'd be mistaken: it had taken up permanent residence in our souls, and we ached for release.

Lora, Sherry, Melanie, Kiki and I exchanged pain-filled glances, desperately attempting to absorb consolation from each other for the loss of our special friend. We had fought valiantly for her, and with her, through the last few years, but sadly were forced to acknowledge many times along the way that the cause might be lost, and much too soon. Certainly, with the passing of the years, the intensity of the grief would lessen, but it would return, inspired by a favorite song once shared, or in a reminiscent moment, rearing its ugly head and inflicting its hideous pain over and over again.

How thankful we were that in our youth, when the time inevitably came to choose separate paths, we'd vowed never to lose touch. And now it was this profound bond of love and closeness that held us emotionally intact. Initially, our hearts and minds became intricately intertwined with the smallest shared hurts from childhood injuries. Then, the bumpy ride of adolescence produced embarrassing moments that naturally accompany inexperienced youth. The turbulent teens followed close behind forcing us to form a common bond of rebellion as we struggled with the innate desire for independence from parental rules, but it also served to secure the knowledge that a friend was always close by when we found ourselves, inevitably, navigating the rough waters of a new or lost love. But the deep blending of our souls was anchored with the late night talks where secrets of the heart were confided. We shared intimacies that only innocence and lack of self-awareness can produce. Evolving from this collective relationship was a fiercely protective attitude for one another. The love we shared was unlike anything I'd ever experienced. It was as deep as, but different from, the love of siblings. The bond was so strong as to be visible to outsiders, deterring them from attempting to infiltrate such a tight group. And what an odd group we were.

Lora's soft but frantic murmuring penetrated my thoughts as she jabbed an elbow urgently into my side.

"Rainey! Rich's family! Nine o'clock!"

Turning to the direction she was discreetly signaling, I froze, gasping. It was Rich, or rather his clone, only twenty years older. Who else could it possibly be but his father? Extraordinarily handsome, but immediately noted in his demeanor was the absence of Rich's air of arrogance and hostility. A pleasant looking woman was clasping his hand to her side; we presumed it to be Rich's mother. Accompanying them was an attractive, twenty-something young lady fitting the description of Rich's sister, Junie, whom Juliet liked and had spoken of on several occasions. She was busily scanning the area in sweeping glances, shifting back and forth from one foot to the other in an attempt, perhaps, to stave off boredom or the cold, or both. They appeared to be evading the lot of us, staring instead directly at the sky or Juliet's casket throughout the service. I know it to be so, because Kiki reported it later, her eyes, boring holes, never left them.

"Uhhh!" It was Mel gasping as she, too, spotted Mr. Vanderling.

Oh great, I thought, *just the thing to set her off again.* As it was, she hadn't stopped crying for more than ten minutes at a time for the past four days, I guess except when she slept, and I can't be certain about that. Was it really only four days? Or was it four years? Then, again, it seemed like only moments ago that we received the hateful, life-changing call from Ellen, Juliet's sister. Time is a strange variable. Usually fleeting or interminable, depending on the circumstances in which we find ourselves. But in this instance, it seemed to be a confusion of both, and our mental faculties were totally discombobulated with nothing making sense. We were struggling to hold our own, doing our best to…just be. Humans seem to be a mass of contradictions, and a good case in point was Mel, whom we believed to be one of the toughest, dealing with medical school and all its ramifications, including death, on a routine basis. Yes, she explained, as a student of medicine, she was being taught to disassociate from pain and grief, not only for her own preservation, but it was imperative to be strong for the surviving families with whom she would be forced to deal and console. But there was no disassociating from the horrific scenario set before her, nor did she want to. She placed a lone wisp of lovely heather, Juliet's favorite, atop the coffin next to a gorgeous spray of white roses. This was Juliet, her friend, a confidante. She'd represented a part of her past, her present, and always, her future. *And now*, she thought, *the least I can do, all of us can do, is grieve, grieve desperately for her, allow the tears to flow freely, to cleanse our hearts and minds of the ugliness in her life, and hopefully, leave behind, only the beauty.*

And we were succeeding for the most part, until the blatant reminder of Rich exploded into our minds by his father's presence. And Kiki, only with the utmost restraint, barely refrained from screaming, "My God!! the nerve, I can't—"

Sherry gripped Kiki's hand with enough force to stop her abruptly. "Please Kiki! Don't start," she whispered. "They're not intruding, they have every right to be here. They knew and loved Juliet, too. And they have to know how we feel, have to know we'd probably be thinking exactly what we're now thinking. But how do you think Juliet would want us behaving right now? So out of respect for her, let's not do this, okay? In a few minutes it'll be over, and we'll never see them again."

"Damn it, Sherry!" squawked Kiki, "you missed your calling…you should be negotiating peace treaties somewhere, at least anywhere but where I am when I'm pissed."

Kiki's hatred for Rich in particular, and men in general, ran deeper than the norm. Even with years of counseling, remnants still surfaced from time to time. Sherry sighed, though forced to agree with her in this instance. It was easy enough to understand the hurt and anger. Ugly, scattered thoughts were running rampant and uncontrolled through each of them. There, standing within our reach at this sensitive time when Juliet's body wasn't yet cold in the ground, stood a sickening reminder of the intense pain she had suffered at the hands of their son. The adage "one rotten apple in the barrel taints the whole batch," came to mind. Were they part of the batch? Was that unfair, unjust, and strictly theoretical? Or specific where they were concerned? Juliet had never uttered a negative word against any of them. Of course, neither did she mention anything positive, so the best and worst we were left with was guilt by association. But bottom line, none of it mattered, none of us cared. They could have embodied the character of Gandhi or Jesus Christ, himself, but we'd never know. We just wanted every particle, every trace of Rich, to be erased from our minds, forever. But oh, what a futile hope that was. One of life's cruel jokes as it turned out…we were more likely to forget Juliet than Rich. For my part, any interest or fascination for him above and beyond his association with Juliet was strictly academic. Being the psychologist wanna-be of the group, I would've loved to have picked their brains in an attempt to understand him. What motivated him? What made him tick? Obviously, I was attracted to that "abnormal" branch of psychology. And allowing myself a dab of levity, I realized that the attraction was partially responsible for my friendship with Kiki.

Sherry interrupted my thoughts this time. "This is so tough, it's agony," she continued, speaking more to herself than to us, really, her words trailing off, feathering into theological meanderigs. "Looking at this beautiful, shiny mahogany box, now her home for all eternity, I'm comforted with the belief that her spirit is freed, living on; she's watching us now, whispering and sending words of consolation and love. We only have to be still for our hearts to hear. And though I'll always ache for her, I am, momentarily, at peace."

At least her words seemed to soothe her, and they served well as a momentary distraction, long enough for us to say our final goodbye. More importantly, Rich's family, who remained standing at the edge of the tented area, was temporarily shoved to the back of our minds.

CHAPTER II

Sadly, we began the lonely walk back across the well-manicured cemetery. I was struck suddenly by the irony of the surrounding beauty…the immaculate grounds and the soft, green grass. Beautiful live flowers of every color and variety adorned the tombstones, many of which were sculpted in shapes of angels or arches, with cherubs and flowers, beautiful enough to rival works of art seen in museums. And it was all here, in this "dead" place, the residents of which could not see or appreciate. Hopefully, I thought, they had each tasted at least a little of it during their lifetimes. Juliet certainly hadn't enjoyed it long enough. And with that thought, came suddenly, a painful resurgence of survivor's guilt. Something about which we had talked incessantly and knew sooner or later, we'd work through. I prayed for sooner.

I'd opened the floodgates of my mind and the morbid musings spilled out. Oh, how I hated the thought of Juliet all alone in a cold, dark hole in the ground. And why was she chosen from among us to be the first to go? And following close behind those disturbing ponderings, came flittering through my mind the delightful little tidbit: which of us would be next?

Thankfully, my moroseness was mercifully interrupted, but unfortunately it was by Lora, erupting into another marathon of sobbing. She had visited another gravesite, hours before meeting the rest of us, and was feeling overwhelmed. For death to have touched someone so young for a second time seemed cruel and unfair, and the memories hit hard. She stood by helplessly as they came flooding back.

Lora came from the same traditional upbringing as the rest of us, except her family was well off by comparison. Her father, Henry Ellis Garrison, inherited a high-end furniture store and he, with his only son – Lora's elder brother by three years – Terry, had expanded the business into a chain of three stores which were located across the northeastern part of the country. They, of course, operated the one in Milton, which Terry eventually was to manage. But fate had other plans, and with death, wealth holds no sway. Terry, by all accounts, was happy and well-adjusted, beginning his second semester as a freshman in college. He was active in sports, an honor student and popular with the girls. Lora idolized him. His life seemed ideal, and one most men his age would enjoy and envy. But the human mind is undeniably complex, and sometimes the body that's housing it, disguises soul-wrenching pain unknown perhaps even to the host, and it may surface suddenly with such anguish, becoming unbearable, as it seemed with Terry.

One evening, he had had a minor disagreement with his parents over his choice of friends and their insistence he adhere to a curfew. But the squabbling ended harmlessly enough, with parents and Terry cooling down and talking compromise. He sulked a while as do most teens when denied something they desire, and had gone to his room. He declined the invitation to dinner with the rest of the family, choosing instead to hang out at home. They were disappointed, but understood and respected his feelings, not insisting on his participation. Returning around ten, they found the house unusually quiet. Terry invariably had the radio cranked up, and eventually, another family member whose tolerance for noise had reached its limit, would bang on his door requesting he turn it down. This evening, in particular, his parents wanted to chat briefly with him, make certain their differences had been settled, and to bid him goodnight, as was part of their nightly ritual. His bed was empty. Kitty, Lora's younger sister by two years, headed immediately to the kitchen, thinking with Terry's humongous teenage appetite, he must be partaking of a late night snack, and with the transistor radio plastered to his ears hadn't heard their arrival. But what she found was her brother lying on the floor dead, his body as still and lifeless as his favorite hunting rifle which lay beside him. Her screams reverberated throughout the house, and inside Lora's mind forever after.

He left no note, and an adequate answer was never found for his decision to end his life. There were rumors flying about connecting him with drug use. Certainly, drugs were prevalent in the bigger cities, and their popularity grew in proportion to the new wave of permissiveness flooding America. College students had easy access, with pushers everywhere – from the sleaziest dealer on the corner to the argyle-socked young man living in the next dorm room. Unfortunately, information about the dangers of their use was not as prevalent.

And even if there was any truth to the rumors, it was irrelevant. Terry was gone, and no one would ever know the reason for his senseless suicide. It was a horrible loss for which a devastated family was forced to contend.

We marveled at Lora's continued enthusiasm after experiencing such a catastrophic event. And although it was temporarily shaken, her innately positive outlook on life in general couldn't be quelled. But Terry was her idol: she adored him, and of course she grieved. She spent hours in the privacy of her bedroom over the next couple of months, much of it alone, as the grief and depression ripped away at her innocence, as she struggled, desperately, to repair the holes in the special place in her heart where Terry's love and image resided. She ranted and screamed at God, at the unfairness and senselessness of it all, saying all the things that grief-stricken people say under such horrific, illogical circumstances. She talked endlessly about him at every opportunity. She shared his favorite music with us and poured over photo albums as she reminisced. He'd teased her unmercifully about her big boobs, out of the earshot of Mom and Dad, of course. His advice to her – an edict, actually – was to demand enough respect from potential beaus, and herself, to never be mistreated. And, ironically, he encouraged her most of all to enjoy every day as if it were her last.

We knew these sessions were cathartic for her, and were pained by the inadequacy of our comfort. But it was times like this, we realized, when real friendship was so valued. Unbeknownst to us, it would be just one of many opportunities we'd have to reach out for emotional support from one another.

But Terry needn't have worried about Lora's attitude. Enjoying life came naturally to her as she effortlessly emanated and displayed a *joi de vivre*, and thankfully, without Kiki's careless abandonment.

Being lost in my thoughts, I almost tripped over a stone marker, and my thoughts were immediately riveted back to Juliet. Where had we gone so wrong? We'd had our lives mapped out so carefully. Yes, of course we knew there'd be bumps in the road, we weren't that naïve. But we'd worked it out so we'd meet our knights or princes in shining armor, we didn't care which, and live happily ever after. But as we were finding out, and as every idealistic young person has learned eventually from the beginning of time, life is hard! Life is callous and has a way of interrupting and disrupting our dreams without regard for feelings. But we also learned that without that same idealism, there'd be no great accomplishments. And therein lies one of the fascinating dichotomies of life.

CHAPTER III

Speaking of dichotomies, there was Kiki, beautiful but deadly. Her mother assigned her the unique name immediately at birth, as she *kicked* her way into the world, and indeed, it proved to be a portent for her life. She was the wild one of the group. Not that each of us didn't have our own special areas of beauty. I was blessed with great-looking skin and beautiful hands, although I never realized how pretty they were until it was brought to my attention. After that I wore nail polish, albeit soft colors, to make people notice. But it seems nature works diligently to maintain balance in every aspect of life and beauty is not exempt, if for no other reason than to keep us humble. And in my case, it was my nose: distinct, yes, with the upper middle part housing a bone protrusion which I was convinced initially began as another digit and, realizing its mistake, stopped in mid-development. It wasn't noticeable, looking dead on in the mirror, and I quickly learned never to subject myself to a profile shot when examining my appearance. Consequently, it never bothered me. Otherwise, I was attractive enough and wouldn't have traded my looks for Kiki's if I could have if I had to be burdened with the rest of her personality quirks. But, nevertheless, we all agreed that standing next to her immediately exposed our every wart, mole or inadequacy. I realized, years later, that I viewed Kiki the same way I viewed beauty pageant contestants. Their beauty was elusive, ageless. The personification of grace, the quintessential woman. Then I discovered I was their age. Who needs that kind of revelation when you're the tender age of eighteen, when we're still so uncertain of our value and worth? But, unfortunately, Kiki only had to open her mouth to destroy the illusion of perfection. She cursed like the proverbial sailor, and her soft beauty belied her aggressive nature.

She chose to wear her beautiful raven hair in a short, wild-looking bob, if for no other reason than it was not the popular thing to do. It didn't matter how she wore it, the blue-blackness of her hair combined with her sky-blue eyes was a killer combination. Ironically, we laughed, her eyes inspired thoughts of heavenly angels, and it was entertaining to watch people's reactions when Kiki entered a room. First, there was the double take, and then the secreted glances as long as we stayed. The reactions no longer held surprise for any of us. Her beauty simply demanded attention, and it was never disappointed. And if that wasn't enough, she possessed a figure we all admired, other women envied and men drooled over. Especially Sherry and I. We found the term *hope chest* especially meaningful, and we'd lament that we'd seen guys prancing around the beach with larger breasts, so we winced every time Kiki whipped her shirt off in front of us, exposing full-to-overflowing C cups. And though we knew her intention was not to add hurt to our already badly bruised egos, she loved flaunting them in front of us. And with very little encouragement, usually from Lora, who was also well endowed but modest about it, Kiki would hum her favorite stripping song, and as we positioned ourselves on the bed, she'd proceed to gyrate, strut and thrust about the room, stripping down to her day of the week underwear. But usually, long before that, we'd stopped seeing anything; our eyes blurred with tears of laughter as we rolled around on the bed, holding our aching stomachs. Sherry and I settled for enhancement with ugly, forever white and well-padded bras, announcing in mock snootiness that our gifts in life lay, obviously, in our brains. That really wasn't consolation, but it was the best we had.

But Kiki's day-to-day behavior could only be described as *beyond ugly* and had been a source of bewilderment throughout our adolescent years. And as bizarre as it sounds, I suppose we were attracted to her precisely because of it. She activated our dark side, that little dab of wickedness lying dormant, inherent in each of us, that we carefully and dutifully keep tucked away. God knows we tried, and succeeded, for the most part, to be discerning of the decadent activities in which we participated. But oh, she could be persuasive. And with the enthusiasm of young teens full of hope and endless energy, accompanied by the innate attitude of immortality, there were a few very interesting and even frightening chapters in our young years.

"What the hell's life good for, if it's not to have a good time?" she'd ask. She definitely kept us on our toes in our feeble attempt to curb her wildness, for we admitted, if not for her, many of our parties would have died of ennui. As it was, she'd arrive mid-party with her stud of the moment accompanied by several other cuties of whom she knew we'd approve, and a good time would be had by all.

Unfortunately, she transferred her mischievousness as a youth (which garnered a lot of attention from her peers, good and bad) to an insatiable need as an adult for attention from men. And there was a never-ending flow at the ready to fulfill that need. And we stood in amazement that in spite of her aesthetic endowments, her self-esteem soared, but off the bottom of the chart, manifesting itself loudly by her choice of men. She chose and dated the dregs of society: men upon whom most young women wouldn't cast a second glance, either because of their slovenly appearance and lack of motivation for success in any endeavor even at the most elementary level, or men loaded with money but teetering on the peak of their golden years. She was attracted to the former, whose defiance of anything resembling establishment suited her rebellious side perfectly, and the latter, who puffed with pride at being seen with a winsome young trophy and were appreciative of any crumbs of attention they received. In turn, Kiki enjoyed the money and attention they so willingly lavished on her.

Kiki's destructive nature became apparent in our elementary years. Minor incidents: destroying erasers, carving initials in the tops of desks, but nevertheless considered vandalism. Her aberrant behavior prompted the desire on our part to examine the dynamics of her home-life, and we discussed the possibility of perhaps abusive parents as the source of her hostility.

But after our first sleepover, and witnessing the love bordering on idol worship oozing from her doting parents, and the respectable surroundings in which she lived, the enigma only deepened. Perhaps when thrust into a society that failed to continue to fulfill her high expectations of adoration, she felt justified in resorting to her own methods to obtain it. Whatever the reason, we watched helplessly, filled with awe and anguish at her unending antics, her rebelliousness and unequivocal disregard for the establishment. Eventually, the outward destruction did lessen, but sadly, was turned inward.

But every prank she ever pulled, from the most inane to the most severe, and every lie or misdeed she accomplished, paled in comparison to an incident instigated by her, and yes, one of which we all took part voluntarily, and without coercion, but accomplished, nevertheless, because, I believe, of her forceful influence. It was a topic stored in the recesses of our minds, hopefully never again to be broached or even recalled. But, of course, it was impossible. Being alive and functioning in society, we were doomed never to forget. And, as has happened from time immemorial, the chickens eventually would come home to roost."

CHAPTER IV

We came of age in the turbulent sixties at the beginning of the "sex, drugs and rock and roll" era, and our home town of Milton, located in western Pennsylvania, was not immune to the consequences of the radical changes including, in no small way, the Women's Lib movement. Lines were crossed that hadn't been crossed before, and rules heretofore adhered to without thought were suddenly being thrown aside like yesterday's newspaper.

Our generation of women was raised with a profound and strict set of values and mores, with virginity being a prize valued above all others. And we aspired to the apex of womanhood, learning and perfecting the arts of cooking, sewing and child care in order to become a suitable mate for a "good man," defined as such by his choice of vocation. Marriage was the ultimate and desperately sought-after goal, followed by children and living happily (or not) ever after. A little ditty from childhood days comes to mind that emphasizes the infiltration of this traditional school of thought into every aspect of our lives. Juliet and I, living next door to one another, participated in all the various childhood games, i.e., marbles, jacks, hide-and-seek and jump rope. Ditties, silly, little songs, were designed for jump rope to sustain the rhythm, and Juliet made one up of her own: "right—now we're—lit—tle la—dies—but some—day—we'll—have—some—babies, 1, 2, 3, 4," etc., etc.. Just an innocent game, seemingly, but oh so profound. The conditioning had begun.

The term "good girl" seems archaic now in view of today's relaxed mores, but it was an age of innocence then and the standards were set high. The double standard was alive and thriving, and we were trained to cater to the male ego. The goal was simple…we were to become our husbands' virgin brides, and sacrifice our lives for them and the children. Goals that perhaps women were content to strive for at one time, but that time was passing and the resentment and dissatisfaction of the limitations set on our options had been roiling and boiling for years, creating a pressure-cooker culture ready to blow at any time. That time was now. Suddenly before us was a frightening – yes – but liberating opportunity to trade the kitchen and all its restraints and limitations for a college classroom and the vast opportunities it promised.

The time had come to shuck off the girdles and bras and throw them in the faces of our dumbstruck parents and the establishment they represented. And while this revolution afforded women freedom not experienced before, there was also, interlaced within it, an extreme sub-culture. An entire generation rose from the ashes of the burning bras and girdles…young people living without rules or restrictions of any kind. A generation of children who, heretofore, had been taught to speak only when spoken to were now expressing their discontent with such repression with wild abandonment. Suddenly, the inmates were running the asylum, and the climate was perfect for the misfits and rebels floundering in what they viewed as an overbearing and oppressive society. A perfect environment in which Kiki, being one of its most faithful followers, could flourish and reach her full dysfunctional potential. No culture could have been better suited for her character. It was what she prayed for and dreamed about. Complete liberation. Liberation not so much from her family, for she seldom allowed their curfews and rules to stifle her activities, but restraints from society's inhibitions. The puritanical philosophy was being tossed flagrantly aside and the Victorian chastity belt was not only loosened but completely discarded. "Free love" became a favorite catchphrase of the day. It sounded too good to be true, and ultimately proved to be so, with old established diseases and brand-new frightening ones running rampant. But for now, it was no holds barred and society was running amok with "flower power."

Kiki was thrilled with society's transformations. It wasn't that she needed or desired a stamp of approval from anyone…she was just ecstatic that the world around her had finally awakened to the hedonistic smorgasbord laid out before it. And as she rushed headlong into enlightenment, it was inevitable that we too, being pulled in her wake, would share some of the excitement, sometimes objecting and remorseful, and sometimes laughing. And although those years were filled with good times and the boundless energy and idealism experienced only by the young, still most of us lived within designated boundaries. The expectations of living and functioning within society's rules created a safety net and security for the conformist in each of us. But Kiki, being true to her free spirit, rejected and abhorred rules, except that good times "ruled."

She drank and smoked to excess when the opportunity presented itself, and if it didn't, she found a way to do it anyway. Both became staples in her life. She seemed always to be teetering on the edge of out of control, and we pleaded with her to be careful if she was going to fool around: a term filled with mystery and fear which we used to define the sex act itself. But we were forced to face the reality that, as reckless and carefree as she was, serious consequences were inevitable. Anytime we broached the subject, her response did little to allay our fears. Searing us with a look of disgust and temper flaring, she'd rail, "I swear, sometimes I feel like I'm hangin' out at the old folks' home instead of with eighteen-year-olds. All you do is worry and nag. And not that's it's any of your damn business, but I use protection when it's necessary."

Realizing we were speaking out of love and concern, she'd regain her composure, and in an attempt to assuage our fear, switch to persuasion mode. "But hell, I don't care enough about most of the jerks I go out with, anyway, to do much more than some heavy petting. And the rich ones don't want much of anything from me but some stupid stuff."

That knocked our interest up a few notches, and we quickly exchanged puzzled glances, almost afraid to ask for an explanation, but our curiosity couldn't be contained.

"I really am a little frightened of what you're going to tell us, Kiki, but I know I speak for the rest when I say we're dying to know what in the heck that means. And try to remember, there are virgin ears listening."

A spattering of laughter was all that could be heard for the next few seconds as Kiki put us on hold. She had us right where she wanted us. Oh, she enjoyed our naivete and nothing pleased her more than to watch us squirm when she regaled us with a bizarre episode or some sexual exploit in particular.

"Well, what I mean is, there's more than one way to satisfy these old guys."

"I don't think I want to hear this," Juliet said. "I just know its going to be something disgusting," and she promptly clapped her hands over her ears while humming softly.

"Oh no you don't," Sherry laughed as she reached over, and tugging at Juliet's hands, pulled them down from her face. "You know better than that. We share everything, the good and bad. Besides, I know you'll just ask one of us later to tell you what she said."

Juliet replied sulkily. "I'd certainly rather hear it from one of you, that's for sure."

"Okay, okay, can we get on with this?" Lora said impatiently. "Kiki?"

"It's no big deal," said Kiki. "One old guy bought me a pair of white majorette boots and a baton and just wanted me to march around in his living room humming that song about the 'Halls of Montezuma.'"

"What?" We squealed in unison. If we thought we were going to hear something naughty, she missed the target, certainly, but we were dumbstruck. We had no idea what she was talking about.

"Majorette boots and a baton?" Mel actually said it more to herself, mulling it over in her mind in hopes of making some sense of it.

"Okay." Again, it was Lora impatiently shushing us with her hands. "Be quiet so she can talk. Then what?"

"That's it. Usually he falls asleep about halfway through the third time around the floor, then I just change my shoes and leave."

"That's it?! You're not leaving anything out, are you, Kiki?" asked Juliet suspiciously.

"No! I'm not, Juliet. What? Suddenly it's not naughty enough for you?" Kiki screwed her face up in a malicious grin, taunting Juliet. "I can tell you what I did last night with some shoe string and silly putty."

"Oh! You're disgusting," responded Juliet.

"Stop egging her on, Kiki. Juliet, please just laugh at her. You know she's just having fun with you, why do you allow her to get to you?"

"Pleeease! Can we get back to this morbid story?" It was Mel. Evidently her cogitation bore no fruit and now she wanted more information.

"Naturally I'm fascinated," I said. "This sounds like a great case study for a psychology student, huh?"

"Hell, if you like that one, I've got a bunch more—"

Bingo. All eyes zeroed in on her face. She slapped a knee and laughed uproariously, enjoying the five mesmerized faces staring back at her. "I feel like a puppeteer, pulling you guys' strings."

"Uh huh, that's great; I'm glad you're enjoying this as much as we are, now just get on with it," urged Lora. "This is incredible, assuming, Kiki, you're telling us the truth."

"I swear to God above, I wouldn't lie to you about this shit. Why would I? I don't think it's anything worth lying about. You're the one making a big thing of it. It's just some old men having a good time in their own way. What the hell do I know? Or care? I take care of them and they take care of me."

"So you're not lying already, so continue," said Lora.

"This one's kinda sweet. Mr. Franklin, the old buzzard, likes for me to wear flannel pjs and sit on his lap and read to him." Not skipping a beat, she added,

"Damn I'm thirsty. Anything to drink around this place?"

"You're really scaring me, Kiki," said Sherry. "I mean, these kind of things aren't normal for grown men do be doing. They're twisted. Aren't you the least bit afraid?"

"For one thing, how would you know? How many old farts have you spent any time with? And these men aren't normal, they're old men in their eighties with nothing left from yesterday except memories, and nothing to look forward to tomorrow but dying, and if what I'm doing gives them a little bit of pleasure, it's okay with me. It sure's in the hell ain't hurtin' anyone. Maybe they miss their mother, or maybe a high school sweetheart was a majorette and she died or something. And what in the hell would I be afraid of? These guys are about to fall into a grave. The only thing I have to be afraid of is dying from boredom from being with them. You're making way too much out of this. I think it's funny as hell. Now, can I have something to drink?"

"I don't know how you could be bored," said Lora, in astonishment. "Do they tell you in advance what they're wanting from you?"

"Naa, but it's always something just as dumb, and they take care of everything…all I have to do is be willing."

"Yeah," said Juliet sarcastically, "and we know you're always that."

"If that was meant as a smart-ass remark," retorted Kiki, "you missed your mark…I take it as a compliment."

"Oh my God," Juliet moaned, rolling her eyes to the ceiling. Kiki laughed, knowing the torment she was producing for her.

Kiki also realized by our response that we obviously didn't find it as lighthearted and humorous as she did, and shooting us a withering look, sneered. "Oh, come on, pleeease, when are you guys going to join in the fun? Look around you. This country is finally relaxing its stiff-assed morals shoved on us by those spooky puritans two hundred years ago, and I'll be damned if I'm gonna sit around and let life go swirling right past me. There's a—"

"First of all, Kiki," Juliet interrupted, eyes flashing and her cheeks flushed with indignity, "being liberated doesn't mean trashing everything that's decent, everything moral and taking part in orgies and, and, whatever you call what it is you do with those old men. It's supposed to mean we now have choices, the same choices the men have always had. The double standard is being torn down, but even all men haven't cast off every ounce of decency just because they can."

"Well excuse me for living, Juliet! Are you through!? I didn't need a sermon, especially from you, and you can get off that damned high horse anytime! I've watched you flirt like hell for years with all kinds of men! At least I'm up front and honest about what I like. You tease the guys half out of their minds with your come-ons, and what the hell is that all about anyway? You trying to prove that men are attracted to you? Hell, any man will take it if he can get it, no matter what a woman looks like, so you're not proving anything. Unless, of course, that's your sexual quirk, and maybe you get off on that, more power to you, but don't give me that holier than thou crap."

CHAPTER V

Kiki had been simmering with anger for quite sometime because of insidious comments directed at her by Juliet. She felt not only justified for her remarks, but momentarily satisfied by her venting. But riding parallel to her moment of gratification was remorse. She was truly sorry for the hateful outburst, seeing tears spring to Juliet's eyes. In spite of Kiki's brashness and aggression, she possessed a soft heart and loved Juliet in spite of her critical attitude towards her choice of lifestyle. We were all aware that beneath this veneer of hostility towards one another, there was a deep abiding love. Otherwise, we would have had no choice but to eliminate them from the group years ago, no matter how devastating the split. But the absence of maturity, not being a staple of youth, prevented Kiki from displaying the magnanimity or humility necessary for an apology. And Juliet, slapped so insensitively and indelicately with what was the truth, had no reply.

"At the risk of having you turn your wrath on me next, Kiki," said Lora, "I have to admit I'm appalled by what you just said. Now don't get me wrong, I'm not judging you, it is your life, that's true, but I don't agree that what you do with your life is none of our business. Don't you think that the fact that we love you and care about you, makes you our business?"

"Yeah," Mel chimed in, "We have an emotional investment in each other. You know what I mean? I mean I worry about each and every one of you. I hope and pray for the best for you, not that I believe I should get paid back for that, but it seems to me it's like a trade of sorts. Oh, I'm not explaining it very well."

I shot a cursory glance at Kiki and almost busted out laughing. She sat, legs crossed with one swinging almost violently, one arm bent with the palm of her hand supporting her chin and eyes rolling; a posture she consistently used to show she was tuning us out, which she did often.

"I know what you mean, Mel," volleyed Lora. "It's like our parents: through the years, they spend time, money and most of all, love, on us. Do they do it because they expect to get paid back for their efforts? Though they hope, of course, they've helped their children grow into self-sufficient, loving adults, but no, that's what love is, giving and loving, just because."

"It's called unconditional love, I said, happy to contribute something new I'd been reading. "And Lora, you're exactly right, true love is loving someone no matter how they behave… of course, that doesn't include abuse." Casting a glance at Kiki, I added, "good thing, too, but we don't have to like it, or accept it.." Kiki, who had placed her fingers in her ears, was humming in response.

"Love definitely makes the connection, makes it our business," added Mel.

"Kiki!!" we laughed as we attempted to get her attention. She never budged.

"That's right," chimed in Sherry, not willing to give up the torment just yet, "answer me this. Is it the business of the husband's, what the wife does? Or vice versa?"

"Okay, okay, okay! I get the point. My business is your business!! Okay?! But if I never tell you another damn thing, don't be surprised… I won't have to be lectured again."

"Kiki, you can tell us everything or nothing, just don't tell us it's none of our business!" Lora said, stifling a giggle.

We started laughing as we all scooted forward on our seats, staring directly at Kiki, and within seconds, in spite of herself, a slight smile broke through the pout on her pretty face.

"Whatt?!" she threw at us. "I've heard all this a thousand times before."

Instantly, a look of recognition replaced her poutiness as we prepared to defuse her as was done with each of us on many occasions when we began to boil over. In unison, we announced, "We lovvvvee you!" as we peppered her with the multitude of soft pillows lying about the living room.

Did this end it? Yes, for Kiki's injured pride, but overall? No. Now we were off and running on one of our tangents. We loved a good discussion and as much as Kiki regretted saying anything, just as each of us had on occasion, it certainly wasn't the first time and surely wouldn't be the last that she or another one of us would be assaulted for what the rest of us felt was a dumb comment.

We were, after so many years spent in each other's company, fully aware of our strengths and weaknesses and loved each other in spite of them, and maybe even because of them. But Juliet and Kiki tested us, and each other, on every occasion.

Juliet was indeed moody and brooding. So much so that at any given moment, she'd switch inexplicitly from a lovely smile to instant tears. We were convinced it was hormonal. Perhaps an internal battle, at that age, was being waged between the mind's desire to remain a girl child and the body's unstoppable evolution to reach its ultimate goal of becoming a woman. This battle combined with her profound need for the consummation of her father's attention and love, produced an emotional, volcanic seething. Bubbling close to the surface, there were unexpected eruptions every now and then and, seemingly to us, without provocation.

Juliet's father, Pastor Charles Coombs, and his dutiful wife Kate were raising eight children, not an unusual number in the fifties. But Juliet often complained of getting lost and forgotten in such a large family. Most of her father's spare time, which was minimal at best, was spent with her five brothers. Her two older sisters, Ellen and Sheila, shared the commonality of age, which helped to dilute the neglect the girls would have otherwise felt.

"Rainey?" she asked wistfully during one of our many teen talks on her porch swing. "Do you know how lucky you are to see your father every day? To sit down to dinner with him? Does he kiss you good night? Does he yell at you once in a while? I know how lucky you are…very lucky!" She answered before I had the chance to respond. "Ironic don't you think?" she continued, "that the reason I never see my father is because he's off ministering to other families, other little girls, maybe even my age? Not only does he not see the irony in it, he's reprimanded me for having an unchristian attitude toward others and tells me I need to spend more time with God and less time with my own selfish thoughts. Is it possible I'm being selfish? I don't know how much time fathers should spend with their children, but I would think they should see them at least a couple of hours a week. Is there something wrong with me? Sometimes I think…well, I think if my own father doesn't want to be with me, why would any other man?"

Tears began flowing unashamedly over her full cheeks, and any attempt to quell them would have been futile. Being devoid of the wisdom inherent in one so young, I was not equipped to answer. The best I could do was try to console her. And I was well aware my comfort was not ultimately what she was seeking or needing but at that moment, succor from any source, I knew, would be welcome. Her sadness and pain wrenched at my heart and I slid my arm around her, drawing her to me as the flood of tears soaked my shoulder.

"Someday," she sobbed, I'll marry a beautiful man who loves me and wants a house full of children to love…someday, Rainey."

Juliet didn't possess the conventional characteristics of beauty, but she carried her five foot, six inch frame with an air of dignity and mystery and the consistent aura of melancholy surrounding her, showcasing her vulnerability, was enticing to men. She wore her strawberry blonde hair shoulder length, allowing it to fall loosely in waves with small ringlets escaping here and there. Her otherwise beautifully shaped nose was a little short for her long face, but her large, round, brown eyes and extra full lips lent her an innocent look, and she used them to flirt outrageously, successfully distracting a man's attentions from any flaws he might otherwise be drawn to.

Whatever the reason for her extreme mood swings, we prayed they would soon dissipate, or better yet, disappear forever. We loved her but we walked on eggshells when we were with her, hoping to avert any conversations or actions that might precipitate a spell. Strangely enough, in spite of her sometimes overwhelming melancholy, she had a terrific sense of humor. Though, as with all her emotions, it was erratic and unpredictable. One minute she sat sulking in her own brand of misery as our conversations seemingly whirled around her unnoticed and then suddenly, without warning, she'd respond with a witty remark, timed to perfection, indicating she had in fact heard every word, reducing us to tears of laughter. She never realized how great her deadpan delivery was, but our joy and attention would bring a lovely smile to her sweet face. And we reveled and appreciated those rare moments of normalcy. We learned early on to focus on and enjoy her strengths, her sensitivity to others, her generosity and her loyalty.

I lived closest to Juliet and we spent a lot of time at each other's homes. Her mother, Katie, was a wonderful seamstress and I was in awe of the clothes she made for Juliet and her siblings. She even made the suits that her sons wore to church. There was no shopping center available then in our small town, and everyone bought their clothes from the same few stores or catalogs and often ended up wearing the same items. But Juliet's were originals, and she was the envy of a lot of young ladies. Katie decided one beautiful summer afternoon, when we were the tender age of eight, that it was a good time to transfer her sewing expertise to Juliet. I could take advantage of the lessons since I spent so much time there. And a good time it was. Although Pastor Coombs didn't ban music from their home, neither did he find it reverent and insisted on it being enjoyed only in his absence. With him gone much of the time, Juliet and her brothers indulged themselves in a teenager's passion for music. They had acquired a large selection of popular records and played them often, at the highest volume to the delight of our friends living close by. We sang and danced on the wide, long porch which extended around three sides of the house and generally enjoyed being young and energetic. To this day, a song from that period can instantly transport me back, filling my soul with the wonderful, freeing nostalgia of childhood.

Katie had decided on a simple blouse pattern for us and we were feeling very grown up and excited. Katie went over and over the initial pattern cutting with us, but was determined to let us go it alone and learn by our mistakes. Over the swinging sounds of her favorite music from the "Big Band" era, we could hear the insistent "sst, sst, sst," of the pressure cooker tenderizing an entire chicken into a mouth-watering entrée, smothered in its own gravy. Katie was a wonderful cook and always displayed a table full of delicious homemade desserts on Saturdays. She was constantly baking and cooking out of necessity, in an attempt to satisfy the appetites of so large a family. Two large family cats came in and out as the kitchen door opened but usually could be found curled up on the porch, snoozing away in the lazy warm afternoon sun. I followed Juliet's lead in pattern cutting. I concluded that even though it was her mother who had the talent, surely some of it had seeped into Juliet's gene pool. We worked and worried the material, snipping and sewing for the next two hours. Katie checked our progress every now and then, unfortunately, tossing a cursory glance in our direction instead of a studied examination of the tortured cotton fabric which would have revealed the ineptness of her protégés. But we were having a good time and perfection was not the sought-after goal. Juliet, inspired by a particular beat of a favorite song, would leave her work area, and dance with the abandonment of the young, and the abundant talent she possessed. Of course I joined in, and the unfinished blouse, or what was potentially a blouse, lay waiting completion. Dinner was announced and the sewing project would have to wait for another day. But we were anxious for Katie's opinion and approval of what we'd accomplished and held them up proudly. But instead of the expected nod, an expression of approval, and words of praise, her hand flew to her mouth to cover a grin which had indiscreetly appeared, but more importantly to stifle an outburst of laughter. As hurt and disappointment instantly stabbed at our sensitive hearts, she cleared her throat in an attempt to retract the expression and replace it with praise for our efforts, but it was too late. We were crushed. Juliet and I exchanged sad-eyed looks as we actually examined the results of our childish efforts. The look of shock registered on both our faces and we exploded into fits of giggles. They were unidentifiable gobs of material, at best. Seams were running everywhere, and neither of us left an opening anywhere. We even managed to close the neck hole securely. That was our first and last attempt at sewing, but it has served the purpose to evoke a good laugh when we reminisced.

CHAPTER VI

There were a number of memories on which to reminisce, pleasant or otherwise. Juliet was the epitome of capriciousness, fun one minute, morose and whining the next. I remember on more than one occasion running to her house, teeming with enthusiasm over a new doll or toy I wanted to share, but when she appeared at the screened door, one quick look would tell me my visit was for naught. My joy would instantly dissipate into the hot summer air, knowing she was not coming out to play nor was she going to invite me in. I would turn dejectedly to seek out another playmate or return home.

But Juliet was stuck with me, and we managed to accumulate a lot of time together in spite of my pushiness and her moodiness. Being normal children, we enjoyed playing, rain or shine. And although sunshine is designated for time spent outdoors, Juliet and I found a way to enjoy the wonderful summer rains. All the houses built at that time proudly displayed long, deep porches. But Pastor Coombs had added a huge, wooden swing, hung by thick chains from the porch's ceiling, designed to perfection for a rainy day refuge. The banister ran half way up the entire length of the porch, all the way around to the front door. When a beautiful soft summer rain was imminent, we would, with the help of her older brothers, quickly adjust and hoist the swing as high up to the porch ceiling as possible. Then, climbing onto the banister, we'd grab the swing and work our way onto it. Blankets that we'd placed on it earlier were now waiting to cover our chilled bodies, and provide warmth from the coolness produced by the rain. There we sat, as two princesses on their throne, singing and talking innocently and naively as only children do. The rhythm of the rain and the moving swing, combined with the sweetness of a dear friend, provided a sense of security and contentment that has yet to be matched. That, then, was the Juliet I knew and enjoyed as a child. Though our friendship didn't end, neither did it blossom further into adolescence. The chemistry between two people is one of life's great mysteries. And though Juliet and I shared many enjoyable hours shopping or just chatting on her porch, these times were due more to the proximity of our homes than a desire for each other's company. Instead, we each were innately drawn to the ones who complemented us, filling the vacuum in our own unique personality.

Lora, the animated, happy one, infused lightness in Juliet, whose quiet, moody characteristics, in turn, kept Lora's feet on the ground. Sherry's calmness and sweetness balanced Kiki's wild, cavalier attitude, and Melanie's shyness and seriousness was in direct contrast to my extroverted personality. Those differences, though we appreciated them, were responsible at graduation from high school for our inevitable separation.

And with that chapter of our lives coming to a close came a flood of conflicting emotions. Life as we had known it for so many years was ending, and although it was a time for celebration, it was also a time filled with tears of trepidation and sadness. We walked about happy but dazed, experiencing the epitome of surrealism. The umbilical cord was finally and officially cut, and the world was now ours to make of it what we would. But before we ventured out into the big, wonderful world, which we believed was waiting with open arms to envelop us lovingly and serve our every need, we were going to have one last summer blast! No homework, no worries, just fun — fun — fun!

Except for Kiki. She proved to be the only downer, suddenly becoming more remote and distancing herself from us at every opportunity. It became her modus operandi to show up at a club where we were, inevitably and noticeably tipsy, only to leave minutes later with a guy unfamiliar to us. Attempts to keep her close and out of trouble proved futile for, without booze, we had nothing to offer and as she so succinctly put it when we questioned her about it, "we cramped her style." She was hurling out of control at a high rate of speed, heading straight for disaster.

And so it was one very early Saturday morning, mid-summer, after a particularly late night of partying, the phone rang. Groaning and moving like a slug, I forced my body into motion. Not having the slightest idea what time it was and my eyes not being capable of opening yet, let alone focusing, I had to guess the time. And from the way I felt, it had to be no more than five minutes after I went to bed. Not wanting to wake the family, I stumbled as quietly but as quickly as possible through the darkness, directly to the phone. After eighteen years, I knew the pathways of the house like the back of my hand. I picked up the phone and Mel's frantic voice virtually exploded through my fog-filled brain, practically knocking me back as she faltered and stammered, finally rattling out bits of information that my unassembled brain was attempting to assimilate.

"Rainey?!!! Are you there?"

"Mel?—Yeah, yes, what's happened?!"

"It's Kiki, she's been in an accident!"

"Oh, God, no!" I gasped, lucidness replacing the haze in my mind miraculously. Kiki had done it. She finally managed to self-destruct. "How bad?" I asked, tentatively, terrified of her response, and her next words did nothing to soothe my fears.

"I don't know. Sherry just said to get to the hospital, A.S.A.P., no details…only that it was bad."

The door was left open, giving some horrific scenarios an opportunity to race through our minds. I knew we'd all meet there; it was just dealing with the minor details of who was driving whom. I quickly threw something on…I'd see what, exactly, when I got to the hospital, which was usually a twenty-five minute drive but being in the middle of the night, with less traffic, maybe fifteen or twenty. Whatever it was, it couldn't possibly be quickly enough. Mel picked up Juliet and me, and we failed in our attempt to keep each other calm.

"Don't worry about her, huh?" Mel grunted. "Boy, if this doesn't prove our case to her, nothing will."

"Yeah," I agreed. "Isn't it the middle of the night? Shouldn't we still be sleeping, peacefully? Oh, but what she does is none of our business, right! I swear, if she's alert, and not seriously injured — Oh God, please let her be okay." We alternated between fear and anger.

"All the talking in the world's not gonna help," added a frustrated Juliet, "she just thinks about herself."

We simmered and bitched, venting our feelings in snippets until we arrived at the hospital. It served to diffuse us. Otherwise, with our nerves so on edge, we'd have lost it, totally. The roads were extremely narrow, loaded with sharp curves and perhaps even a trickling of the Friday night crowd driving home with brains saturated with booze. In our haste to get to Kiki, we didn't need to be involved in an accident ourselves. But it was tough keeping it together, and we prayed a million sincere prayers on the way. Sherry and Lora resided near the hospital and would be there to comfort Kiki, if in fact she was conscious and in a physical state capable of being comforted. We knew she'd be taken directly to the emergency room and headed straight there. We saw no staff to answer our inquiries but spotting Kiki's distraught parents, Donna and Walter, we rushed to them, hoping for good news. Unfortunately, they knew nothing other than she was alive and tests were being initiated. There were, naturally, obvious cuts and bruises, but the extent of internal damage, if any, would not be known for a while. Waiting was a nightmare, but there was a plethora of unfortunate distractions as ambulances came and went with sirens screaming on an all-too-regular basis. People of all ages and all walks of life with all manner of injuries were being pulled in on cold metal gurneys by hustling, burly men and taken directly to the emergency area to be poked and prodded and kept alive, hopefully, to live and play, and some, to drink and drive again, on another Friday night. Some were paying for their lack of sound judgment alone, but some had taken innocent victims with them. It was a depressing scene and the beeps and buzzing of the different machines was incessant, but the inherent rhythm produced a calm and if not for my jangled nerves I could have been lulled to sleep. Instead, we paced for what seemed like hours before the doctor finally appeared, motioning for Donna and Walter to join him in a room off the emergency area. Again, the waiting was insufferable. What was the average time for relating someone's medical status to another? Either there was hope, and the prognosis was good, or they'd died. We believed she hadn't died; Donna and Walter would have appeared quickly, since doctors aren't reputed for belaboring, emotionally, while communicating a patient's demise. Pitiful consolation that, but it's all we had. Finally, Donna appeared, distressed and crying. Her demeanor deepening the fear in our already frightened hearts. Walter followed close behind and the doctor vanished. We walked over to console and, hopefully, be consoled. Sherry, being a surrogate daughter, was elected without hesitation as spokesperson. We huddled in close to hear the answer to the question she tentatively and desperately asked, "Is– is she going to be okay?" Her words came out perhaps a little harsher and louder than was her practice, but emphasized and echoed our sense of urgency and fear. Donna mumbled, but failed miserably in her attempt to speak.

"Please…what? What?" we implored her. Our heart rate at her faltering words was rapidly approaching and exceeding a speed limit which the human body could endure. Finally, Walter filled in the blanks. Kiki was in one piece, was presently sedated, as to be expected, and had been moved to intensive care. She'd suffered a severe concussion: her head had taken the brunt of the impact, but thank God, it wasn't head on; she'd hit the windshield with a glancing blow, or she probably wouldn't have survived. Her right eye had been dislodged partially, sitting on her upper cheek when she entered the emergency room. She'd badly chipped a couple of teeth, some were loose and she'd sustained a broken ankle. Of course, she was covered with inescapable bruises, accompanied by cuts and scratches of various sizes. The real concern at this time was internal damage, however. If there was any, it would be determined over the next twenty-four hours. Donna held Walter's hand tightly, sobbing pitifully. Their little girl was badly damaged and their world shaken.

"Thank God," cried Sherry. This was bad. Horrible! But nothing from which she couldn't recover. Tomorrow, hopefully, with negative test results, this tragic episode would have been nothing more than a hideous lesson, albeit a hard-learned one, for Kiki. We were staying the remainder of the night, of course, and wouldn't leave until we saw her. We found semi-comfortable chairs, removed the discarded magazines and candy wrappers covering them and collapsed, giving at least some physical relief to our overstressed systems. And now, with a modicum of tension released after hearing some positive news, I eagerly invited the humming and beeping into my brain to work their magic, to transport me into a transcendental state if not a mind-numbing sleep. It worked, on and off at least, for the next couple of hours. But when the new shift of workers came pouring in, invigorated with the restoration of a good night's sleep and, inadvertently, jarring our numbed bodies with their enthusiastic conversation, we struggled to upright ourselves into a comfortable sitting position before rising to stretch and headed for some strong, hot coffee to hopefully clear our minds. It was a new day, and hopefully, a new beginning.

Time dragged, of course, and accompanying these circumstances were dialogues of introspection which seem to flow unrestrained from the roots of pent-up, nervous energy. Always, without fail, inane conversations will follow and with exhaustion riding on the progression of the hour comes silliness, couched in the form of unseemly comments and jokes. They served, I suppose, to release tension and preserve one's sanity. And between fits of giggles I questioned rhetorically: "I wonder just how much of the pain and misery Kiki is feeling is due to her head injury, and how much is due to a severe hangover?"

CHAPTER VII

At seven thirty the next morning, Dr. Massey arrived with the wonderful news that Kiki was stable and her prognosis looked good. However, she was to stay in ICU until the results of the full range of tests confirmed his opinion. To verbalize our relief would have been impossible, so we cried, hugging each other, releasing the anxiety of the last several hours.

We were granted permission to visit Kiki, and of course we deferred to Donna and Walter.

After what seemed like an eternity they finally reappeared, and lord how nice it would have been for them to have prepared us for Kiki's appearance. She, who epitomized life and living, was lying so deathly still and it was incongruous and frightening. Certainly only sedation could accomplish that feat, I mused. But more horrifying was her face. She was unrecognizable. Shock waves ran through us as we studied it, now horribly swollen, cut and discolored. Her beautiful face! With the prognosis for her overall health looking good, my thoughts concentrated on the cosmetic aspect of her healing, and if the disfigurement which we were observing was any indication of the seriousness of the injuries, our old Kiki was gone for good. How would it affect her? I needed to speak with Donna and Walter and request she not be handed a mirror for at least several days. It surely would improve with time. Our hearts ached and it took every ounce of reserve to hold back cries of anguish seeing her so badly broken and hurting. We administered gentle loving touches to any area that wasn't covered with tubes and bandages, kissed her gently, and reassured her of our love, hoping she could feel our presence. Oh, the anguish and sympathy we felt, but as we slowly exited the room, our anger began to grow in proportion to that anguish and sympathy…anger because of her reckless, irresponsible behavior. We understood she lived her life on her own terms, and we were supposed to accept her in spite of them. Didn't we just have a discussion about this? It was small comfort now, seeing her lying there bandaged and battered and watching the suffering her parents were enduring. They deserved better. We were angry because we knew we were impotent where she was concerned. We were nothing more than loving, helpless spectators watching her selfishly destroy herself, and knowing all the love in the world could do nothing to change her. We ranted and raved about her to each other until our anger was spent and our tears dried then, dog tired, we arrived home hoping to sleep for a week.

Details of the wreck surfaced the next afternoon when one of the two men with her regained his senses. They too were banged up pretty badly, but neither as severely as Kiki. Richard Gaines professed to be the most sober of the group that night and related it the best he could, solemnly and quietly, gulping after every few words to, successfully for the most part, hold back tears. After all, these were young men too, eighteen and nineteen years of age, and terrified now with the overpowering realization of not only how close to death they had come, but also with the possibility of taking innocent lives with them.

They had partied into the wee hours, liberally partaking of free drinks being offered at several different friends' homes. And even then, it wasn't Kiki's idea to quit the evening but with the realization everyone else was leaving, she left with Richard and his brother Web. They took an unlighted back road, reasoning that even though more narrow and dark, it was also less traveled. They had been driving recklessly and were quickly approaching a small bridge over a little stream with the tiniest of bridge abutments rising up on either side to keep cars from going into the creek. When the car's high beams shone on the abutments, Kiki, in her inebriated state, was convinced it was an impossibility to get through the tiny opening and screamed, "We're going to hit the bridge," and of course nobody will ever know; she could have been correct. But, correct or not, on a pitch-black night, being drunk and disoriented and coming upon it so quickly, she panicked, grabbed at the driver's arm, and jerked the wheel. His foot instinctively hit the brake; how much this helped or hindered, who's to say? The violent braking consequently thrust Kiki into the windshield. The passenger's side of the car, where Kiki sat, took the brunt of the impact, and the car careened off into the creek, turning over, God alone knows how many times, ending upright along the bank. The limberness of their bodies produced by the alcohol probably was, in no small way, responsible for their survival. Damaged and bleeding, they managed to climb out of the crumpled vehicle. Stumbling and crawling, they roused several dogs whose barking guided them to one of the few houses sitting at the very edge of the road. The ambulances were called, and then here we were. After hearing the details, we felt extremely fortunate that there were no fatalities.

Kiki was fully alert the next morning, feeling ravished after having not eaten for a day. But all too quickly, she realized her breakfast would have to be carefully and painfully sucked through a straw. It took a little practice and a lot of wincing, but she managed to consume enough at least to extinguish the hunger pangs gnawing at her. She was informed by one of an ant-like, relentless stream of nurses coming and going through her room to expect Dr. Massey that afternoon. Kiki experienced mixed emotions about his visit. She was anxious to hear a good report, but feared that the number and thoroughness of the tests would disclose another diagnosis responsible for symptoms she was experiencing and didn't want known. So she was stuck, and forced all her thoughts and energy on escaping the sterile and sickly environment as quickly as possible to put this mess behind her. She had barely gulped down the last sip of her lunch and was wiping away the sweet residue of a coma-inducing, unidentifiable blob of dessert from her mouth when Dr. Massey arrived. "Good afternoon, Kiki," he smiled. But it was an unsuccessful attempt to disguise his dispirited heart. "Hello," Kiki returned softly and painfully. Even with pain pills her face ached terribly, and speaking was extremely difficult. She struggled to sit up straighter, not taking her anxious eyes from his for a moment. His countenance and the undeniable sympathy he held in his dark eyes sent a sudden chill through her, and she began nervously gathering the covers tightly around her for comfort. *He's going to tell me what I don't want to hear*, she thought frantically. *God no, please don't let it be so.*

He helped settle the white, thin, hospital blankets over her, patted her arm, and with a sincere smile brightening his face and temporarily replacing the compassion in his eyes, delivered the good news. "Well, young lady, you are very lucky indeed. The test results show no internal injuries. You're young and strong and your body can withstand a lot, but please, let's not put it to the test again, okay? And if you continue to show improvement over the next couple of days, I don't see why you can't be released the first of next week. How does that sound?"

"Great," she said, nodding her head gently. Even the slightest movement sent lightening streaks of pain through her face. But her lack of enthusiasm over such an exciting announcement was evident. Under other circumstances, she would have found the strength to bound out of bed at that moment, throw on her clothes, and leave nothing but skid marks where she'd once been. But being distressingly aware his eyes had not left her face, and with a dead silence suddenly hanging heavy in the air, she felt certain there was more to come. It was though Dr. Massey was gathering the courage to continue.

"How do you feel, Kiki? Really?"

"Good," was all Kiki would allow. Even if she'd had the strength to expound, she wasn't going to volunteer any more information than necessary, besides, it hurt!

"Kiki, are you sure you've been feeling okay? I mean, before the accident? Any unusual aches or symptoms of any kind?"

Oh, God no! she thought, as the hair stood on the back of her neck, and instantly feeling the heaviness of the world settle on her heart. *It can't be. But why is he asking me that? Does he know something? Am I being paranoid? I don't want to say anything to incriminate myself, but, oh God, this cat-and-mouse game is excruciating. If there is something, why doesn't he just come right out with it?*

"Kiki?" He moved his head over toward the windows, more into her field of vision where her misery had allowed her eyes to drift, and abruptly and unmercifully interrupted her thoughts. "Have you?"

"I…I don' know what you mean, what kind of aches or symptoms?" she said, evasively, trying hard to avert her eyes.

"Kiki, I'm trying to maintain a sensitive bedside manner here. I don't want you getting upset," and reaching over tenderly, he began rubbing her soft, smooth hands as they twitched and pulled subconsciously at the covers lying across her lap, "but is there something you'd like to talk about, something you need to tell me?" Kiki's head dropped slowly to her chest as she expelled a huge sigh of resignation, being overwhelmed emotionally only because her weakened mind and body was succumbing to the stress of the accident, and because, she was just eighteen. Dr. Massey barely heard at first the sounds of anguish before he noticed the small stream of tears falling over her swollen cheeks. He handed her a tissue and she had to dab quickly to stem the flow. After a few swipes at her dripping nose, she cleared her throat, preparing to speak, but words failed her.

"Kiki," he said tenderly. But as he focused his kind eyes on her wet ones, and with her faltering words, her full awareness of her condition became clear to him. "We're on the same page here, aren't we? I wanted to be certain you were strong enough to talk about this. I didn't want to add more stress if you didn't feel up to it." He was such a sweet, caring man, and he wasn't a stranger to Kiki. She had seen him on many occasions over the years, he being her family's doctor. His silver hair and gentleness lent him a grandfatherly air that calmed his patients. God knew she could use all the calmness she could get right now. Lifting her head slowly, she looked at him pleadingly, almost willing him to speak the words to make everything right. He placed an arm gently around her shoulders, the compassion of which resulted in another eruption of sobs. Even though just a few moments passed before she regained her composure, it seemed like an eternity. He gently placed his hand under her tear-streaked chin and, lifting it to look squarely and sympathetically into her once beautiful face, stated, without equivocation, "Kiki, you're pregnant, but then you know that, don't you? Or did you just suspect?" Not only had she suspected, she was ninety-nine per cent sure, but oh, how she burdened that slim one per cent with a thousand fervent hopes and prayers. Now, that thin thread was violently severed. What now?

CHAPTER VIII

Kiki proved strong enough to return home in the promised two weeks, but though healing nicely on the outside, we realized she wasn't rebounding to her old irrepressible self. She went through the motions of living but remained in a deep funk which we chalked up to post-trauma and medication, not being privy to the other condition. And one of us visited her every day in an attempt to uplift her sagging spirits. She seemed to be mumbling to herself continuously, as though working through something. And over and over again she apologized to her parents and to us, begging forgiveness for the hurt and anxiety she had caused, but never for the actions that had produced them in the first place. When we apprised her delicately of this omission, a spark of the old Kiki, consistent with her former personality except for the slight speech impediment produced by her injuries, rose up sharply from her depression, long and strong enough to retort with an almost belligerent shrug of her pretty shoulders. "Shit happens, okay?" But of course we forgave her, we always did. She took it for granted, and rightly so. But there was something different about her since the accident. It wasn't just depression. She was in a constant state of edginess…a relentless bubbling just under the surface that we couldn't identify. We were convinced she wasn't drinking. Dr. Massey warned her that drinking combined with her medication would only exacerbate the situation, and we knew it was possible that medications could produce slight changes in her behavior, but still we watched and questioned her, and she only fired our suspicions by hedging with her responses. Granted, she had a difficult time talking, but if Kiki wanted to talk, nothing would stop her short of a coma or death, and she pleaded exhaustion every time the questions began. We felt certain she was withholding something. But what? Did Doctor Massey hand her a death sentence? Was she wanting to spare our feelings? We weren't medically astute enough to understand the intricacies of the human body or the possible complications from the trauma she'd experienced, so maybe it was possible she wasn't out of the woods yet. Naturally, our lives were on hold until this was resolved to our satisfaction. Hopefully, our suspicions borne of misconceptions and ignorance were unfounded and she would soon be a better, calmer version of her old self, with the lessons learned. We doubted that, but one could only hope. At any rate, we resolved to try harder to get her off the booze and get her life together. Unfortunately, as one day led to another, the enigma continued and it became all too obvious she was wrestling with something bigger than even Kiki was able to handle. We finally devised a plan to encourage her to confess this "thing" to Sherry and decided the best tactic was to have Sherry spend some quiet time with her. Having a group of people, friends or not, sitting and staring intently at you, waiting impatiently for an explanation, had to be more than a little disconcerting. Sherry and Kiki were bosom buddies, soul mates, and we were convinced that with a little nudging from Sherry under the right circumstances, she would feel secure enough to unload the undoubtedly painful burden. We arranged a quiet evening for the two of them the next Saturday. Sherry convinced Kiki's parents to take the night off to enjoy themselves. They agreed readily, revealing just how exhausting this whole episode had been and exposed our insensitivity to their needs. Our mental capacities were not exactly cooking on all four burners right now.

Sherry arrived promptly at seven, filled with anxiety mixed with a large dollop of optimism. Maybe tonight would prove the mystery innocuous after all, nothing more than lingering symptoms of trauma, and we could reenter the world of the living. The evening started off smoothly as we listened to music and chatted, although Sherry realized she was doing all the talking while a distracted Kiki sat, as usual these days, lost in her own thoughts. Sherry plumped and plopped some soft down pillows strategically behind Kiki, stroked her soft hair lovingly and asked if she needed anything before she sat. Kiki gently signaled no, sighed deeply and suddenly, without encouragement or prodding, began talking, agonizingly slowly, as if more to herself than to Sherry, about the accident and how it wasn't an accident. Nothing was making sense to Sherry and she felt a little frightened, thinking Kiki was showing signs of delirium. Kiki continued. "I just want it to all be over, done with. I think I'm well enough do take care of things now." She looked up at Sherry, who was standing in front of her with a confused, concerned look on her sweet face. "I want it to fade into just a bad patch, you know? I've gotta plan in the works."

"Kiki?" Sherry knelt gently in front of her with her hands resting on Kiki's knees. She looked into her eyes, but could plainly see Kiki was elsewhere. Sherry motioned her hand back and forth in front of Kiki's eyes to break her focus. It worked. "What are you talking about, honey? Are you okay? The accident is over, and you're going to be fine. Dr. Massey said so." But instead of pacifying her, the words proved to incite her. "Damn, damn, damn, I can't believe I've been so stupid! Ow!" She winced, as pain shot through her jaw at her flare up. "Me, Kiki, the wise-ass know-it-all. Yeah, some wise-ass I am." She paused and Sherry, believing she was engaging in self-reproach, hastened to soothe and console her, though actually thrilled at Kiki's words of self-condemnation…it was a good sign. Maybe she'd had an epiphany or something. Sherry had read about things like that. Anything positive would be a step in the right direction. "We all make mistakes and we'll continue to make them, Kiki," Sherry whispered softly. "But it's all behind us now, and I'm just glad you feel this way ab—"

"Ah crap, Sherry," exploded Kiki as she sprung from the chair, looking at Sherry with a half-glazed look before continuing. "Would you stop talking about the damn accident?! Ow!! You don't have a clue what's taking place inside me right now." And suddenly becoming unnervingly calm, she began to unfold the startling revelation to Sherry, whose body had instantly stiffened, and any trace of her previously felt optimism, slipped away in an instant. "I wanted the accident…no, let me rephrase that, It's not that I wanted the accident, exactly, but, but I'm certain I made it happen. I didn't wanna' die, but I hoped, I hoped maybe I'd kill the baby!" Her voice softening in mid sentence because of an attack of residual pain, she plopped back into the chair with pitiful resignation and lamented. "Of course, if it had killed us both right there on the spot, I guess that would've been okay too…I wouldn't know it anyway." Sherry stood frozen, staring wide-eyed, attempting to absorb the horrible words. It was too much at one time. "My God, Kiki, what are you saying? Are you certain that you're pregnant? How do you know? You wanted to kill yourself? You knew you were pregnant? How long? Oh my God, Kiki! The accident!" Sherry dropped into the nearest chair, hands going to her dazed head, eyes darting back and forth across an unseen floor. Surely this is a dream. Silence filled the room as she tried desperately to incorporate Kiki's words, make some sense out of the impossible things she was relating, and Kiki afforded her the grace period, fully aware it was needed. Finally, Kiki sighed. "Dr. Massey confirmed it, and yes, I believe I did cause the accident. No, I didn't set out that night with it all planned, but I've thought of nothing else but how to get rid of this, this *it*, since I found out, and the very first thought that raced through my brain that night when I saw those bridge abutments coming at us was hope, blessed hope that the baby at least would be killed right then and there, and this hideous nightmare would be over." Her voice rising again, she continued. "The worse part for me is, I can't believe how stupid and careless I've been. And believe me these tears aren't in any way sympathy for me but anger. And my main concern, here is not to ever, and I mean never, let this touch Mom and Dad! But I sure's in hell am not going to let this ruin my life! And before you ask, don't! 'Cause I don't have the slightest idea in all of creation who the father is. Not that it matters anyway," she added as a sad afterthought. Sherry wasn't shocked or surprised about that, not with Kiki's track record. Finally, Sherry rose, shakily, to console her. "Kiki, we love you, and you know we're in this with you. How…how long, how many weeks are you? Do you even know?"

"No, I suspected something wasn't right for several weeks, but I was afraid to actually voice it, even to myself let alone anyone else, thinking that that might make it real." Kiki reached for more tissues and dabbed gently at her still partially swollen face as she continued. "I kept hoping and praying that the symptoms would just disappear – Ow!! – but they didn't, and Dr. Massey confirmed it right before I left the hospital. I'll figure a way out of this, Sherry, I just can't let it hurt Mom and Dad."

While on the one hand Sherry was filled with indescribable relief to have fears of Kiki's impending death smashed into eternity, on the other, pregnancy was listed only after death as the biggest tragedy for a young, unmarried girl of our generation. *Well*, thought Sherry, *she didn't lose the baby. Now, dear God in heaven, what was she to do?* How do you tell your parents a thing such as this? The shame would be almost unbearable. Although, if the truth be known, with Kiki's behavior over the last several years, it was doubtful anyone would be surprised but in fact would wonder why it hadn't happened sooner. Nevertheless, her family's world would be turned upside down with the disgrace of it. For Kiki's part, she never once thought about the actual experience of the pregnancy itself…everything was overshadowed by shame, guilt and fear. But not shame for her. "I couldn't care less what in the hell anyone thinks about me, you know that, but it would kill Mom and Dad! It would just kill them!"

If ever there was a time for a meeting of the minds, it was now. Over the years, when faced with overwhelming problems, we gathered as a group, had open discussions until we distilled them down to a successful conclusion. However, now, I couldn't muster enough hope to be even cautiously optimistic about a resolution to this one. We'd never faced anything remotely resembling anything so monumental. Our most horrific dilemma to date aside from dealing with Kiki's general wild behavior, was discussing the incessant rumors part and parcel to the pettiness abounding in teen circles about one of us and who started them, or something else – in retrospect – just as trivial. Oh, how upset we could get over such minutae. How sweet to revel for just a moment in those passed few months, to the carefree days when pettiness, homework and what to wear for a hot Saturday night were our biggest concerns. For dead certain, the innocence of youth vanished with this pregnancy, not just for Kiki, but for the rest of us as well. So this is what being grown up was all about. This was what youth rushed headlong to achieve and experience. Making monstrous decisions about monstrous problems and learning how to, hopefully, successfully cope with them. Life didn't seem very forgiving at this moment, as we attempted in vain to formulate an immediate solution, a reprieve for all of us. But no one could have wanted a do-over more than Kiki, to begin again, to be given a second chance.

Dr. Massey wanted to examine Kiki as soon as she felt well enough, and an appointment was set for two weeks. And though there were few signs of lingering physical damage, including the frightful damage to her face, thankfully she remained in a constant state of distraction; her irritability gathering momentum with each passing day. Even for arrogant, invincible Kiki, the pregnancy proved daunting and the battle to maintain her composure showed in the constant working of her facial features. She was obviously thinking, planning, and contemplating her options. Kiki was a survivor, and ultimately, no matter how thoroughly we discussed the situation, or what conclusion we came to, we knew deep down her decision would prevail.

Phone calls were made, assembling the group and we were to gather in Kiki's bedroom for the meetings. She requested Sherry drop the bombshell on the rest of us. She wasn't up to it yet, mentally, to cope with our reaction. And a bombshell it was. We felt that If Kiki, with all her savvy, could screw up, no girl was immune and it served well to heighten our attitudes of moral restraint, even though hating at the same time, it was our Kiki serving as the sacrificial lamb.

When it came right down to it, there were few options. Having the baby in Milton was actually an option in theory only. It wouldn't happen, and wasn't considered, and there was never a question of Kiki keeping the child. The only viable solution was for her to move discreetly to another town, or better yet, a big city, and give the baby up for adoption. But the logistics of such a move was well beyond our abilities to comprehend, let alone execute.

Kiki's doctor's appointment was in four days and a first for us. She wasn't the least bit nervous about the prospect of an examination. Under these circumstances, probably for anyone, embarrassment would be overshadowed by the pregnancy itself, but any momentary crack or weakness in Kiki's mental stamina surrendered without a fight to her temerity. She was proud of her body and if the truth be known probably in other circumstances would have enjoyed displaying it once again for the eager eyes of yet another male.

That weekend, we had a pizza get together. It served well as a pleasant distraction for our tortured states of mind. We talked and laughed for hours, reminiscent of numerous carefree evenings we'd spent together, enabling us to forget, for a little while anyway, the ordeal that lay ahead over the next few days and beyond.

CHAPTER IX

"Piss on the doctor and his orders not to drink...I'm not taking the damn pain pills anyway," Kiki mumbled to herself on the evening before her doctor's appointment. And consequently, she'd downed at least two six packs in a successful attempt to obliterate her misery and satisfy her need, even for just a few hours. The next morning, she dragged her unwilling body out of bed and peed for what seemed like the hundredth time. Now, as she stood looking in the mirror, she couldn't believe she was only eighteen. Physical and mental health being the barometer, she felt at least eighty and at the moment looked every bit a well-used forty. Bloodshot eyes peered intently back at her in an attempt to focus, a condition not totally resulting from the alcohol, but partially from a sleepless night. She had tossed and turned relentlessly between the bathroom trips. "Damn! How in the hell did I get myself into this mess?" Anger and frustration exploded out of her as she hit the sink with the side of her fist, and then yelped from the pain of it. She pulled herself over to the full-length mirror hanging on the back of the door, and forced her unwilling eyes to focus on her belly. Was that slight swell the beginnings of the new life inside her? Or was it just beer? She couldn't be sure. What the hell did she know about being pregnant? Nothing! And she didn't care or intend to find out anything more than she knew right now. Not for a second did she allow any sentiment about the baby to enter her mind. She couldn't. She had no intention of having it in her life any longer than possible. And at that thought, she checked the time on the tiny crystal clock on her bedside table. Ron, "the Neanderthal," as she liked to call him, would be there in thirty minutes as prearranged. She had her appointment with destiny in just a few hours and was filled with anxiety, fear and relief all at the same time. Ron was coming through for her now in her time of need, making all the arrangements, providing the transportation of sorts, and offering his companionship and moral support. He was one of several guys Kiki kept on a string, and priority-wise, he was tops on her list. He was good-looking enough, once you got past the usual grunginess, but as was expected his lifelong ambition was to be worthless, a consistent trait in this particular category of Kiki's men. With one notable exception: Ron had discovered a form of martial arts months ago and was completely captivated by it. I personally believed it was nothing more than his transparent super-macho ego attracting him like a magnet to a new and exciting defensive form of fighting. Yes, it was touted to be strictly defensive, but knowing Ron, he would be anxious to display his talent at the drop of a hat and would be more apt to use it offensively. Nevertheless, his excitement and enthusiasm for the sport was contagious for Kiki, who was not only ready but more than willing, to try something different, especially if it would garner her more attention. And over the next couple of months she drove us to distraction asking, no, insisting, that we allow her to teach us the women's self defense moves. Poor Sherry. Since Kiki spent more time with her than the rest of us, she became Kiki's partner and protégé. And in spite of herself, Sherry took to it naturally, doing it at first to pacify and certainly help her best friend, but the more she participated, the more she enjoyed it. It was great exercise and was responsible for more giggling sessions than sleepovers as a little girl. And succumbing to her constant nagging, the rest of us practiced from time to time, with each of us gradually dropping off after a few weeks, confident we were proficient enough to overcome a predator on a dark night. Assuming, of course, he was smaller than we were and himself more than just a little frightened, perhaps crippled, and too drunk to resist. But Kiki stayed with it and was determined to acquire some type of colored belt or two. Well, if it kept her from the booze, more power to it. We were excited and happy for her.

So Kiki had prevailed upon Ron, naturally, to be her partner in crime, and they dedicated themselves to her plan of action. She lied to her parents, telling them she was spending a few days with Sherry and the rest of the gang, a big last get-together, she said, before we departed for different parts of the country. She could tell them anything and their unconditional love and blind trust made them avid believers, but she hated lying to them and was filled with terror that somehow, someway, the pregnancy would show on her face, in her eyes, or she would misspeak and give herself away. They adored her and she hated the deception where they were concerned. Over the years, they'd been overall unaware of the extent of their daughter's aberrant behavior. They bragged to friends of her lively spirit and were thrilled with her zest for life. Yes, she got into some trouble from time to time, but they viewed this as healthy for young people, as long as the reins were kept tight. Little did they know just how loose Kiki's reins really were.

She intended to call Sherry later with some concocted story to free her up from another group meeting. That was the most difficult part, since they stuck to each other like glue, but Kiki was nothing if not resourceful; she'd come up with something. Working out the details of her plan with Ron superceded every other thought in her mind the last few days, even a thought of her doctor's appointment on this very morning. Kiki had hazily placed it as being further in the week and was unconcerned, since she had every intention of canceling it anyway, telling Dr. Massey she was moving to another town and would find an obgyn there. That bought her time, and the rest would be figured out later.

Ron was nothing else if not punctual. And true to his chauvinistic nature, he sat in front of the house honking the horn in his beat-up '55 Chevy. In actuality, Kiki's biggest fear at the moment, considering that vehicle, should have been whether she'd reach her destination safely, if at all. It spent more time in the shop than on the road, and when it was running, it banged and rattled so much that Kiki kept a pair of sneakers in the back seat, prepared to walk on any given outing. But because Ron drove such a clunker, it proved to be serendipitous once again for Kiki to be dating him. On more than one unfortunate occasion, the car did break down, usually in the middle of nowhere because they'd parked in some dark lover's lane area on the outskirts of town. However, Kiki's personality didn't allow her to sit in the car as a helpless damsel in distress. She was right beside him, flashlight in one hand, screwdriver in the other, exploring the rusted inner depths of the old car, probing and testing each part in hopes of discovery and a quick solution. And almost without exception, they succeeded. Ron couldn't afford anything better, so had driven nothing but junk cars, and consequently had virtually rebuilt a few of them over the last several years. Kiki was a quick learner, and never let it be said that car maintenance or repair was a waste of time. While it was true she didn't have a license at this time – none of us did – Ron had taught her to drive and her parents had already committed available funds for a car, but the thought of Kiki turned loose on the highways struck pure fear in our hearts. But all that aside, this was the day it was imperative it kept running.

She yelled down to her father to tell Ron she'd be out shortly, requiring her to push her sluggish body a little faster, and forcing her to forego the last and favorite step of her dressing ritual…applying one of her favorite fragrances, liberally and lovingly. She had a thing for perfume, and a long bathroom shelf housed and sagged with the weight of at least twenty beautifully shaped bottles of different sizes. But much to my chagrin, she was obsessed with the scent of musk: heavy, nostril-flaring, lung-clogging musk. She wore it almost exclusively, and joked that if could bring down a deer, what must it do to a man? But her momentary disappointment was replaced by a cavalier revelation, "what the hell, I'm sure not needing it where I'm going," and with a sigh of resignation, took one last look in the mirror and for the first and only time, showing compassion and awareness of an actual baby growing inside her, whispered softly to her waistline. "Sorry, it just can't be."

CHAPTER X

Sherry was a tall, willowy redhead with porcelain skin. She kept her naturally wavy hair free and easy. Huge, round, blue eyes that screamed innocence were surrounded with long dark lashes and to emphasize her youthful look, each cheek accommodated a giant dimple that looked as though, when she smiled, a small raisin could reside snugly in each of them. Snowy white teeth often exposed by a flashing, engaging smile along with her optimistic personality were responsible for the illumination of her surroundings, competing competently with the sunshine. But Sherry's beauty secret was her *laissez-faire* attitude regarding her looks. She was of the opinion that they were secondary to what she held in her heart, and consequently carried herself with an air of confidence which the opposite sex found quite appealing.

It seems unfair, then, that she was seemingly chosen to harbor Kiki with her problematic and unpredictable behavior. But ironically, her very nature dictated that inevitability. And here she was. She arrived at Dr. Massey's office promptly at nine. Kiki made it clear to Sherry when they'd discussed their plan that Ron would be dropping her off and Sherry would take her home. Sherry wasn't surprised that Kiki wasn't there yet. She rarely was punctual, she thought as she perused a magazine. At nine thirty, though, she became concerned and checked with the receptionist. "Excuse me, did Kiki Woods call in and cancel her appointment?" Checking the book which lay directly in front of her, the pleasant, middle-aged lady looked up and smiled sweetly. "No, she didn't, but give her more time. This isn't unusual for a first-time visit. Young girls are always nervous, and try to postpone it as long as possible." *Well,* Sherry thought, with a half smile tugging at her pretty lips, *if she only knew, that sounds good, not like Kiki*, but at this point, she'd buy anything. And certainly they'd never been involved in such circumstances, so it was possible. She called Kiki's house thirty minutes later, only to be informed by Mrs. Woods that Ron was supposedly dropping Kiki off for their weekend get together. Sherry's mind was racing as she barely mumbled goodbye. There was no get-together planned. And how in the world could she forget something as important as this appointment? How indeed? Suddenly, horror flashed through her. In retrospect, she realized that though Kiki had seemed preoccupied, she also had seemed strangely upbeat for the last couple of days; Sherry had chalked it up partly to edginess and partly to relief from disclosing her secret, which, undoubtedly, had laid heavily on her heart. But that wasn't it at all. Oh, how could she have been so stupid and blind! She knew Kiki was determined to get out of this mess. And what she set her mind to do, she accomplished. Her heart sank and the cold hand of terror gripped her as never before. *Where did she go? Oh God, Ron took her, and being aware of his street savvy and unsavory contacts, she knew beyond a shadow of a doubt it was a done deal. So this was her solution all along. She wanted it over and done with now! Not months from now. Patience was not a favored virtue of Kiki's anyway, but especially when there was so much living to do,* Sherry thought angrily. Yeah, that's one thing Kiki was definitely good at, living life to the fullest, spontaneously and impulsively, regardless of the consequences to her or friends and family, and in this case, another innocent life. She was confident she could always fix it later. The important thing to Kiki was to live in the moment.

Sherry was furious, but even more than that, she feared for Kiki's well being. But she knew she was the only one between the two of them that did. For all of Kiki's sophistication, she knew nothing more than the rest of us about abortion, but that would be but a minor concern for her. She would dive in, head first and if there was another problem, dive in head first to solve that one, and on and on. Later, when Sherry updated the rest of us with the disturbing news, the phone lines grew hot with discussions, voicing our fears and anger at Kiki's decision.

We didn't see her again for a week although Sherry kept us abreast of what was happening with her, and to our dismay and never-ending astonishment where Kiki was concerned, nothing had changed. Well, except the obvious...with her burden lifted, she'd bounced back with more enthusiasm than ever before.

Lora, Mel, Juliet and I were aggressively demanding a meeting with Kiki, Sherry being the intermediary, of course. We believed that our group being what it was deserved a question-and-answer session in hopes of relieving the almost unbearable fear and anxiety which had reached a level capable of producing heart attacks and strokes in weaker victims. Sherry agreed, and the get together was set up disguised as a pizza get-together. Not that Sherry used deceit to entice Kiki. It wasn't necessary. Kiki would be eager to disclose every aspect of the abortion. And as innocent young girls and her best friends, we were bubbling over, not only with curiosity, but every other available emotion.

Lora, Mel, Juliet and I drove together and arrived thirty minutes early in anticipation of the cathartic discussion. Sherry served iced tea and cookies and we chatted about nothing as we munched, distractedly, painfully skirting the main topic, not wanting to dilute the subject even to the smallest degree.

Kiki came in, almost flaunting, we felt, her wicked accomplishment. I guess the dark parts of Kiki's mind took pride in handling and solving a serious problem on her own. I have to say we were impressed, but only to the extent she had visited forbidden territory and came away unscathed...at least, at the time, it seemed to be so. It would be years later, when she became pregnant, that mental storm troopers from hell would bear down upon her, tormenting her relentlessly, filling her with guilt that she had taken her first child's life. But for now, she was happy and free, once again.

As soon as Sherry handed Kiki a glass of tea and she settled back in her favorite chair, the verbal assault began, questions flying across each other like bullets whistling at a police shoot-out. And eventually, not only was each one answered to our satisfaction, but very quickly the horror of it thickened and swirled around us, reducing us to tears of sadness. A pall settled upon the room, the gloom of which hastened the end of the session and our departure.

That was the end of it, at least for the rest of the group. However, for me, a memory best forgotten resurfaced instantly of Mother revealing to my sister Vicki and me how she had attempted to abort us immediately upon discovering she was pregnant. I realized in later years that, subconsciously, every move and decision I made since that revelation was driven by a mission to validate my very existence. As the years unfolded, the dearth of Mother's maternal instinct was proven time and again, and as hard as I tried, I couldn't recall her ever initiating a hug, kiss or affectionate cuddling of any kind. A perfunctory goodnight kiss on the cheek – not to be mistaken as a loving ritual, mind you – was performed and initiated by me through the years. But one evening when I was thirteen, after a minor disagreement, she denied me that small kiss as punishment. It was not until years later on a visit home that the routine kissing began again. Vicki, three years older than I, turned off emotionally completely to Mother, transferring her love and attention to academics. Sadly, Vicki and I weren't close…those three years being enough, at that crucial age, to create a chasm between us. She left home for the west coast after graduation and it would be a while before we had the opportunity to finally connect as sisters.

I've learned in my life, if we have the desire, the ability is available for changing and growing. And in later years, I realized Mother, at that time, loved us as much as she was capable. But, unfortunately, when we needed her most, she was completely self-absorbed, making it virtually impossible to include anyone else in her small circle of emotions. In my adult life, I've often pondered the relationship between my parents, realizing it was dysfunctional at best.

My father, being the traditional male, wanted the model traditional housewife and not working outside the home, expected that home to be kept immaculate. But to his great dismay and unbridled disappointment, Mother couldn't have cared less. She preferred jeans and bare feet, and I don't recall ever seeing her with a broom or cleaning cloth in her hand except to shoo off a neighbor's straying dog or cat. The household chores were assigned to me and Vicki as soon as we were big enough to wield a broom and with the gene for a strong work ethic inherited from our father, we took to it instantly. And we do remember, well, life being a constant battle between them. They consistently and diligently concentrated on their differences, with criticism and sarcasm being their choice of weapons with which to bludgeon each other unmercifully. I remember overhearing talks of divorce up until my graduation. There seemed of late, however, to be a compromise of sorts and peace reigned. As the years progress, the aging process slowly translates to physical degeneration, and perhaps is as responsible for promoting an attitude of peace as much as maturity…with limited energy, it's less desirous to spend time on worthless activities such as squabbling. Whatever the reason, somewhere between the anger and resentment apparently, a little wisdom, determined and aggressive, forced its way into their psyches. Dad hired a cleaning lady once a week and learned to accept pants on his woman on occasion, and Mother consented to a stuffy housedress once in a while. They discovered a shared love of travel and fishing, which had lain dormant but thrived in spite of the repressing environment in which they forced it to remain for so many years. I keep in constant touch by phone and visit at least once a month and sincerely enjoy my visits. We are closer now that the burden of parenting is no longer a barrier. I love them with the desperate love of a child for a parent which, I believe, is inherent in us and transferred through the umbilical cord. I wish them every kind of happiness. I can only pray I come to a full and complete understanding of the strengths and weaknesses in myself as well as those I love, and accept and forgive compromise with life and find peace sooner, rather than later. Although I believe most of us will travel through our entire lives searching for our "why was I born?" That being one of my favorite topics, and analyzing – a strong point – I attempted to engage the rest of the group in a hot session at every opportunity. And while discussions were always happily anticipated, the desire for heavy psychoanalysis was not, and complaints came in on a regular and consistent basis. But for the most part I ignored them. We each have our burden to bear from the others, and my penchant for psychobabble was theirs.

So it was with all the usual angst and confusion thrust upon adolescence by hormones and parents, compounded by the antics and predictions Kiki subjected us to, we felt we were more than prepared to enter the world of adulthood some of which, thanks to Kiki, we had already experienced. Future plans had been discussed on many occasions and though we knew our lives would never be quite the same, nothing could have prepared us for the trials and tribulations which lay ahead.

CHAPTER XI

Lora, Mel, Juliet and I were departing for different parts of the country at the end of summer, and Kiki would now have only Sherry to look after her. And the only weapon left in our arsenal of sisterhood, for Kiki, was prayer.

Lora was moving to West Virginia to attend the university in the fall. Lora was the effervescent follower in the group. She had a head full of blonde, naturally curly hair and was five feet three inches tall of giggles and fun. But what she lacked in height, she made up in bosom and we teased her about defying gravity as she walked about. She was never without a cute guy hanging on her arm…not that she was boy-crazy, but her happy, bubbly countenance attracted them, and certainly the expansive bosom didn't hurt. Although some males may have misinterpreted her ebullient, flirty personality as promiscuity, they were mistaken; she entered each relationship with seriousness and reverence. She was steeped in the tradition of serious husband hunting and declaimed to anyone who would listen that her matriculation at the University was intended as the next step in consummating that tradition and would by no means be sidetracked by any desire for, or attempts at, achieving academic excellence. Where was there a better female hunting ground? And the sooner Lora found a mate, the better she would like it. The biggest challenge in her life was wrestling with the new "sixties" sexual furor, as it was for the rest of us. It was exciting and confusing to suddenly have all sexual taboos erased, but the awesome responsibility inherent in this liberation was also frightening. So her revelation at one of our last get-togethers before our separation, still held some shock value but was not altogether unexpected. It seemed that one by one, the layers of our biblical morality, which we thought was thick enough to carry us through these sudden and volcanic changes, were being stripped away little by little.

"Whoa, did I have a night last night," she said, glowing.

"Lord," said Sherry, "not again. This is the third time this month, alone that you've said that, and each time it's been about a different guy. Who is it this time?"

"This one's different..."

And with, "yeah, yeahs" all around, Lora responded, shaking her head. "No, Bain is the one. I'm sure of it."

"Lora," I said, amused. "You say that every time."

A wicked smile spread across her face, suddenly deepening into one of her irrepressible giggles, and looking towards the door in case a parent was eavesdropping. Satisfied we were alone, she continued in a conspiratorial whisper. "Maybe so, but last night's the first time I ever really wanted to," and giving a nod to Kiki, since it was one of her favorite expressions, continued, "give it up." Emissive sounds of curiosity filled the air, and Kiki couldn't resist a satisfied smirk spreading from ear to ear. She wasn't surprised that young people were falling like flies to the prevailing sexual attitude. Our culture was, after all, being suddenly submerged in it, and applying a powerful intangible force to be reckoned with. Kiki was amused because another of us was caving, and she scooted in a little closer, practically slavering, not wanting to miss a single detail. We pressed Lora for more information, and the perfunctory giggles were followed by a complementary color of pink rising in her cheeks, not from embarrassment but from the reveries of her sexual excitement experienced the previous night. "I'm not ashamed!" she stated emphatically. Protestations pregnant with guilt and spoken to no one, for no one had responded. "I'm tired of the double standard. The guys are having all the fun. Do you have any idea how much masculine cuteness there is strutting around the campus? The smell of testosterone is heavy in the air. It's like turning a kid loose in a candy store. Oh, the upperclassmen love to tease us with accounts of the exciting parties they go to and who's doing what with the sexiest guys. I just sit there mesmerized, getting hot and bothered. It was okay when no one was doing it, but now, everyone's doing it, and I'm not only feeling the pressure, but more than that...damned deprived. Besides, it's beginning to sound sillier all the time when I attempt to explain that I'm saving myself. I'm not sure what that even means. I feel like I've been thrown into a den of iniquity and I'm less and less sure all the time I even want to be pulled out; the rules are gone, everything's changed, and my head's spinning, but I have to admit, I'm loving it."

Kiki laughed. "Damn Lora, it sounds to me like you're trying to justify. I sure's'n hell couldn't care less. I'm just glad someone else in this group is finally showing some signs of life. But just learn from my stupid mistake, be careful and use something."

All eyes turned to Lora with a long enough pause of anxious anticipation for Melanie to interject a question. And being the almost neurotically shy one, asked in an awestruck whisper filled with disbelief, "you really wouldn't go…I mean do it just with anyone, would you? Wouldn't you want it to be with someone special?"

"Yes, of course that's what'd I prefer, what I want and oh, it would be so easy with Bain. I want to so badly it's painful. But Bain said it's nothing compared to what a guy suffers. Well, of course I can't dispute that, but it just doesn't seem normal that we should stop when something feels so good and so right, and he says—"

"Wait a minute, Lora," said Juliet. "Now just think about that a second. I was reading about a serial killer being interviewed—"

"Oh lord," moaned Kiki. "Here we go."

Juliet ignoring her, continued. "And you know what he said, when they asked him why he killed?" Of course we shook our heads no, and our eyes riveted on Juliet's face in anticipation of the answer and even more curious to see the connection between having sex and killing someone.

"He said, it felt right and very good and those feelings compelled him to do it again and again."

"Hell, Juliet, what's your point? You think Lora's planning on killing off a bunch of men by having sex with them?" We laughed with Kiki in spite of ourselves. We knew she understood perfectly well what Juliet was saying, but enjoyed teasing her.

"Kiki," said Juliet, "can't you be serious for even a minute? I'm trying to have Lora see the flaw in her reasoning, not that I'd expect you to understand it; it's academics, not 'monkey sex' we're talking about."

"Okay you two, that's enough!" said Sherry, getting more than a little weary of their constant bickering.

"Juliet," exclaimed Lora, "that's certainly profound, what in the heck have you been reading?"

Juliet nodded in my direction. "Rainey has a stack of psychology magazines a mile high; there's always something worthwhile to read," and casting a sly grin at Kiki, she went in for the kill. "Of course you have to be interested in reading once in a while, instead of spending all your time screwing around with perverts."

"Okay! That's it! I've had it, Juliet! I'll be damned if I'm not—"

The rest of us jumped up, separating the two. "C'mon guys," begged Sherry, "You two are going to have to come up with some kind of compromise. I mean we can't ever get together anymore without you two getting so hateful, and I'm sure I speak for the rest when I say, I'm getting darn sick of it. Enough is enough."

Mel spoke up. "Maybe you two need to sit together without the rest of us and hash out your differences, then, whichever one survives—"

"Cute, Mel, real cute," Kiki slashed back.

We actually acted on Mel's suggestion, or a modified version, anyway. Every time thereafter when we were together, we more or less forced Kiki and Juliet to sit beside each other, and engaged them in a dialogue in such a way they were forced to communicate with each other. It seemed to help, a little, anyway. We discussed their personality conflicts, and wondered if perhaps the resentment rose from each envying some character traits in the other. We each had witnessed Juliet's flirting: not the normal, silly kind engaged in by most teens, but flirtation filled with an intensity seemingly bent on producing intentional torment to its victim. We'd called her on it, delivering our objection and concern with sensitivity and love, but she chose not to discuss it, right then, anyway. Perhaps she envied Kiki's ability to be so free and open. Kiki conversely, envied Juliet's ability to tease without consenting to every Tom, Dick or Harry. And as we examined their arguments, every one of them, without fail, ended up eventually, at that very topic.

"Anyway Juliet, that – what you said – makes a lot of sense. But I guess because my mind was only concentrating on something positive, like, hmmmm, sex, I didn't relate it to anything negative." Then, thinking aloud, Lora half-mumbled. "Yeah, just because it feels good, doesn't necessarily mean it's okay to do. Interesting."

"Or eat," I chimed in. "If that were the case, I'd weigh three hundred pounds." Everyone agreed.

"Well," Lora said, jumping back on track about last night. "Bain suggested birth control pills, and said he can easily get them for me. And Kiki, believe me, I would never go through what you did, so I just can't get pregnant."

We'd never used the word abortion in the course of our conversations since Kiki's experience. And when the subject surfaced, it never failed to produce a few moments of disturbing silence; an uncomfortable, almost visible aura would fill the room. Our feelings and emotions had been distorted, put out of balance, and we were too young and immature too properly deal with such a traumatic event and our mental equilibrium had yet to recover.

We were shocked by her revelation that she was actually thinking seriously of having casual sex. Of course we wanted her to be protected, but it would make it so much easier to give in that first time, and then, again, and again. What was happening to us? But Melanie, a first year nursing student, was concerned first and foremost about the medical aspect of it. "You need to see an obgyn first, and not just pop some pills some stranger gives you."

"Mel, this is Bain, not some stranger, for goodness' sake."

"Lora, he is virtually a stranger! How long have you known him? A month? Please, just don't make a hasty decision about something as serious as this, at least talk to a doctor first."

"Do you really think you're going to use them?" asked Juliet, "I mean, Rainey's right, if you don't take them, it'll keep you from going too far, but if you start taking them, then with the fear of pregnancy gone…you know what I mean?"

"Yeah, believe me, I understand, that's exactly my dilemma. But I'll tell you what – oh, I don't know, I'm so confused. You know? I've dated a lot of guys, but I've never felt this emotionally involved with any of them. It's different with Bain, I don't want to stop…it's the hardest thing I've ever done. You know I was raised to believe in God and go to church and everything, but, and how do you know if it's really love? Besides, I think if I don't do this, he can so easily find someone else who will, and the thought of losing him is almost unbearable."

"Maybe he's counting on you thinking just that, Lora." I said, adding my two cents. "I hate to sound so cynical…maybe he really is 'the' one for you, but to give him the benefit of the doubt: if you can't distinguish love from lust, what makes you think he can? Besides, answer me this," and, without any conscious thought on my part, the traditional values ingrained from childhood, surfaced, sex without commitment? Unthinkable! "Is this guy's actions synonymous with marriage in your mind? Has he given you any reason to believe he's serious about this relationship?"

"No, no, not really, I mean he hasn't said he loves me, but maybe that's not his style. You know most guys have a hard time expressing themselves verbally, I don't know, I guess, bottom line, I just want to give in. And lord, I found out the further you go, the more difficult it is to say no. I just don't know what to do," she lamented, obviously in emotional turmoil, but unfortunately with our collective lack of experience, Kiki notwithstanding, she was drilling a dry hole with this crew.

Certainly if pressed, we would admit, we too were tired of the double standard, and we also believed Lora was correct in her assertion that the field of sexual exploration shouldn't be designated exclusively male territory. We knew exactly what she was going through. Hormonally speaking, we had all experienced the physical and emotional pain she described, each to her own degree. And for certain, the thought of getting pregnant was as good as any chastity belt, most adept at curtailing progressive sexual activity. This was great fodder for a sexual debate, and for the next couple of hours we did just that, revealing feelings and opinions, ad nauseam, striving to arrive at a conclusion we could learn from and hopefully implement in our lives. Actually, we'd created a coming-of-age sexual support group and didn't know it. Discussions were the backbone of our relationship, no matter how big or small the problem, but in this case, it turned out to be a moot point for Lora, after all. She discovered, before making her heart-wrenching decision that Bain was hitting on Judy, her college roommate. Her love for him died at that moment. Confirming, of course, it wasn't true love in the first place for either of them. And Lora, as was expected for her personality, moved happily back into the dating cycle and as she said, the wiser for the experience.

CHAPTER XII

Sherry was starting classes at a local college, studying criminology and related fields to enhance her private eye aspirations. And for all her serenity and quiet ways, she could hunker down with the best when it came to a good murder mystery. She had also exhibited a natural bent for writing, for turning a phrase. We teased but seriously encouraged her to contemplate combining the two talents to write crime novels or become a seductive sleuth with a romantic penname like "Veronica Foxx." We whiled away more than one evening making up names and murder plots, thoroughly enjoying the potential of such a career, even if she decided not to pursue it. But by a stroke of good luck, (if you are inclined to believe in luck, which I'm not) after graduation, Andrew Carpenter, a young man in his mid-twenties and a mutual friend of the family, had been residing in Virginia for several years and claimed journalistic connections. He contacted Sherry and with just a few phone calls hooked her up with a local newspaper. Small time news for sure, but for Sherry, an opportunity to apprentice with a veteran reporter, doing some actual hands on reporting. She hated the idea of being so far away from family and Kiki, but Virginia was beckoning with great promise, and she was excited about obtaining such valuable experience. She was also excited about being on her own, even if it meant calling two tiny rooms in a boarding house "home," conveniently located within walking distance of the newspaper office. Her excitement reached atmospheric levels and was contagious. Only a change in Kiki's lifestyle to what she believed to be that of a normal functioning woman her age could have made her happier.

Kiki couldn't imagine life without her best friend being close at hand and had planned on moving with Sherry, but was offered a job as a cocktail waitress right outside Milton and as Kiki put it, "I'll be bringing down some bitchin' big bucks." Suddenly she imagined life without Sherry just fine, at least for the time being…only time would tell, but one thing for certain, Kiki had proved she could take care of herself, whether we liked her solutions or not. We just hoped she didn't self-destruct before permanent help arrived, and it would be interesting to follow her life over the next few years. She's a bundle of energy, a dynamo, and I wondered what she'd end up doing with her life. She was the only one never to mention goals or dreams during our discussions of what the future might hold for us. And if we probed, she'd say, "having a helluva good time and living out whatever comes my way."

Melanie. Ah, ambitious and shy but brainy Mel. She left for Colorado, supposedly to visit family but enjoyed the climate so much she decided to stay awhile and work in her aunt and uncle's dry cleaning business. Mel's very attractive; a brunette with beautiful brown eyes surrounded by black eyelashes and thick eyebrows. She's as slim as a reed, never having to consider calories, and if we didn't love her so much, we could easily hate her for it. She, too, is unaware how beautiful she is, and her naturalness is a great part of her appeal to men and women alike. Women don't feel threatened by her, and men find her shy innocence endearing. She's taking advantage of Colorado's wonderful ski slopes, many of which seemingly begin at the front door. We laughed when she informed us she was taking lessons, since we can't think of anyone less inclined toward athleticism than Mel. As long as I've known her, she's been tripping over non-existent things. Neither can we imagine her being instructed by a stranger, since she's so shy and exhibits a meandering kind of walk, almost a sidestep, with head bent downward, seeming in an attempt to hide within herself, but ironically drawing more attention. We believed any man attracted to her would have to be super-attracted to her physically and aggressive enough to overcome her shyness, in other words, bulldoze his way into her life and pounce! Otherwise she'd probably never even have a date. We also wondered where the time for recreation would be found. Her heart at first was set on becoming the world's best nurse, but she later confided to us her dream of ultimately becoming a doctor. She had been forever curious of the inner workings of the body and medicine for as long as we'd known her. And her parents had encouraged this inclination with every age-appropriate medical and anatomy book available. And oh, did we suffer from her medical preoccupation. Throughout her entire academic career, I don't remember successfully completing a conversation with her without it being peppered with little toss-off comments like, "I have the strangest twinge in my chest…it feels like it's deep inside my pleural cavity." Or once when I complained of a headache, she quickly remarked, "Exactly where does it hurt? There are so many reasons for cephalalgia...it helps to know exactly what kind—"

"My Goddddd!" screamed Kiki, "did you forget to talk like a normal person in that damn school?" Melanie was hurt, sometimes not realizing the extent of her usage of medical terminology. And it had, much to our dismay, expanded by quantum leaps when she entered medical school. But she apologized, as she always did. And Kiki accepted, offering an apology of her own. Melanie explained that conversing with classmates twelve hours a day, seven days a week, she even dreamed in medical terms. It was an automatic response. "You know," she said, smiling playfully, "like being part of the autonomic nervous system." Lori threw a pillow, landing a direct hit to the side of her head. We believed what she said to be true. Mel didn't have a pretentious bone in her body, not the ulna, pelvic, phalanges...and we agreed that if it caused her discomfort to change her mode of conversation, forget it, we would adapt and learn, and be all the better for it. If she became Dr. Melanie Matheny, and with her dedication and love for the profession I couldn't think of a reason she wouldn't, she would be my choice for medical care.

Juliet was heading for Maine. She loved the romantic idea of surviving a cold winter there, and her sister Ellen informed her she surely wouldn't be disappointed. Although Pennsylvania didn't exude warmth through the winter months, it couldn't hold a candle to a Maine winter. Ellen invited Juliet to stay with her as long as she liked and was looking forward to having her as a roommate. But though Juliet was excited about the visit, her heart and dreams were Florida-bound. She had dreamed of living there since, as a small child, an aunt returned with tales of alligators, swamps and even stifling heat. Details and descriptions which might discourage the heartiest of souls produced and stoked the fire in Juliet. Her ambition was to operate a small beachside business, nothing elaborate; she wasn't intellectually equipped to handle anything more substantial, but that was okay. She loved the idea of a small shop filled with unique items for which she'd shopped and chosen from distant places all over the country. And with this dream in mind and the opportunity at hand, she enrolled in night school, taking two business classes. Just the basics, but a good start. We were extremely proud of her. Maybe this was the outlet she'd been looking for and we'd been praying for. Would it prove to be a temporary distraction or a serious career move? Only time would tell. But at the very least, we hoped for a noticeable change in her spirit, even temporarily. We'd take anything.

This period of our lives was proving to be an evolutionary as well as a fascinating time for all of us…discovering our wants and desires, as well as learning and reveling in the goals and experiences of the others.

I certainly was burdened with my own fair share of wants, desires and idealism, and sufficiently motivated to begin moving and shaking to realize, at least, some of them. On a mad impulse, I made arrangements with two other "on the fringe" friends, Corina Linkett and Sheila Brown, to take on New York City. We pooled our graduation money and applied for bus tickets through a local newspaper from a New York-based company advertising for maids for the New York burroughs. Why not? Sounded exciting and certainly different. And if it didn't work out, we'd find something else. Well, the bus trip turned out to be an eye-opening experience for three hayseeds such as we were. We arrived at the depot at the scheduled time, only to discover the bus two hours off schedule due to anti-war demonstrations, blocking and virtually closing many of the city's streets. It all proved to be a little unsettling for traveling novices and we scurried to secure seats in the proper area. Finally relaxing, we began scanning other passengers around us. We giggled in amazement at the wide array or rather disarray of the various styles of dress and hair with matching idiosyncratic mannerisms. And after thirty minutes of ekeing out every ounce of enjoyment from every oddity we could find, we dared to venture away, perusing the book and magazine racks, and snapping pictures in the little draped boxes set up for the patron's amusement. There is definitely something mystical about those little draped boxes. Once inside, I've yet to see anyone sit primly and settle for a normal picture. Not on your life. Magically, once inside, a personality transformation takes effect, unexplainable by the participants themselves, but one which encourages the most outrageous behavior…let's see who can contort their face into the silliest forms! And because of limited space, faces are juxtaposed or squished just inside the picture, and always, there are the hands or fingers over someone else's head. And this foolishness which, at best, is only mildly humorous under other circumstances, suddenly becomes hysterically funny once inside that booth. Step over the threshold when finished, and we return to normal humans once again. Where else can you have that much fun for twenty-five cents? Once we'd exhausted the supply of entertainment on the inside, we strolled up and down the sidewalk directly in front of the depot, not exploring further because of the danger and the imminent arrival of the bus. At least not until our stomachs alerted us we'd not eaten for hours and so we approached and examined the snack bar menu. But with one look at the charred, wrinkled wieners rolling, rotisserie style, over and over, the piles of french fries lying cold and lifeless on a side table, and the paper thin hamburger patties curling up on the sides speckled with white pieces of something unidentifiable, we decided to play it safe and opted for candy bars and chips from the machines. Finally our destination was announced and as we retrieved our belongings from the temporary lockers, we started the short walk to the bus, actually exclaiming our disappointment to each other that this unexpected adventure was over. Little did we know, this was just an appetizer, something to tide us over until New York City.

CHAPTER XIII

Exhausted after a long, exciting day, we boarded the bus happily, anxious to get settled in. It was going to be a long trip. Much later, after resigning ourselves to the overwhelming smell of gas fumes, and realizing that chances were good that that was the most fragrant odor we'd be confronted with, and giggling and groaning over the plethora of sounds emanating from the various oral cavities of our fellow passengers, we decided to risk a trip to the bathroom before attempting to sleep. My bladder screaming for relief, I went first, and it was a stringent test of one's agility and balance, a gymnastic feat, to complete the mission. And feeling proud of the accomplishment, I was hurrying back, hanging on as best I could as I bounced from one seat to the other, experiencing the physical maneuverings of a staggering drunk, when a leg, suddenly and without warning, appeared in front of me. I tripped, of course, stumbling and flailing five seats forward before successfully regaining my balance. I ended up with a few strands of dark hair intertwined in my fingers. I'd heard a few yelps of pain and surprise as I'd made my way down the aisle, so I turned and apologized to everyone and especially to the older lady, rubbing her head in a soothing manner. I proceeded, humbly, back to my seat. Of course, Corina and Sheila were shrieking with laughter. The young lady, over whose leg I had tripped, was standing next to my seat, waiting to apologize. She had dozed off, she explained, and her foot extending into the aisle was the result of her tired body relaxing. Her name was Trish Walker. Trish was short for Patricia, a name she hated, she explained because a fourth grade boy, whom she found disgusting because of his constant nose picking, had a serious crush on her. At every opportunity, he would rub that same nose picking hand up and down her arm while he mewed her name, "Pa...trici...a, I love you." When she began fifth grade, she changed her name to Trish. Fortunately for her, he had moved away, but the nickname didn't. She was a three-year veteran of New York, and explained she was on the bus because her parents refused to fly. She hated it for the same reasons we'd been discovering since departing the station.

For the remainder of the trip, we were to hang on her every word. She was a very pretty twenty four-year-old, and knew the New York City ropes. We desperately wanted to know everything she knew, and disclosing our immediate plans, she gladly offered advice. "I've got the best job going, and I think you should give it a shot. I tried the waitress thing and menial jobs when I first got there, but kept looking for something better. Well, I found it, and maybe you'll be able to bypass all that small stuff." She had our attention.

"Is it legal?" I asked. "What you do, I mean?" Trish laughed.

"Well, sometimes I think it shouldn't be because of what they pay me, but thank God it is." We were nearly exploding with curiosity.

"What do you do?"

"Okay, okay." Trish motioned with her hands for us to calm down. "I model." Our mouths dropped open. She was pretty enough, to be sure, but I guessed her to be about five foot five and I didn't recall seeing any model less than five nine. Trish deliberately hesitated before expounding, enjoying to the fullest the perplexed looks on our faces. "Yes, I know I'm too short. But what you don't realize, just like I didn't, is that there's all kinds of modeling. Advertising agencies use every part of the body, with the exception of the obvious parts, of course, for ads and television commercials."

"Of course!" said Sheila, "that's right. Just think of all the ads in magazines...those feet, knees and hands belong to someone, even the back of people's heads to show hair. Corina! Your hair! Everyone's always talking about your beautiful hair!" Her excitement rose, and then suddenly fell. "I think my best bet is still to be a Nanny." Sheila was blessed with many friends, but unfortunately for her, they were all female. She felt deprived in the looks department; although I believed it was not necessarily nature's doing but just more of a lack of attention on her part. And Corina, too, though possessing beautiful, olive skin and yes, long, luxurious, raven hair, seemed to be just missing it. Both possessed even, unimposing features, but did nothing to enhance them. Lora and I spoke many times of inviting them to a get-together so we could operate, beginning with the simplest of beauty tools...tweezers. Sheila was almost a uni-brow. I was aware that large department stores offered free makeovers and was determined and looked forward to those two taking advantage of them.

Looking down at my own hands, I felt a wave of excitement rising. Could it be possible? The remainder of the trip was spent obtaining every detail regarding this modeling thing the where, who and how of it. I was definitely ready to give it a try.

If we thought Pittsburgh's depot had a monopoly on weirdness, we were quickly brought up short when we entered the New York terminal. As tired as we were, even the thought right now of seeing the sights of New York didn't produce much adrenaline. We sat down to organize our thoughts, and determine with whom to consult about directions to the "women's" hotel where we had reservations. But before we managed to get comfortable, a middle-aged man wandered slowly toward us carrying a lunch-type brown bag, opened at the top, and held snugly to his chest. We instinctively cringed, closing in tightly toward each other. Unfortunately, this created just enough space for him to squeeze his filthy, crumpled, raincoat covered body into the seating space next to me. He stank of booze and cigarettes. His gray streaked, shoulder-length hair lay in oily, flat strands across his whisker-stubbled cheeks. But what drew my attention more than his slovenly appearance was the soulful, resigned look in his huge dark eyes. Eyes filled with hopelessness for, and death to, any future dreams. Unfortunately, staring directly at me, I was presented with an opportunity to linger, with sadness, at the vacancy where once life had resided, when he offered me a bite of the mysterious contents of the brown bag. At my polite refusal, a smile, resembling a sneer, crept up the right side of his face revealing a mouth full of rotten, nicotine stained teeth. And shrugging his shoulders nonchalantly, he methodically and lovingly, reached into the bag, carefully retrieving a huge jar of...applesauce! We sat spellbound, but only momentarily, as our hypnotic state involuntarily erupted into fits of giggles. We attempted some semblance of control and discretion but needn't have worried; he was so intent on his mission that he never noticed. We realized later, amusingly, that neither did the majority of the patrons seated around us. But even before the applesauce man had completed his performance, we were confronted with Act II on the opposite end of the terminal. An explosive rush of air whooshed through the terminal doors, which had been violently thrown open by two police officers on horseback! As we attempted to regain our crumpled composure, we realized a young man, diminutive in size at first glance, until we realized it was only in comparison to the size of the massive horses, was running through the terminal, with the hope of outrunning the policemen. He didn't, and within minutes he was handcuffed, led back out the doors he'd so recently exploded through, and secured in the back seat of a waiting squad car. We had no idea what further adventures lay ahead, but if this was any indication, we were in for an exciting time. I've decided that for anyone born with a minimal amount of people curiosity, a bus depot is a voyeur's paradise.

By the time we checked into the hotel, we were exhausted to the bone, and for the first time in memory I dropped into bed without a shower. We slept till ten the next morning, and awakened only by the obnoxious screeching of brakes right outside our window. The next few days were spent, frenetically, looking for an apartment in Flushing and Brooklyn; Manhattan rentals were way beyond our ability to pay. We settled for Brooklyn, renting the bottom half of a family's home. It was nice enough, I suppose. None of us had experience with apartments anywhere, so we had nothing with which to compare, and only time would tell, of course, how strange the family was, and from what we'd witnessed already, it was a given, just to what degree? Axe murderers? In the meantime, we cleaned and enjoyed our newfound freedom.

Touring Manhattan, we were duly impressed by the numerous skyscrapers, our necks feeling the strain after only a few hours of sight seeing, but we walked for miles in an attempt to cover every little nook and cranny, not wanting to miss anything.

Our funds were limited, of course, and getting jobs took top priority. Our rent was paid for the month, and we were confident of finding something as soon as we began looking. Sheila kept her appointment for employment as a maid, but I pledged to reimburse the bus fare as soon as possible. I called Trish and she set an appointment for me with one of the company's agents. I was so nervous I needed Corina and Sheila both help me prepare for the interview.

Trish met me in the lobby and escorted me to the appropriate room, leaving me to enter alone and handle it from there. She had given me a pep talk on the elevator, and boosted my confidence enough, I hoped, to see me through. I entered an immense office and the secretary promptly announced my arrival. My nervous system was quickly reaching the meltdown point as the young lady opened the door, ushering me inside the appointed meeting room. My eyes landed on the biggest executive's desk I'd ever seen, covering half of one side of the room. Green plants of the hanging and potted kind practically covered every available space with the exception of the pathways surrounding the desk and doorway. I felt as though I'd entered a rainforest. Perhaps the plants were part of an ad campaign. Whatever the reason, they provided a refreshing, clean fragrance to the air, and I hoped to maneuver myself through, gracefully, not bumping into, or knocking down, any of them.

CHAPTER XIV

Two gentlemen immediately approached me. The first was intimidating, and his eyes began scanning me from head to toe the moment I entered the room, sending my confidence plummeting. And as he neared, hand extended, to introduce himself, I felt like a bug under a microscope. I think he saw every part of my body, except my eyes. His face was angular and made sharper by a pair of square, black glasses. They failed miserably in an attempt to cover his piercing blue eyes, which complemented his chopped short, wavy, black hair. I realized later it was his immense presence that was overwhelming, not his size; he appeared to be no taller than five foot seven or eight. I, at five foot five, didn't find it difficult to look almost directly into his eyes. Mr. Peyton Goeble, or Pate, as he preferred to be called by his associates, informed me of the casualness of the company and the interview, itself, and requested I address him as such. I have to hand it to him, he was trying hard to exude warmth and friendliness, but it wasn't working. Turned out, he was one of three partners and, as he mentioned, made it a point to meet every potential model. Shaking my hand once again, he introduced me to Michael Dreason before making his exit.

Thank goodness, Michael, as he requested I call him, was the designated interviewer. Lighting up the room with his pleasant smile and openness, he was a delight, and not just in comparison. His beautiful gray eyes were quite engaging, and I found it difficult to stay focused on the questions he asked. To say he was handsome was an understatement. I was a great fan of the movies, and with a goofy smile creeping helplessly to my face, I wondered, as I sat soaking him in, why I'd never seen him on the big screen. Somehow, I managed to stumble through with the appropriate answers, and then it was time to audition my hands. He reached across the desk and with the lightest touch I've ever felt from a male, lifted them, turning them over to examine them firmly and carefully. Suddenly, any romantic ideas were dashed as I realized he was, of course, handling, literally, a potential product, but my heart remained hopeful. When I looked up, our eyes met, and I knew, definitely, there was more to his interest than just dollar signs. The chemistry between us was undeniable and obvious, and he suddenly released my hands, cleared his throat, and with all the corporate authority he could muster, declared them acceptable for assignments. I cannot recall, no matter how hard I try, even a miniscule amount of excitement at those words. My head and heart was roiling and teeming only with heat for this Michael Dreason, and when, oh when, would I see him again.

Corina interviewed, on my insistence, and passed her hair audition, and within three weeks, we were both called upon for magazine ad assignments. It was exciting and the pay was great. This New York thing was working out better than I could ever have imagined.

Sheila began her job as planned and was quite happy, and with the money we were making, we visited some of the better salons in the city and all of us, in fact, took advantage of the makeovers offered. Corina and Sheila, whose faces had remained naked all those years, gazed into the mirror and were newly introduced to two very attractive young women. Ah, the magic of makeup. We splurged on shopping sprees that would make every female proud and the apartment was filled with clothes and shoes, shoes and more shoes. We wore the same sizes, give or take a half size, so had a pair to match every outfit. Oh, we were enjoying life and all the young men we were meeting at company parties, but even though they were our age or a few years older, we agreed they seemed immature, and their hormones kept them in a constant prowling state, and us on our toes. Sexual exploitation not being a major part of our agenda, it was a constant battle of the sexes. Our moralistic roots ran deep and even hundreds of miles, and a new culture away, much to the young men's disappointment; we still would not relax our knees. I remember vividly asking Mother once what she would do if I came home with the news I was pregnant. Without a pause, she looked me squarely in the eyes, and stated, "I would kill you." I believed her. And even now, with all the miles separating us, I believed she would find a way.

But yet, after only a few weeks away, and with my new life and all the excitement it contained, I was missing everyone back home: feeling isolated and somewhat disconnected. I was forever thankful I was an avid reader, and a good book always succeeded in chasing away the blues. I was just settling in, book in hand, when the phone rang, disrupting my ugly mood. Unfortunately, as Kiki responded to my dismal hello, sounding distressed and agitated, I realized my blue mood wasn't going to improve with the immediate conversation, and my heart sank. "Kiki, what's going on? Tell me quickly so my mind doesn't have a chance to start fabricating something."

"It's about Sherry," she said, then paused long enough for the fear to intensify. "I mean, she's okay, but, well it's a long story and distressing, but really damn funny at the same time." She had just spoken to Sherry, who was still upset and shaken over an incident that even though she had handled it successfully, was nevertheless, frightening. Seems that Andrew, the mutual friend of the family in Virginia, turned out not to be so trustworthy, after all. He was very charming and sweet, and certainly came through on his promise to connect her to the right people. But he obviously became enamored of Sherry's charms, or was just a creep to begin with. Anyway, he decided he wanted more than just a friendship. One evening, after what she thought to be nothing more than a casual and friendly movie date, Sherry allowed a perfunctory kiss on the cheek and bid him good night at her door. But he was insistent, smoothly inviting himself in, just to chat, he said. The evening was still young, "let's get to know each other a little better," he said. Too soon, however, Sherry discovered to her horror, he was more interested in pillow talk, and when she rebuked his romantic advances, he became angry, and an ensuing battle followed for her honor. Surprisingly and thankfully, she won. So much for our poo-poohing the women's self-defense moves we'd practiced. In the midst of her struggle, she forced her feelings of panic to the recesses of her mind and regained her composure. She desperately hoped and looked for that small window of opportunity, in this case, just enough room to draw her knee back, and once found, shot her right leg and foot out violently, and with the accuracy of a laser guided missile, connected dead center in his crotch. Sherry related later that she couldn't decide which hung open wider, his mouth or his eyes; she was too busy concentrating on his ultimate touchdown. He was headed for a newly acquired, beautiful vase, she, just that day, had filled with a lovely bouquet of spring flowers, and hoped desperately he was going to miss it. *Bam!* went his body as it slammed, instead, into the door leading into the hall. Unfortunately, the noise brought out the other two tenants, who were left staring bug-eyed at Andrew's distressed and perplexed face as he expanded his quick exit to the hall and beyond. Sherry assured them she was fine; the noise was just the television turned up too loud. But their knitted eyebrows and expressions filled with doubt and curiosity, loudly questioned the validity of her statement. With apologies all around, she retreated inside, shaken to the bone, and quickly assessed what had just taken place. She smiled broadly, and smacking her hands together gleefully, felt pride well up inside her as she had never felt before. "I am woman! Yeah!"

I thanked Kiki for being such a pain in the butt about that martial arts thing, after all. It was phenomenal, shocking and wonderful all at the same time. But even more than that, it reminded me of a similar experience Lora had, just two years ago. As Kiki related the story of Andrew being so smooth and sweet, another handsome young man's face instantly flashed across my mind. It was a Saturday night, and all of us, except Juliet who was with her steady, Stevie Beltski, were at a regular dance club, where we felt very comfortable and knew just about everyone, just about. Justin Riggs asked Lora to dance almost immediately upon our arrival, and being attracted to him, she acquiesced when he invited himself to our table, which raised some verbal protests from the rest of us. We had a "no pick-up" policy for obvious reasons. But for the next three hours, until the remainder of the evening, they talked and danced and she felt, perhaps, she'd stumbled into a potentially serious relationship. And though every conceivable argument was used to persuade her later not to leave with him, to escort her home, she didn't listen. He was wonderful, she said, after all she'd just spent three hours learning about him and his family. Sometimes you had to use common sense and go with your instincts, she said. And at the end of the evening when she approached us, revealing her plan, we of course objected vehemently. And even I, with my much admired, but unpracticed gift of ESP, couldn't dissuade her, our words falling on deaf ears. The rest of the tale has been told and retold, and we laugh uproariously every time, but Lora couldn't find a thing to laugh about that night. Just one half mile from the club, Justin suddenly turned into a vacant gas station, squeezing between the station and the little grocer next door. It was the dead of winter, a very cold, moonless night, with just a dusting of snow allowing for a minimum of illumination. Lora was momentarily perplexed, but believing he wanted to "park," felt giddy and looked forward to their first kiss. But somewhere during the long delicious kiss, she realized his hands were forcing hers down, down to his crotch. Not being frightened but angry, she fought to retrieve them, but not before her hand brushed across warm, hard flesh. Struggling as quickly as possible toward the passenger door, she screamed she was getting out, and ignoring his pleas of forgiveness, did. It was five miles to Mel's house, with whom she was spending the night. Five miles of snow covered, slick highway, and she was wearing three inch heels. We interrupted her story then, emphasizing this not so small detail in light of the long, treacherous walk before her. She enlightened us. "I couldn't think past getting away from him at that moment. I guess that's the way it works with survival: it's one step at a time and when that step's accomplished, you can think about the next one." And it didn't take long for her to think about that next one. As soon as she removed herself from any potentially imminent danger, she only had to lay eyes on the icy highway looming ahead of her to realize, perhaps, she had stepped out of the frying pan into the fire. But, nevertheless, with her pride bundled up warmly and smoothing the wrinkles from her dignity, she began to slip and slide down the darkened road. Within seconds, Justin pulled up alongside her, pleading with her to get back in, promising he wouldn't do any such stupid thing again. Well, she was thinking, it's possible, of course. He could've been testing me. Any creep looking for sex would certainly try, but now he knows. So with those comforting thoughts supporting her, better than the three inch heels were, she slowly and cautiously climbed back in. Well, it turned out that Justin was not only a sex creep, but a liar, too. For just three miles down the road, he pulled off the road onto a ball field. And although it lay at the bottom of a well populated community, everyone was certainly asleep at this late hour, and not a car had yet passed them on the highway. So much for hitching a ride...and maybe she'd end up getting picked up by another creep like Justin or worse! This time she didn't give him an opportunity to get near her, but instead, began screaming at him with threats of severe violence against his body, and especially that crotch area, if he didn't get the car back on the road and get her home...*Now!!* She'll never forget the look of pure fear that registered in his eyes. Or the feeling of control and empowerment she felt at that moment. It was inspirational. She was intelligent enough to realize that only because Justin was not a psychopath, she succeeded, but when it's the only weapon you're packing, use it. Not another word passed between them on the way to Mel's. Now, you'd say, that was enough indignities for one night, except the night wasn't over. Mel lived on a very steep hill, at the bottom of which were steps leading up to the house. Lora requested to be dropped off there, but she certainly didn't mean it literally. Justin pulled the car up to the steps, and because the two lane highway was so narrow, and Mel's house sat in a curve, his vehicle tightly hugged the edge of the road. A deep ditch lay between the road, for which Justin's car was hugging the edge of, and the bottom step. Lora was thrilled to be safely home, and that sense of security suddenly rose up, filling her with a sense of smugness that she was anxious to flaunt squarely in Justin's face. She could hear him still mumbling apologies and did she hear him actually asking for her phone number? Unbelievably, that's what he was doing. *Well*, she thought, *I can certainly tell him a thing or two more, now that I'm within walking distance of the house.* She had to walk up to the driver's door, to reach the first step, as Justin had not moved, and she placed her hand on his opened window for support before spanning the ditch onto the waiting step. But before she could open her mouth, her foot, slipping off the slick edge of the road, disappeared into the ditch and the remainder of her body followed as quickly as a lightening flash. Her first thought was to feign death, but it was too damn cold and wet to stay put. And much to Justin's credit, he didn't laugh, not that she heard, anyway, but offered assistance, to which Lora screamed, "*No!!* Just get the hell outta here!" which he did. Neither she nor any of the rest of us ever saw him again.

She was left shaken for days, reliving the incident and imagining other potentially horrifying endings to an otherwise harmless night. And armed with the knowledge of the after effects of such a violation, I was concerned about Sherry's present state of mind, but Kiki placated me. Not only was she not suffering any residual trauma, "it's inspired her to do some interviewing on college campuses; snooping around to see if she could find other young woman who had experienced such a thing and turn this whole episode into an article for the newspaper."

"That's wonderful. It may prove to be even more serendipitous than that. Being the romantic that she is, this gives her an opportunity to cull out all the creeps and maybe she'll meet someone. Wouldn't that be ironic? God does work in mysterious ways, and to hear Lora talk, all you have to do is appear somewhere near the campus, and men of every type magically appear for the taking."

CHAPTER XV

Sherry discovered, much to her dismay, that she wasn't alone in her unfortunate experience. One out of every five girls interviewed stated that their dates didn't respond quickly enough to "no," but had to gently but firmly be fought off. And consequently her findings, in the form of a three-part series, produced and written by our very own Sherry, were carried not only by her paper but two other newspapers as well. Proud as a peacock and feeling like a celebrity, she bought papers for everyone, and we too were as proud as parents with their first born. The telephone lines were kept humming between the states as we called her with congratulations. Never a week went by without our updating each other on our successes and/or failures anyway, but it was nice to call and share something so spectacular with a friend. And although Sherry wasn't successful at producing her knight in shining armor from the campus, it turned out to be unnecessary, as he literally turned up on her doorstep.

Almon Moon, a gentle young man of east Indian heritage, had graduated high school with honors and was attending the local college on a football scholarship. The scholarship, along with his independent nature and strong work ethic would prove to be all that was necessary to complete his college education.

Almon was the eldest of five children, a big family, but one his father had successfully supported for many years as a plant manager in a large cannery. An out-of-control fire on a cold, winter evening led to serious burns over thirty-five percent of his body, forcing him into early retirement. Almon's mother was an accomplished seamstress with a loyal following and with the two incomes, they managed to take care of their growing family quite well.

The Moon family had lived comfortably in Milton since Almon's birth and

Mr. Moon planned on each and every member to be buried there. It was a wonderful place to live, but every city and small town, at that time, was divided into segregated areas, each carrying its own set of traditions and values. Milton was no exception. And it was expected each generation would carry the torch of those values, and to do so with pride.

Though Almon loved his family deeply, the fires of his torch began to dim noticeably during the course of his journey into manhood. Enlightenment took a firm hold during his college years and the reflection of his family against the backdrop of his revelations, blatantly revealed the prevailing attitude of prejudice. Many hours were spent in hot debates, escalating to hateful arguments between Almon and his father, who was devastated by his son's radical thinking. They'd reached a stalemate. Almon was saddened by the turn of events, but was determined it would not affect him or his future. That future included the partner with whom he would choose to spend the rest of his life. But as Mr. Moon had disclosed to Almon, his family not only assumed, but expected the children to marry one of their "own," and settle down within the confines of the neighborhood.

Ironically, he'd also been emphatic with his teachings, encouraging them to think for themselves…this was America, after all, anything was possible. Anything, Almon came to realize, as long as his father agreed to it.

Sherry, too, was raised in a traditional, hard-working family and happily so, but small towns such as Milton rarely afforded opportunities for contacts with other races or ethnic groups. And her parents were in agreement with Mr. Moon that the socializing needs of their children should be met within their own community. But as diligently as the parents worked to ingrain the cherished traditions of their respective cultures into the lives of their children, a dilution was inevitable with the ensuing generations, and as sure as the sun rose each day, rebellion, too, would follow.

Kiki was visiting Sherry on a rare weekend off, and spending as much time in a bar as she did, had no inclinations to go bar hopping… neither did Sherry, as she grabbed at any opportunity to stay at home since her job entailed driving all day. So having pizza delivered sounded great. Visiting, not food, after all, was the priority. They hadn't seen each other for at least a month and were excited at the prospect of quiet time and catching up. Kiki was still Sherry's only friend. Sherry devoted herself to her job, completely, and had no desire to take the time and energy necessary to develop new relationships. She was still feeling the flush of success with her dating article, when her supervisor, Chris Whitley, surprised her with news it was time for her "christening," the newspaper's term for the rookie's first exposure to a murder scene. Sherry was apprehensive. Her experiences with murder, to this point, had been in books, and facing the reality of it, was a sobering thought, but, nonetheless, an exciting one, and she proceeded to mentally prepare herself.

It was gruesome…she expected nothing less, and as she succeeded in remaining upright and stable to the end of the investigation, and kept the contents of her lunch intact, Chris gave her the thumbs up sign.

She'd nearly filled a notebook with what she saw and heard, and looked forward to studying it with the anticipatory thought racing through her mind that she would extract a piece of the puzzle which would, ultimately, solve the case. That was the brass ring, after all, and it was more exciting to her than anything she could imagine; but then, her pizza hadn't arrived yet.

Kiki hadn't eaten since breakfast, and was glad when the doorbell rang, announcing food, and with her usual exuberance, threw the door open wide. Her eyes grew large and a seductive smile spread eagerly across her mouth at the sight of the gorgeous man standing before her. And being Kiki, she immediately set her sights for another trophy to add to her collection.

"Well, hellllooo….hellooooo!" Kiki said, not taking her eyes from his. "Don't just stand there, bring your beautiful self in."

Sherry, hearing Kiki's flirtatious comments, rushed to join them for the protection of the young man. But the moment Sherry looked into Almon's huge dark eyes, she came to an abrupt halt. She heard bells alright, not just ringing, but clanging. Her temples actually began to ache from the explosive and rapid pulse of her heart. Gulping for a breath, she collected herself enough to whisper, "Hi."

Almon smiled self-consciously, having two attractive ladies standing there staring at him so intently. But as Sherry stated later, she believed the feelings running amok in her heart and mind, were mutual. It was obvious he was in no hurry to leave, but when Kiki invited him in, and without taking his eyes from Sherry's, he mumbled quietly that he had to get on with his deliveries. Kiki was experienced in the art of love, at least more so than Sherry, and was well aware she was witnessing something marvelous taking place.

Almon finally turned slowly, but managed to look back three times before finally driving off. Sherry stayed, hugging the door, reluctant to leave the residual, aura of their first meeting, and watched until his car was out of sight. Kiki laughed, as she pulled her friend away in order to close the door and watched Sherry walk, dazed, toward the kitchen.

Sherry confided to Kiki later that looking at him, her brain seemed to suspend momentarily from thinking or speaking. She was a neophyte where love was concerned and the giddiness and warmth found a lovely place to rest inside her as she discussed with Kiki the possibility of "love at first sight." They talked into the wee hours, and as Sherry reluctantly climbed into bed with Almon's handsome face filling her mind, she was lulled into a night of delicious dreams.

It was the uniting of two sweet souls, and sherry found herself ordering pizzas on nights when she didn't want pizza. After each delivery, Sherry would call Kiki, keeping her posted on the progress of the relationship, but, ultimately, a long discussion would ensue regarding Almon's heritage and the prejudice of their respective families and communities. Of course, Kiki would never let it bother her. But Sherry wasn't Kiki, and she knew she was letting herself in for a battle…one she'd be powerless to stop.

What an example of the ultimate irony. Sherry was the conformist, the devoted daughter who volunteered for community projects and hospital work, and never sought attention. It was obvious to everyone who knew her that she'd been blind sighted by cupid.

So began their relationship, tentatively, and discreetly of course, for obvious reasons. It was weeks and weeks of long talks, getting acquainted when he brought her pizza, before she agreed to see him publicly, and even then, it was in a secluded hideaway. Faithful Kiki played chaperone to prevent more tongues from wagging, and could be found sitting right beside Sherry at every outing. Sherry's life to this point had been wonderful, and the few nasty bumps had been overcome with great success. But alas, the pendulum will inevitably swing back. This time the nasty bump came in the form of Sherry's Aunt Jessie. She made a surprise visit one weekend, and though Sherry made a feeble attempt to explain Almon's presence, the sexual heat generated between the two left no room for doubt they were romantically involved, and Aunt Jessie wasted no time in calling Sherry's parents to break the distressful news.

Almon had a sweet spirit and judged people's worth by what they carried in their heart and was disheartened momentarily knowing the rumors would run rampant affecting all parties involved, and he braced himself for what he knew would be an onslaught of anger and frustration from his family because of his "disgraceful" behavior.

What a match these two were. If the world were full of Almons and Sherrys, and love, gentleness and caring could solve life's problems, we'd be living in Utopia. But for now, there was no utopia, not for Sherry and Almon or anyone that loved and cared for them.

Sherry bombarded her mother and father with phone calls, pleading with them to meet with Almon, to trust her instincts and judgment and take that opportunity to discover for themselves, what she had found…a kind, generous and loving young man. But they were unrelenting. It was, thankfully, an easier road with Sherry's friends, who were optimistic her parents would eventually conclude it was better to have their daughter under any circumstances, than not at all. Oh, how she cherished their support, and she tried to share their optimism, especially since she made it very clear that her love for Almon was not a passing infatuation or an act of rebellion. But the continued rebuttals and refusals were taking a toll, and Sherry was terrified she'd be forced to surrender her parents to their prejudice. Her heart was breaking because of the chasm, but to give Almon up was unthinkable. They would just have to yield. Some way, some how, she would make them understand.

CHAPTER XVI

After a hectic but exciting weekend of partying and outings, it was back to work for me – but I was loving it. The first several weeks had been spent learning the ropes and getting acquainted with the sets, the terminology, and the people with whom I'd be working. Everyone was patient and wonderful and I looked forward to a long and successful run with the agency. Funny thought that in the mornings, as I stood before the mirror, taking stock of my hair and the little makeup I wore, I realized that, on the job, no one really cared. It was my hands that kept their rapt attention. I wondered, laughing to myself, if anyone even knew my eyes and hair were dark brown. But this Monday, for some unexplainable reason, unless a little of the ESP thing was sneaking in, I had taken more care than usual with my appearance. The girls I worked with were either knockouts or knew the art of making up, and so every once in a while I'd be inspired to add a touch of glamour to my otherwise casual look. And it wasn't easy for me, preferring the natural look. Ribbons and lace were not my style: give me leather and denim. Nevertheless, I spent extra time powdering and coiffing and I was ultimately satisfied with the end results, but that satisfaction nearly caused me to miss the subway, and it only reinforced my priorities… why I didn't do this routinely. I hated being rushed, and liked sleeping as long as possible.

The morning seemed endless, as I was not being shot. Instead, I was subjected to reviewing ads and fighting off boredom. Finally at noon, as usual, I headed for the lunchroom, and also as usual, I headed there alone. A select few of the women had invited me to join them on more than one occasion, but finally stopped asking, since I never accepted. Either I was more of a loner than I realized, or I was aware, innately, that a soul mate wasn't to be found among them. Anyway, I disliked shopping, and for me, spending money eating out every day seemed a waste. I was tucking any extra cash away in my "dream jar," with the intent of someday traveling to exciting places, not only in the United States, but Europe as well. But most of all, I detested the pettiness of office gossip, and since the others had given me the rundown on everyone else, I figured they'd now have the opportunity to dissect me. Plus, I enjoyed the quiet break from my work, and I always found something worthwhile to read while eating. And as usual, spotting an interesting magazine, I picked it up from the table on my way in, got comfortable and had just taken a bite of my sandwich, when I heard the rumble of a man's low, sexy voice. "Interesting?" I first ignored "it," thinking "it" was speaking to someone else. But "it" asked again, so I looked, discreetly, out of curiosity. As I turned, I gulped my food, hurting my throat in an attempt to swallow, and my eyes focused on Michael's gorgeous gray, half lidded ones, gazing back at me. I recognized him instantly, of course, and felt a rush of excitement even though I was, at that moment, filled with extreme discomfort, wrestling with the bite of food still battling with my tongue for position – and, oh my God, I began an uncontrollable coughing fit. I knew my eyes were attempting to pop from their sockets and my distorted face would be frightening even to the most stouthearted of men. Michael, comprehending my predicament, immediately grabbed up the soda, shoving it at me just as I turned my body to head out of the room in total humiliation. Timing is everything. I hit the can full force and watched in horror as the contents literally exploded onto his face and hair. I caught one last impression of the sticky liquid dripping from his eyebrows and nose as I made my exit, hoping I would die before days end. How cruel and insensitive fate could be. Hmmm. I wondered facetiously if I should mark him off my list as a potential date.

Corina and Sheila lamented with me, initially, about my bad luck, but before it was all said and done they laughed until they cried. I wasn't in a frame of mind, yet, to find it humorous, since I might be seeing him the next day. Well, I needn't have worried, I wouldn't see him again for weeks. I wasn't even certain if he worked here permanently, or worked for several different agencies. And oh, my emotions were painfully conflicted. My desire to see him again was very strong, but how I dreaded the thought of facing him. It's amazing the stress such an episode can inflict on the body, and I felt great relief each day as I returned home. Friday couldn't come soon enough as I was looking forward to a fun weekend. Consequently, my mood that morning was a light and happy one. I dressed casually but still with special care in hopes of seeing this gray-eyed, gorgeous man again in person, instead of only in my fantasies. And again, spending extra time with my makeup I was running behind, missed the subway and arrived thirty minutes late for work. Hurrying at top speed to the break room for my much-needed second cup of coffee, I quickly pushed the door open, rushing inside and smacked right into a hard body. The impact knocked me back about two feet and a coffee cup went whizzing in the air and landed with a sickly cracking sound, with coffee flying everywhere. Regaining my balance, I stood frozen, and slowly raised my head, allowing myself to look, remorsefully, into the surely angry face of my victim. And found myself staring into that same beautiful face I'd gazed into with horrid humiliation on that fateful Monday, surrounded by the all too familiar look of shock and surprise. We were picking up exactly where we left off. His gasping sounds from the surprise collision and the scalding coffee jolted me back to reality and I immediately grabbed for napkins to help clean up the mess. My first instinct, after killing myself of course, was to immediately proceed with an attempt to dab at the coffee, which was splattered over his beautiful blue-gray suit, but I was afraid he might strike me. My face was aflame and I mumbled incessant apologies. I just wanted to be swallowed up by the building...transported out of there...*now*! No such luck, and instead, in the midst of my babbling, suddenly, he exploded with laughter. It startled me so, I stumbled back, lost my balance on the still wet floor and barely escaped another disaster by latching onto the door. No one has ever possibly removed themselves more quickly from the presence of another human being. I concocted an excuse to the supervisor, went home, and thought seriously about never returning. Instead, I opted for spending the rest of my life in a bubble bath, crying.

My sweet friends empathized with me this time, and couldn't bring themselves to even smile, or at least they had the decency not to in my presence. They were going out with some new friends and, mercifully, my mind was preoccupied with their preparations for the evening. We laughed and talked as they tried on first one dress than another, but I finally left them, realizing it'd be several outfits later before a decision was made. Besides, my bath was waiting and I burdened it heavily with the responsibility of lifting my sagging spirits, and then to bed to bury my miserable thoughts in a good book.

I lounged lazily in the tub, enjoying the heat as it caressed and soothed my aching mind, lulling me into blessed nothingness. *Brain dead has its advantages*, I was thinking as I gathered my shampooed hair into a towel, turban-style. The phone rang, and I yelled over the loud music for someone to catch it. It was usually for them anyway; their date books were always full to overflowing. I was happy for them, but I refused any attempts to be fixed up, preferring to sit at home rather than go out just for the sake of going out. After the fourth ring, I ran to the phone, quite irritated. My hair, only half in the towel, tumbled back out, cascading over my face. And attempting to blow it aside, while holding the towel in one hand and grabbing the phone in the other, I practically screamed hello with disgust dripping from my voice. Instantly I recognized the low, sexy voice. I couldn't speak. A void had settled where my vocal chords once resided. Michael spoke my name. "Rainey?" It was like the purr of a mountain lion. I hesitantly said, "yes," and mouthed a silent prayer to untangle my tongue. I was not going to have another fiasco. I asked him to please hold a moment, went to the kitchen, got a drink of water, stepped out on our small balcony, screamed as loudly as I dared with neighbors so close, to release the tension in my body, cleared my throat and went back to the phone. By damn, this time I was determined to sound like the self-assured, young woman I knew I could be, but oh how I hoped he couldn't hear my knees knocking or my heart pounding. Then, suddenly, the thought crossed my mind that he might be calling to warn me of a lawsuit for his third degree burns. Hmm, I was curious to know how he had gotten my phone number, and as though reading my thoughts, he quickly explained that as a partner at the agency, he had access, and though it was a conflict of interest to obtain phone numbers for personal use, he couldn't be certain either of us would survive our next meeting, so he decided to "meet me" on the phone, and if I was offended, he said, we would hang up and he'd never call again. Well, that broke the ice and I laughed, embarrassingly, and asked. "Just which accident exactly was it that attracted you?"

"Well," he said laughing, "actually, I enjoyed our first meeting the most… you know, the one where there were no drinks involved?"

"Okay," laughing, I said. "I think we've milked this for all it's worth." And then, suddenly, we were faced with one of those interminably long pauses. We were both filled with a million questions and the desire to ask them, but how and where to begin? Michael, thankfully, filled the gap. "I suspected you were being really hard on yourself and I wanted to talk to you to let you know, believe it or not, I've had worse things happen, and by people who were not nearly as pretty."

This was definitely a man with possibilities, this Michael Dreason. At twenty eight, he was a few years…several years older, actually, than the man of my dreams, but the vision of his handsome face looming across my mind, wiped away any concerns about the age gap. His boyish good looks belied the worldly experience he had tucked securely under his belt. Joining the Army at eighteen, he grabbed at the opportunity to turn a love of photography into a career as a war correspondent, traveling into hot spots around the world. Serendipitously, he discovered the mountains that would soon become the objects of his obsession for climbing. Upon his discharge, he, along with two close friends had immediately begun intensive training, spending weeks at a time, gaining experience trekking over the different mountain ranges, each with its own unique topography. And though he had enjoyed many years of climbing, his dream, his ultimate goal, optimistically, was to conquer Mt. Everest in three years, and the joy and exuberance in his voice as he spoke about it was inspirational.

Other than the mountain climbing, we had a lot in common. For starters, he, too, was a huge rock and roll fan, and discovering that, invited me to an Evil Mind concert in two weeks. I told him I'd get back to him, not wanting to appear too anxious or accommodating, but lord, he had to be hearing the pounding of my heart. We chatted for at least thirty minutes more, flirting a little, and exchanging the superficial information about our families. His father was a retired architect and kept his hand in now and then, freelancing, and his mother dabbled in real estate strictly as a hobby. When Michael's youngest sister left home, his parents fulfilled a lifelong dream of moving to California, and naturally, Mr. Dreason designed their beach home. Michael's happiness for their accomplishment was dampened by the fact that they saw each other only once or twice a year, and except for their trepidations over their son's mountain climbing which was certainly understandable, they enjoyed a wonderful relationship. I had to admit, though, it added an extra, exciting dimension to his personality, and by the end of our conversation, I was floating, dreamily, at twenty five thousand feet myself. Sleep managed to interrupt my dreams a couple of times that night, and it was going to be difficult to wait until Monday, to hopefully see him again.

CHAPTER XVII

I was now thankful I'd been experimenting with makeup the last few weeks. I had become expert at applying it quickly and no longer worried about running late. But it didn't matter, my hopes were dashed as he was nowhere to be seen, and I moped the rest of the afternoon and evening, with monotony relieved, and moments highlighted, only by reliving our conversation over and over. And if I was depressed because I hadn't seen Michael all that day, I emotionally hit rock bottom when I overheard through the rumor mill that he would be out of town as long as three weeks. I was incredulous that he hadn't related this to me during our phone conversation. Maybe he felt it was too early in a relationship for disclosing his plans to me. Well, maybe, but it seemed a common courtesy. At any rate, I was devastated. Well it was time for a visit home, anyway. My assignments were completed and nothing new was in the works for a few weeks. My contract specified that between assignments, I was entitled to two weeks off because some of them ran three or four consecutively. It had been too long since I'd been home and the more I thought about it, the more excited I got. Corina and Sheila wanted to come along, but Corina was booked for the next month, and Sheila wasn't due a vacation for another couple of months. So I caught the next flight out that very evening. No buses, thank you!

It was wonderful reconnecting with Kiki and Sherry, who was visiting for the weekend, and we picked up right where we left off. Kiki was as wild as ever and fighting against her addiction to alcohol daily, unfortunately, losing most days.

I met Almon and he was as sweet and wonderful has he'd been described to me. Sherry was a very lucky young lady, indeed. Almon and I had many controversial conversations regarding politics and the world's problems in general; they were heated sometimes, but never acrimonious. His true interest was politics and his goal was to be Dr. Moon, teaching Political Science in a good college or university.

It was a wonderful weekend, relaxing and catching up on everyone and, of course, ended much too quickly. But my disappointment was tempered by thoughts of Michael, even though he wasn't there, at least I'd be back on his turf. And there was always the possibility he'd return sooner than expected, I could only hope.

It was a beautiful spring evening and Corina and Sheila were meeting with a group of friends trying to locate a new dance club and, as usual, invited me along. And also as usual, I thanked them but looked forward to spending the evening alone after a hectic week away. I felt the need for a relaxing, cool shower, do some reading, listen to music, some mellow classical thing, to help me unwind. I was rounding up the music and being a little distracted as Sheila's Persian cat was rubbing up against my legs. She had consulted with both Corina and me before her acquisition of this new addition to our small apartment, and we saw no harm in it. Little did we know what we were in for. Sheila was an ardent Beatles fan but loved John in particular, so…yes it had to be that the cat was called "Lennon." He was gorgeous, but I, being unfamiliar with the feline family, had no idea how much hair could cover one animal. Nor did I know he would so generously share it with us and the entire house. It was everywhere. So much for having the basic black dress hanging at the ready in the closet. It became evident very quickly we had a choice to make between the cat or any clothing even resembling dark. Sheila begged for time before we threw Lennon out the window or fed him to the Rotweiler living next door that strained at his leash and slobbered profusely every time he spotted him. She bought different brushes and promised that with a good brushing everyday…outside, the problem would be solved. I suggested an industrial strength vacuum cleaner. She didn't see the humor at this point, well, neither did we. We'd know within a few days. But in the meantime, we covered all bases by wearing light color clothes as much as possible and kept all food well covered. I found myself enjoying Lennon's company, in spite of his relentless shedding, and, I had to admit, the purring was comforting. And as usual, as soon as someone headed for a chair, Lennon would be following close behind, jumping and ready to alight as soon as a lap was formed. And we had to be very careful for sometimes his timing was off and he'd light before we sat, and it was quite a sight watching us attempt to suddenly abort touchdown. I have to admit he is one smart cat; it's only taken two good squashings for him to have wised up and lost his eagerness. Now he looked up at me hopefully, ingratiating himself by winding in and out of my legs, as I attempted to not fall over him as I settled in my favorite reading chair. It didn't take but a whimper of an invitation for him to jump, agilely onto my lap. He wound around two or three times before he settled, eyes blinking lazily as he, I suppose, slipped easily into literally a catnap. What a life. Conscious of Lennon and not wanting to disturb him, I was snuggled comfortably with the intention of staying in that position…a while, anyway, and was concentrating on a particularly interesting article, when the explosive ring of the phone disrupted the tranquility, and, startled, I jerked upright. Consequently, Lennon jumped also, hitting my cup, sending a geyser of hot coffee over the pages of my book and down into my lap, but his explosive ejection spared his hide from any burns. He became nothing more than a white bolt of fur flying across the room, and out of sight. I spotted him later in a corner in the bathroom, curled up on Sheila's discarded pajama bottom. He didn't even bother to look at me when I entered the room. I found out that Lennon's personality didn't lend itself well to forgiveness.

Stinging from the hot coffee, I hesitated only momentarily not to answer. It was as though the ringing itself was ominous, an announcement of something urgent on the other end, but feeling compelled to answer, I lifted the phone hesitantly, afraid of what I was about to become engaged in. The moment reminding me again of the moment Mother revealed to me at the tender age of twelve that she'd seen evidence I possessed this "gift," passed down from her sister.

Great Aunt Seddy had the gift or curse depending on one's point of view. She viewed it as a gift as did many in the surrounding communities who had benefited from her divining. Grandmother had recognized her penchant for the supernatural even as a child, and watched at a respectful distance as she practiced her art faithfully. Many evenings as a child, I remember vividly, Mother relating Aunt Seddy's hair-raising stories. I've shoved the spirits and visions to the recesses of my mind and, instead, liked to think about the valuable experiences she had. One in particular stands out. World War I was literally exploding all over Europe in 1916, and Aunt Seddy, born and raised in Sarajevo, lived next door to her best friend Duska whose one and only son was sent off to war months earlier. He had been as faithful as one could hope for with his correspondence, but when several months had passed and not a word had been received, her fear for his safety naturally intensified. Great Aunt Seddy was there, consoling and comforting her as best she could. One night in the wee hours of the morning, Aunt Seddy suddenly sat straight up in bed, hearing Duska's son, Joseph, calling to his mother. The tone and inflection of his summons revealed intense suffering. Seddy, torn and indecisive, was hesitant to rush to her friend, not wanting to terrify her if what she had experienced was nothing more than a release of tension and misery she had been sharing with Duska. She sat, rocking by the window, staring into the yet darkened night, wringing her hands and tears flowing. Within the hour, she realized she could not deny the sense of urgency she felt inside, compelling her to take action, and tossing a heavy, wool shawl around her shoulders, she set off to relate the frightful premonition to Duska. Motivated by love and fear, Duska quickly located two local men friends, and riding horseback for two days, they found her son, who indeed had been desperately injured and lay half dead in a makeshift hospital. She sat at his bedside, lovingly holding his hands, willing him to live, moving only out of necessity for nearly a week. He did survive and healed completely, and the doctor's agreed that without her presence and prayers, he wouldn't have.

I had never had, nor did I want, such responsibility. That may sound selfish and perhaps it is, but I also believed because I possessed such an attitude, I would handle it badly. Leave it to the ones who desire it. I have had a few minor experiences in the past, such as "knowing" what to expect when the telephone rang, and I wanted it to stay that way. Mother attempted to convince me to explore its possibilities, but the supernatural frightened me, and besides, I had difficulties enough dealing with everyday problems, I certainly didn't have any desire to "see" what was coming down the pike. The stories did serve me well as a child, though, socially speaking. There were a few summer evenings when a continuous rain discouraged any thoughts of running and playing hide and seek or tag on the water-soaked ground. Consequently, the entire group of ragtag neighborhood kids would, instead, huddle together under blankets on a neighbor's porch to indulge in one of our favorite pastimes…telling scary stories. I was always the hit of the evening, as I related the spookiest tales. Mine were designated the best, not only because of their content, but because they were supposedly true! And as much as I fought the inclination to believe in them myself, or anything supernatural, it was made extremely difficult, due to a pretty lady who by reputation, was an authentic witch, living right there among us. So what? You would say. Just because she says it's so, doesn't make it so. Sounds reasonable, but her activities, which took place throughout those summer months, lent plenty of credibility and validity to the claim. Many late evenings, too numerous too mention, and always around nine thirty p.m., after full darkness, our playtime would come to an abrupt end as "Callie Browning," a resident of our community, who some claim they had actually seen during the day, would, more often than not, be seen, at night. Spotting her was never easy, dressed all in black as she was and furtively walking in the direction of the nearby woods. The first time we saw her, we innocently began yelling hello, as was normal under the circumstances. But realizing not only was she not responding to our salutations, she never veered her eyes or her steps from her intended destination. A deathly silence descended on the group as we watched her, seemingly in a trance; walk steadily, without wavering, until she disappeared right before our disbelieving eyes, into the pitch black woods. The hair stood up on the back of our necks. Some of those nights, wild shrieking or howling could be heard. On those occasions, a vacant spot would instantly appear, where moments before, several kids had been. Other nights, when we were as sure as we could be that there would be no shrieking or howling, we'd muster up the courage, and walking as one, edge as close to the woods as we dared, for hopefully, a closer look. It was then that we'd see and smell strange smoke, grayish, light wisps, snaking slowly up through the trees, to find an outlet to the dark sky above. Those were the nights without a moon, or at best, a sliver, but a full moon obviously held some special significance, as we would later discover. Although she would be dressed in black from head to toe, as usual, she'd also be carrying a huge, black bag or sack, gathered at the top, and filled full of something which created a "lumpy" look; we were afraid to know what. But strangest of all, on those particular nights, nothing happened, at least that we were aware of. Not a sound, no smoke, no smells and no shrieking or howling. For some reason, we found that to be most frightening of all, and it was during those bright lit evenings, we attempted to find refuge, to seek out a secluded spot from which to view her without her viewing us. At this point, fear of Callie Browning, and what we perceived to be her magic powers, was steeped into our souls, and we would've died from fright at her approach. Thankfully, she never tested us, and after three months of summer, and the stress and fear induced by the mysterious and spooky Callie Browning with her supernatural goings-on, we looked forward to winter nights, when we'd be snugly ensconced in front of a roaring fire as huge, beautiful snowflakes piled up outside our door, gladly leaving Callie to the woods and her witchery. We couldn't tell you to this day, if she ever knew we were there, watching her every move.

CHAPTER XVIII

Tales of the supernatural were as close as I wanted to get to the ether world, but from time to time, it sneaked up on me, as now with Sherry's call. And very quickly she confirmed my premonition that this wasn't a social call. It was difficult to understand her, at first, and either she had to slow down her delivery or I had to speed up my hearing. I think we met halfway, and I finally deciphered enough to know Juliet was in trouble and needed our help, urgently.

"Just hold tight," she said. "I've called everyone else, and I'll call you as soon as I have more information, I just wanted to prepare you in case it's not good."

My heart was racing. "Is it an accident? Has she been hurt?"

"No, no, nothing like that, it's got something to do with the guy she's dating…not a very nice one, from what I'm learning."

This emotional turmoil would be in play for another three days before it was Juliet, herself, who called Sherry, still in a bad emotional state but, at last, revealed her present problems with her boyfriend, Rich. She spoke extensively of his hot temper and verbal abuse. Juliet certainly had no psychological or emotional ammo to defuse or cope with someone else's problems. She hadn't figured out, yet, how to deal with her own. Sherry reassured her we were available to her, not only for emotional support, but would physically rescue her if necessary. Frustratingly, she refused to reveal her location, asking at this time, for a friendly ear only. That was difficult. She wanted to pour out her misery and hurt on us, but discouraged any kind of resolution. It wouldn't be long before there was an emotional explosion from one of us, and the obvious candidate, of course, would be Kiki.

It was during the course of another hurried conversation with Sherry that I discovered Juliet had left Maine permanently the previous month. The last I'd spoken with her, she seemed rather content…for Juliet. She'd been working as a cashier in a small gift shop, and was still taking business classes. She found the cold ocean air invigorating and in conversations with her, she'd described Maine in such glowing terms I thought it had replaced Florida as her decided home state. But no, she still yearned for Florida. And it was becoming evident the rest of the family shared her sentiment. Her parents moved there after Juliet's youngest sister graduated, to live in the same community as one of Katie's brothers and his family. Her father Charles continued to pastor at a small church in a coastal town called Elton.

As the story continued to unfold, it seemed that Juliet met, and apparently fell hard for, Rich Vanderling, a twenty eight-year-old buyer for a string of family-owned gift shops lining the Gulf Coast. He was, in fact, in Maine on a buying expedition when they met. They hit it off immediately and soon Juliet was traveling with him back and forth before settling somewhere in Florida, but no one knew exactly where. Calls to Juliet's sister, Ellen proved to be revealing, at least where Rich was concerned. She wanted him out of Juliet's life, the quicker, the better. Although he truly was disarming at their first meeting, it didn't take long to discover his brooding and misogynistic attitude. And she'd witnessed the barrage of verbal abuse aimed at Juliet on more than one occasion. Although she certainly understood Juliet's initial attraction to him: He was beautiful. His medium brown hair had surrendered to a coup by blonde streaks developed through exposure to the hot Florida sun, and it shone like spun gold. His strong jaw supported a deep cleft and his skin was flawless. But it was his intensely black eyes with dark lashes which pulled you in. When they flashed with vulnerability and sweetness, they could melt ice, but the next second they could fill with a fierce anger, and they did in Ellen's presence. She feared for Juliet. She found it inconceivable and certainly incongruous that something so beautiful could house something so vile and ugly. But any negative comments she made about him to Juliet only encouraged her to defend him, and finally, Ellen, realizing the futility of it, never mentioned him again.

One evening as I sat contemplating our lives since graduation, it dawned on me that fate seemed to be working a "hit list," of sorts. First, Kiki, then Sherry, and now Juliet. I wondered which of us was next, and it was unsettling. I involved myself in an entertaining book for the remainder of the evening to attempt to replace, or better yet, erase such depressing thoughts.

Sherry's call had prompted a telephone marathon that lasted for days. We called every family member we could locate, to no avail. We were feeling helpless with nothing left to do but wait for Juliet to contact us again.

At least it was pleasant revisiting with her family and I especially enjoyed reminiscing with her brother Rob who was only two years my senior. He owned an office equipment business on the east coast, which surprised me. He was never the scholarly type and barely made it through school. But, nevertheless, I remembered him as being ambitious, and I often wondered, without furthering his education, how he expected to reach his monetary goals. He has in spite of it, or perhaps, because of it, and seems very happy. He was the local paperboy when we were adolescents and he was an insufferable tease, and though he was very cute, I never gave him a thought romantically. Obviously, as I found out later, that wasn't true on his part. Often on weekends when we were teens, our parents would permit us to have dances in the basements of our homes, except for Juliet's house due to her father's attitude toward "sinful" music. We all had great record collections, all the "45" hits of the day, and we loved these innocent dance parties. Juliet was a wonderful dancer, and her confidence in her ability showed when she hit the dance floor. All the inhibitions that usually accompany a young lady in her teens magically disappeared. I remember on more than one occasion, dancers stepping aside in the middle of a number, to allow her and her partner to take the spotlight. When I thought back to even earlier times, I realized Juliet sang a lot also. She was very talented, musically. Not that she would ever consider doing anything about it, with her father's religious attitude. He didn't approve of Juliet's making a fool of herself dancing when he was around. But thankfully, for Juliet, his absences afforded her the opportunity to enjoy that outlet for her energy.

It was inevitable that with so many teens coming of age, the hormones would surface at some point and when they did, everyone paired up, seemingly overnight. Juliet was with Stevie, a crush which had turned into a full fledged high school romance, and rarely was one seen without the other. It was very sweet and I was very happy for her. It ended, abruptly, upon graduation, however, as Steve was drafted into the Army. He never moved back and the initial deluge of letters and phone calls subsided to a mere trickle before stopping, altogether.

"We were cozy and comfortable with each other," Juliet told me. "It wasn't like we were in love or anything…and when I think about him, even now, I think of a good friend."

She felt, perhaps Steve was hesitant to contact her, believing she loved him and he wasn't able to reciprocate. It was sad. A great friendship was ruined because of miscommunication. But Juliet felt sometimes the relationship kept her from moving on, and I was proud and happy she handled it so well.

As I quickly scanned the room, the only two people left, were Rob and me. It was very awkward, but only for me, as it turned out. Rob snickered, loving every second of my discomfort, and looking at me, said, "Well Rainey, I guess that leaves you and me."

"Yeah right, in your dreams," I replied lightly, hopefully deterring him.

Rob was a fantastic dancer also, and possessed a dancer's tall lean body, bordering on skinny, and looked great in his clothes. His lithe body contributed to the slow, easy, dance movements, which he executed flawlessly. But I never chose to slow dance with someone I thought of in terms of a brother. Nevertheless, I consented…being the only person left, and when he pressured me, it did seem silly to refuse; it was only a dance, after all. As he placed his arms around me, he drew me tightly to his chest, practically cutting off my air supply. I wiggled a little for breathing room, which encouraged him to pull me even closer. I looked up to tell him to lighten up, but the look in his soft, golden brown eyes stopped me. He softly whispered my name and the sexiness in that small strain of masculinity proved potent enough to activate my, heretofore, nonexistent hormones. A warm, sweet, unfamiliar feeling rushed through my body, instantly flushing my face with sexual heat. I was embarrassed, and felt vulnerable as if I were suddenly half naked in front of him. But I couldn't seem to pull my eyes away from his. He softly whispered my name again, gently lowering his beautiful full lips to mine. We barely touched, but an electric jolt fired off through my system. So this was what it was all about. I was now fully aware of what I'd been missing. He was so sweet, nuzzling and nipping at my neck and ears as the slow sensual music carried us into an, all too short, romantic fantasy and we finished the dance with our feet barely touching the floor. *Wow,* was all I could think, and I looked forward to that feeling again. Rob, fortunately, was accommodating, and every dance, by his design, after that, was slow. The evening ended much too soon, and Rob escorted me home several blocks away, but I don't think my feet ever touched the ground. His goodnight kiss melted over me like warm chocolate and I refused sleep to overtake me until I had relived the evening several times. Now, with a strong physical attraction such as that, one would think a romance would have ensued, but that night stands on it own. We traveled in different circles and I began dating other guys, and rarely saw or spoke to him again. But there have been many lonely nights when I have retrieved those precious memories and relived and relished every sweet moment.

This incident wasn't mentioned as we spoke, now, but we did talk about getting together sometime, and he offered his beach house to us for a visit anytime.

CHAPTER XIX

I was listening to a great radio station as I cleaned, danced and watered the few plants scattered about our sparsely furnished apartment which I'd managed not to kill off just yet. The windows were thrown open wide, and I inhaled the wonderful spring air. The temperature was in the dry seventies, and that was my idea of paradise. The phone rang and, of course, I hoped to hear from Juliet. I had spoken with Sherry, but she had nothing new to relate. It was Kiki, sounding down, but then, she rarely sounded like her old self anymore. She'd regressed back to her old habits of living in the fast lane. She'd experienced more in the last two years then most of us will in twenty, including eloping with some drunk she partied with on a Saturday night, and having it annulled as soon as she sobered up. We hoped it had been a lesson well learned, but of course, with Kiki, it would take banging her head into the wall more often than the average person before wising up. She remarried again within six months. We suspected she was involved with drugs even though we desperately held out hope she was too smart to get involved with the heavier stuff. But she had also pulled away from us emotionally, and we were concerned. Sherry noted that she'd noticed something about Kiki that she'd never thought would possibly happen: the sparkle for life had left her eyes.

We were devising a plan for a therapy session at a date, hopefully in the next few weeks, and in the meantime, intended to inundate her with words loaded with common sense and encouragement with every phone call. Maybe she needed a change, or a new start for motivation, whatever the case, her demons were not giving up easily.

Thrilled with the opportunity to initiate our plan immediately, I was determined to be positive, to keep the mood light in hopes of lifting her spirits a little. I was pleased that true to Kiki's personality, she made a few crude jokes about her soon-to-be-ex-husband, albeit for Kiki, they were low key and perfectly normal. We exchanged pleasantries, and I inquired if she had gotten around to listening to the tapes and reading the material on Yoga I had given her. It was all the rage in California, espousing peace and tranquility to all who practiced religiously, and though we didn't expect miracles, anything that could distract her from the bottle for even short periods of time, would prove helpful. And who knew what the transforming element for her would be? It certainly wasn't any of the men she'd met. And she knew, deep down, the answer wasn't in a bottle, and was amenable to most suggestions. Although we couched every recommendation in delicate terms so we didn't incite her pride or anger at our determination to reform her. And oh, I was thrilled to hear sparks of the old Kiki suddenly come to life as she proceeded to unfold a hilarious tale involving her, Sherry and the tapes. She had promised Sherry an evening devoted strictly to practice, but Kiki, as usual, had had too much to drink. Yoga exercises require the practitioner to slip into low gear, with each move done with slow deliberation, and with full concentration, and even in the best frame of mind, it's difficult to keep one's balance. But with Kiki being tipsy, it was impossible. Consequently, they spent the majority of the next hour untangling their bodies as they lost their balance, falling into each other and onto the floor, laughing. "Hell, I had to actually untie Sherry from one of those damn goofy poses, but I was impressed she got into it in the first place. Of course, I had to force an elbow here, a leg there, until she got it; she looked like a damned pretzel. She started squealing, too, like a stuck pig, for help. Her eyes were bulging out. Oh, I made her beg."

So, she said, though they hadn't necessarily reaped the benefits they were supposed to, they thought it, ultimately, a very positive experience. Except for the above-mentioned for Sherry, of course. And she was seriously considering writing the company, suggesting a little drinking be included while executing the exercises. Kiki said they hadn't laughed that hard in years, and as usual, she had me laughing at a time when she was supposedly hitting rock bottom. Then, her tone changed suddenly to relate the real reason for her call, and it was difficult to immediately acquire the appropriate sense of seriousness. However, Kiki's next few words, spoken softly, and filled with despair, stopped me cold. "Juliet's pregnant." I sucked in my breath, but before I could react, she added, "and there's some kind of problem." I waited anxiously for her to continue immediately, to explain; she didn't.

"Did she get married? To Rich?" I asked. "And do you mean there's a problem with the pregnancy? Or what?" My mind was filled with momentary confusion and a hundred questions.

"Hell no! I hope she never marries that nut case. It's driving us crazy, but that's all I know, or, actually, don't know, except that she's wanting us to get together."

Juliet had called Sherry, unnerving her as she cried through most of the short conversation, speaking quickly and urgently and finally requested an urgent meeting in...*Florida!* Now Juliet knew we were scattered all around the country, so for her to make such a request was an indication it was serious. Being pregnant and unmarried was just about as serious as anything I could imagine. But there was more? Nothing replaces a great imagination, but for the life of us, as we discussed the situation at length, we couldn't produce a scenario or theory to warrant our lives being disrupted at a moments notice. But naturally we'd be there for her, and Kiki volunteered, much to my surprise, to take charge of the travel arrangements, contacting everyone and calling with details later. She advised me to get my airline ticket in the meantime and make arrangements to get off work. Well, I was hoping for a reunion soon, but this was definitely not what I had in mind. And although we were excited at the prospect of an unexpected reunion, it would be impossible to exhibit much happiness and enthusiasm with Juliet's unhappiness uppermost on our minds. We loved her so much and the hurt and pain, whatever it was, and for whatever reason, would permeate our hearts. But I was having conflicting emotions. I was anxious to be reunited with everyone, of course. It had been too long, but what were we facing? My mind was filled with nothing else since Kiki's call. Some sort of complication with her pregnancy was the only viable explanation I could conjure up, but what on earth could we do about it? Surely, she was in the hands of a competent doctor. It wasn't like Juliet to have us go to such an extreme as uprooting our lives for something we could do nothing about. No, this was something so big, so frightening in her life that she found it imperative for us to be there, just as we always shared any event or problem overwhelming us.

Saying goodbye to Michael was very difficult. We'd barely had a chance for a good start, and the relationship would have to be put on hold. Only under such dire circumstances, whatever they were, and only for a best friend, would I go. I knew it would be a short separation, but when I felt attracted to someone as I was to Michael – which, thinking about it, I never had been, I border on possessiveness and doting. I enjoy loving my man, and being extremely affectionate, I have to work at curbing the desire to smother him. These ponderings prompted me to question whether I possessed a latent, unhealthy need for a man, or was it just Michael, in particular, that stirred those reactions? All I knew was that as much as I loved Juliet, and wanted to be there for her and with everyone else, my heart tugged unmercifully at the thought of leaving him.

Lora had taken an earlier flight, so it was Kiki and Sherry and me. Our flight was, thankfully, uneventful, but as usual for me, too long. I'm not a good flier. I'm of the belief it's unnatural to fly, as if we're fighting against nature, which, of course thinking in those terms, physically speaking, we are. And if somehow, for some reason, fear was not loitering in the back of my mind, ready to pounce, there was always time to concentrate on airsickness. My stomach stays at the airstrip at liftoff and returns several hours later after landing, so I nap during flight, if possible.

I'd never been to Florida and conflicting feelings hit again. It was thrilling to be in a new place, but the uneasy feelings acquired during my conversation with Kiki managed to stow away in the back of mind, lingering and nagging, unfortunately, never venturing too far away. Well, I couldn't afford to be concerned at the moment about Juliet. Our lousy sense of direction and lack of traveling experience created a valid distraction…we had to find out where we were going, but presently didn't have a clue where we were. So we wandered around, our eyes diligently searching for signs directing us to the baggage area. Within minutes, relief flooded through us seeing the name of our airline up ahead and began running ecstatically toward the luggage packed, conveyor belt, yelling and grinning from ear to ear, when we noticed someone waving, almost frantically, from the other side. It was Mel. Oh god, it was good to see her. We ran, laughing and squashing each other in a hug rambunctious enough to knock us both off balance. Tears of joy soaked our cheeks. Thankfully, mascara was not a big thing for us, or we could easily have been selected as poster children for a horror movie. She'd retrieved her luggage already, so we left the airport, talking a mile a minute. Of course, taxis were plentiful and anxiously awaiting their next fare. Minutes later, at the restaurant, we found ourselves amidst a giant group hug, jumping around excitedly and squealing unashamedly like a bunch of ten year olds. When the exuberance subsided, and the shouts calmed to a buzz of chattering, the reality that Juliet was not among us settled sadly on our hearts, and immediately following that reality, came the barrage of questions simultaneously. We were anxious to have the mystery solved. It was extremely unsettling and we were too young to be dealing with such drama. Never were we more thankful we had each other for moral support. Sherry led the way, having made the living arrangements. She was bubbling over, describing the small beach house she'd rented in hopes of fitting in some vacation time in spite of the seriousness of the visit. None of us was opposed to a little sun and fun on the beach. And we especially were looking forward to admiring cute, masculine bundles of well toned muscles rippling in the sunshine.

CHAPTER XX

It turned out to be a three-hour drive and though it was a little snug inside the rental car, we were family, and it was a glorious drive down the coast. We laughed relentlessly, making jokes out of nothing and generally enjoying being together. We interrupted each other constantly, pointing and shouting excitedly, not wanting a thing to be missed. The lovely palms lining the beautiful, blue-green gulf waters and white, sandy beaches, swayed lazily in the balmy breeze, as though offering a personal welcome. It was all so new and exhilarating. We kept even the mention of Juliet and her plight out of the conversations. We were determined to enjoy the little time we had before we were entrenched in something, we were certain was going to wreck the remainder of the visit. The beach house looked exactly like we'd hoped and Sherry dreamily had described. And inviting as it was, we couldn't get inside quickly enough to remove our perspiration-soaked traveling clothes, enjoy a quick, cooling shower, and relax in the semi-tropical surroundings. Relax as much as possible, that is, with the apprehension and trepidation we were feeling, sneaking in every unoccupied, mental space.

The second we entered, we threw the windows open to allow the invigorating sea air slip inside, wiping away any sand particles and dust that had had a chance to take up residence since the last visitors. After our showers, we lounged, settled in and sipped cool lemonade. That first afternoon, we chose to walk on the beach, and visited every cute little bar along the way. We decided to let our hair down; we were taking two vacation days, after all, but we'd have to watch Kiki like a hawk. She'd renewed a commitment to stop drinking again, and we didn't want to stretch her will power to the breaking point. We stayed with the lighter, fun tropical drinks, loving the taste because of the heavy, fruity flavor, not the alcohol, so asked the bartender to cut the strength by half. We wanted to make the most of the beautiful day and wouldn't have the impending sunset discover five tequila-soaked, tanned young ladies, wallowing around, incoherent and out of control along a washed-out sandcastle. The beach was heavily dotted with the usual varieties of people and activities, sunbathers, children building castles in the sand, and even a few fishermen trying their luck in the shallow water near the sand's edge. The strains of "island" music pouring from the various ocean front bars, the crashing rhythm of the waves and the incessant screeching of sea gulls, set a perfect, tropical scene. The experience was even better than we'd hoped. Maybe Juliet had something after all, wanting to live here. Although a job is still a job, wherever you live, still the thought of driving to and from work along an ocean highway, with warm, sweet breezes sliding through the open car windows without end, was quite tantalizing. No shoveling snow, and no scraping car windows with numbed fingers in an attempt to separate the frozen ice particles from the glass, sounded great. But then, I realized, neither would there be, breathtaking springs, or the glorious, brilliant palette of colors experienced in the explosion of autumn. Everything balanced out, for me anyway. But in the meantime, we felt like we'd left the states, and were lingering and lounging on some island in the South Pacific. Eventually though, evening intruded, bringing an abrupt and unwelcome close to a wonderful day. But a glorious evening it was. And twenty minutes before the sun began to set, so did we, drinks in hand, and watched as people suddenly began scrambling like ants, setting up tripods and camera equipment to best catch the heaven's nightly performance. And it was worth everything, Juliet's problem, notwithstanding, to get here. It was fantastic, utterly amazing, to watch the sun seemingly get larger with its gradual descent, until suddenly, teetering at the very edge of the horizon, it fell quickly, without remorse, disappearing into the huge expanse of blue sea, patiently waiting below. The residual sunlight, played with the clouds for a while longer, creating a myriad of patterns and colors, turning the sky brilliant pinks and lavenders, to the delight of the appreciative audience filling the beach. The breeze strengthened a few notches the instant the sun made its exit, and we enjoyed the cool feel of it whisking across our sun-heated bodies as we retreated up the short path leading back to the beach house.

We were anxious to shower and remove the sand from every orifice the breeze had blown it into. And it had no shame, seeking out every single one, even the most private and secluded. We chatted excitedly, reviewing the day while setting about closing the windows and enjoyed, instantly, the refreshing, coolness of the air conditioner. The sun and alcohol had worked its magic, infusing us with giddiness, but also a sweet exhaustion, indicative of a day filled with playing hard. And as everyone flitted about seeking a comfortable spot to sit, we looked forward to a relaxing cup of soothing, hot coffee. The remainder of the evening was deliberately left open for girl talk. And since Melanie had been the one heard from the least, we descended upon her to 'fess up. Naturally, we were curious about every aspect of her love life, and insisted she not omit a single detail. Actually, we were anxious to discuss everyone's love life, as we'd been mentally calculating just how many virgins were left. Surprisingly, Melanie was more than willing to share the details with us. And she proceeded to regale us with several humorous anecdotes.

"I dated one guy for eight months before I found out he was gay. I'm glad I didn't fall hard for him, because I don't think it would've worked out." We howled.

"Gayness" not only was a rare topic for us, but rarely seen in the circles in which we traveled, so she had our undivided attention as she elaborated, "I wondered why he wasn't more sexually aggressive towards me, and I was beginning to really feel inadequate as a woman because of his lack of desire. But he was very attentive and loving, otherwise, so I finally came to the conclusion that it was just that he hadn't had his first sexual experience either."

Melanie definitely had Kiki's attention now, for certain. Sex talk excited her anyway, but the stranger the situation, the more she savored it. Actually, truth be told, we all did.

"I'm almost afraid to ask," said Lora, "but how, exactly, did you find out he was gay?"

"Well, I know you'll find this hard to believe coming from me, but…I just asked him, straight out."

"Well, kiss my ass and call me Jack," Kiki shrieked with laughter. "You've grown some damn balls, Mel, I never thought I'd see it."

"Okay, okay, Kiki…sshussh!, and stop being so crude," Sherry reprimanded. "Go on, Mel."

"And?" asked Sherry, with eyebrows raised. "What did he say?"

"It was at the end of a wonderful date, or at least what I thought was a date, and we were back at my apartment, as usual. And after putting on some of my hardcore sexy music with hopes of finally inducing at least a spark of lust from him, I realized he was totally indifferent and after a few minutes of chatting, he suddenly said he had to go. My frustration level had reached its peak, and the words just exploded from my mouth. I said, 'Jason, I've got to ask you this. Why don't you find me sexually attractive?'" The proverbial pin could have been heard dropping, waiting for her to continue.

"He looked shocked and surprised at my question, then, a little smile began creeping across his cute face. He started apologizing, and before I could ask him why he was smiling, he said, 'I thought you knew why, Mel, it's because, well, to put it crudely, but directly to the point, it's because you don't have a "penis."'"

"Shiiitt! He didn't!" Kiki said, mouth gaping. It wasn't often you could one up her, so we enjoyed the moment even more.

"Yes, he surely did, and I stood there looking pretty much like you look right now, Kiki. But as attracted as I was to him, I actually considered a sex change."

She made that statement straight faced and without a crack in her voice, leaving us staring at her, full of wonderment and confusion. And after a few seconds of fully enjoying the moment, she busted out laughing. "I'm kidding, guys, boy you are such an easy mark." We, then, laughed too. It was true. We were an easy mark where she was concerned. I remember when we first met, I thought her very strange, until I realized her sense of humor was very droll. Now I appreciate and enjoy it.

"Anyway," she continued, "I was so ignorant about homosexuality…you know? We'd never known any gays, and it just never crossed my mind. But even worse than that, and I don't know if you're ready for this, he told me he was really shocked by my question, because he'd thought all along that I was gay! He'd explained that he'd never seen me dating, or heard me talking about any guys. Is that just a hoot and a half?"

"What in the world did you say to him? Oh, I think I would've died of embarrassment," remarked Sherry.

"It was pretty awkward at first, but then when I told him how relieved I was to know it wasn't me, after all, the moment passed, and we laughed and laughed, and now, we're good friends." With her innocence for a backdrop, her stories were the best we'd ever heard, and we begged her to please tell more, and she was glad to oblige.

"Then there was a six-month relationship, which I initiated. It didn't last, but I enjoyed it while it did, if you know what I mean?" she said with a leering smile.

"Uh, wait a minute, Mel," we interrupted, and I asked, "You're telling us you made a move on a guy?"

"Yeah, there's a lot you don't know about me, I'm not the same timid little thing I used to be. I finally got bored of just school and work, school and work, and forced myself to start going out with some friends. Although I'll never be a 'Kiki,'" she said, shaking her head and laughing as she looked at her, "but I'll never be the same boring Melanie, either. And I'll tell you what, after being around the hospital and dealing with all kinds of nut cases, you learn very quickly to get a little aggressive or some of those guys will take advantage of you. I've been pinched, smacked on the butt, and one old guy actually kissed me square on the mouth, because, as he said, I reminded him of his mother and I took care of him as well as she did. I asked him, in utter amazement, if he kissed his mother like that. He threw his head back, almost falling over backwards, laughing, but he didn't answer, and I still wonder about that one."

We laughed eagerly, enjoying her stories, not only because they were shocking, coming from Melanie, but they were so funny. She had come out at last, and we couldn't be happier for her. She related a few more amorous escapades, and as we sat there, mouths hanging open, she said, "I know it's hard to believe this coming from me, but I wasn't born rooted in my personality, you know. I've been growing all this time, and, let's not forget, I am, after all, part of this sixties sex revolution too."

"Yes," said Kiki, motioning with her hands for Melanie to spill all. "We're hearin' you…but come on, have you given it up yet?"

"Kiki!" Sherry said, "I hate when you say that…it's ugly and tacky."

"What the hell?" responded Kiki, "we all want to know, I just ain't gonna pussyfoot around like you all do."

Melanie laughed. "Ahh Kiki, I've missed you. You may be a pain in the butt, sometimes, but we never have any doubts where we stand with you, and to answer your question, since you're insensitive enough to ask, no, I haven't. I have to find that special one to share that gift with."

"Hell, it's always Christmas with me," said Kiki.

Sherry threw a pillow at her. "We don't want to hear about any more of your sorry, worn out stories, Kiki, they're old hat…and with some of your dates, they're very old hat!"

CHAPTER XXI

"Well, I'll tell you," Lora began, her seriousness changing the tone of the conversation, but only momentarily, "sometimes, depending on the guy, I'm glad I'm part of this sexual thing, and then sometimes I'm filled with sadness that I chose to join the cause. But for the most part, I'm enjoying it." She giggled. We were aware of Lora's affairs, and the shock value had diminished, but Melanie was a different story. We were fascinated by her revelations and watched her demeanor the remainder of our stay. Her funny, meandering walk, sure enough, was replaced with a confident stride and she demonstrated an extroverted side of her personality not seen before. She was working hard at her second year studies and also worked evenings and some weekends, to supplement the meager allowance from her parents. They were doing their best, and Melanie appreciated it. She missed Pennsylvania, and was happily planning her move back to Milton at graduation, and we looked forward to having her closer.

Now all eyes suddenly turned to me, since very little was known about this mystery man they knew I was nuts about. I filled them in on the little bit of dating that I had done, but when I mentioned Michael's name, they watched and laughed as I instantly went all dreamy eyed and mushy, they said. And when I recounted the horrible incidences of our first meetings, we laughed uproariously and I was, at that moment, very glad they happened. We needed to stock up on all the joy and laughter we could hold, as it would be in short supply just several hours later.

Now it was Lora's turn, and she was more than anxious to tell all as well as share something new she'd experienced. She was currently in her second year of Special Education. We thought it a perfect field for her. She eagerly revealed to and shared with the world the child qualities inside her, and that joy and innocence easily connected with the children and consequently was ultimately responsible for a positive contribution to their development. She'd had no serious relationships yet. Terry remained her model and not until a guy met the high standards he himself set for her would she consider escalating a relationship to the next level. But that was not to prevent her from enjoying other aspects of the relationships while they lasted. Right now, she was taking full advantage of the hedonistic smorgasbord set before her. Nights were filled with football games, bonfires, parties, all-night gab sessions, and best of all: guys, guys, and more guys. What more could a young, single, attractive woman ask for? Even though I wasn't particularly thrilled with Lora's sexual attitude otherwise, I was happy she had, as with Melanie, found a place for herself.

"Okay, okay," Sherry said, revealing a rare display of impatience. "What's this new thing you're so anxious to share with us."

"Oh…oh, let me grab my purse." She hurried across the room, dropping small giggles as she went, as four sets of inquiring eyes followed her, full of puzzlement.

She squirmed back into her chair comfortably, smiling all the while, and dug deep into her bag. Finally retrieving the mysterious contents, she looked up at us with black eyes glowing as two small lumps of polished coal. "This," she said, holding up a cigarette as if it were the coveted object responsible for winning the blue ribbon at the county fair. "This is the something new I've discovered."

"Hell, that's what you're so damn worked up about? asked Kiki, recognizing the "cigarette" immediately. "Big deal! And, why in all mighty hell are you showing it to this crew? You believe for one second this bunch of puritanical poops are gonna go for it?" Kiki laughed. "I've been trying to turn Sherry on for months, and she looks at me like I've asked her to murder someone, and says the same damn thing every time," And in a whining simper, she quoted Sherry, "'I don't do druggggssss.'"

"Well, I don't do drugs, either, Sherry," said Lora. "But this is not the hard stuff. You know? It's just like getting a good buzz from a few beers, for me, anyway, and whewwww, talk about relaxing, you guys have got to try it. The campus smells like a marijuana field being burned for clearing. Everybody's doing it and nobody seems to care."

Mel injected her two medical cents into the discussion, enlightening us regarding information she'd read in a few medical papers, proclaiming the potential health benefits of marijuana for cancer patients. The studies were just in the budding stage, and consequently, she wasn't convinced yet and believed, as we all did, ingesting anything like that into your lungs couldn't be healthy.

"C'mon, guys, loosen up a little. I'm not asking you to get hooked on drugs or something…this is not 'dope.' Anyway," and this was the point that easily won us over, "we're going to be dealing with Juliet the next day or so, and—"

Enough said, we all laughed sadly. So it was. Our introduction to the mysteries of marijuana. And for the neophytes of the group, it remained just that. It didn't do much for us, and perhaps that's the reason we weren't attracted to it in the first place. But now that this particular "can of worms" had been opened, Lora and Kiki reveled in the freedom to indulge in our presence. And if I'd had any inclination to partake on a regular basis in the future, witnessing the transformation of Kiki and Lora from normal demeanor (if Kiki's demeanor could ever be considered normal) to one of a bowl of jello, with half-lidded eyes staring unfocused, would've frightened me back to reality. But that evening we enjoyed it, oh yes we did, but not from smoking it, but watching those two. Everything, suddenly, was hysterically funny, and though I never believed it possible for Lora to giggle more, she did, and if ever I needed more convincing to not share their enthusiasm for it, watching them eat everything we'd brought with us, stamped a negative exclamation on it. I would've gained ten pounds after a couple of sessions. We decided to let them have their fun until tomorrow afternoon, and then, scare them straight with threats to "sic" Juliet on them, alone, if they didn't stop.

We bummed around the next day, strolling at our leisure, visiting every delicious boutique and seaside shop we came upon. Together, we must have purchased a shopping bag full of interesting and quaint gifts for ourselves and family members.

Kiki and Lora readily agreed to abstain from smoking. We needed everyone's brain operating at peak condition for this…meeting with Juliet, whatever it was going to be. A sky writer advertised a restaurant that sounded interesting and we lunched there at noon, enjoying more tropical drinks and strolled the beach or sat in rented beach cabanas until dinnertime. We decided to dine out early instead of having food delivered. None of us was anxious to give up the day. The seafood was excellent, and with the heat, the drinks and a full stomach, I wondered just how much alertness was going to be available for Juliet; we might as well have smoked. But being relaxed and calm before meeting with her was a necessity, and we were definitely on target, so far. We headed back, showered and gave ourselves an hour for resting or napping, if possible. Her arrival time was seven thirty, but of course, the tension began building long before. We'd discussed and covered every possible scenario for her visit, and came up empty. There was nothing left to do now but wait.

It had been almost three years since we had all been together. And the anticipation of joy it should have inspired was replaced by pure dread. The best we could hope was it not be as ominous as we feared. I had momentary regrets I hadn't attempted to stir up my latent esp talents, but if it was disturbing news, which, of course, we knew it would be, the blissful time we'd spent these two days, wouldn't have been. I was blessed, indeed, with wonderful friends; they respected my desire to not dabble in the supernatural, and never pressured me, even now, when the curiosity was almost unbearable.

Juliet arrived, and though we were thrilled to see her, we wanted to be sensitive to her situation, whatever it was, so we welcomed her, but used an unusual amount of restraint.

We were shocked at her appearance and our hearts ached at the sight. She looked terrible. Quick glances were exchanged among us, and I was certain we were entertaining the same sickening thought: Juliet had been diagnosed with a terminal disease.

Her body bore witness to it, clearly. She'd lost at least ten pounds, which she couldn't afford to lose in the first place, and lost it not in the best of places. Dark circles emphasized swollen, puffy eyes which were resting all too comfortably in a hollowed, gaunt face. A no-brainer for me, if I had to guess…extensive crying. Her posture was slack, and worst of all, she exhibited an overall physical demeanor of apathy and lethargy. Something had gone terribly wrong…this was not our Juliet. Yes, she could be somber, quiet and moody, but this was somber and quiet to a frightening degree. Not just moodiness, and if not a disease, then a deep injury of the soul. God, it hurt to see her so troubled. What calamity had befallen her, and God help us, what were we expected to do? Looking at her, I had doubts there was a doctor alive that could remove the layers of pain evidenced there. A feeling of helplessness was settling heavily around my heart.

We arranged the chairs in a semi-circle around her, got as comfortable as was feasible, with so much tension permeating the room, and exchanged the perfunctory pleasantries.

Melanie served the "house wine of the south," iced tea, and we exchanged the perfunctory gripes about dreadful traveling experiences until we had exhausted the subject.

As close as we were, we'd never experienced a situation as serious as this obviously was, and waited for Juliet to take the lead. We hated rushing her. But suddenly, as a deathly silence permeated the room, we realized all eyes subconsciously had focused squarely on her, imploring her to relieve us of any further anxiety. But much to our anguish and dismay, she exploded into great, shaking sobs. We surrounded her immediately, and her torment produced tears all around, about what we didn't know, and at this second, it didn't matter. We offered our love, hoping to soothe, even a little, the ravages of the deep wounds exposed before us. After what seemed like hours, the crying subsided, but I was certain, before all was said and done, there would be buckets of tears to dump into the already teeming ocean outside our window.

CHAPTER XXII

After several minutes, calm prevailed. Juliet's sobs reduced to sniffles, and we began to gently encourage her to talk, to disclose this horrible thing of torment for her and to us, for that matter. Being so close to unveiling the mystery, and the suspense stretching our frayed nerves to the breaking point, I feared one of us, probably Kiki, was going to blow any second. And it wouldn't be pretty. Enough was enough!

Juliet began. First, she said, it was very important to her for us to understand the depth of her love for Rich.

Kudos to each of us for using the utmost restraint at that pronouncement. God knows that any one of us could have expounded for an hour about the many reasons, we believed, she shouldn't love him. But if we had responded negatively at that moment, she would have bolted. We knew her well enough to be convinced that to be so. However, she obviously wasn't as astute where our feelings were concerned. I realized a hint of a smile was making its way across my mouth, in spite of the seriousness of the situation, as I thought of Kiki. Surely she was biting her tongue at this moment. After sifting all this through my mind, I then began to wonder what, if anything, her love for Rich had to do with the problem. Well, I had no choice but to wait.

Juliet continued for the next thirty minutes extolling Rich's virtues and his kindness and devotion to her, except, she said, for the few times she'd provoked him to verbal and physical abuse. Shock waves ruffled the air around us at the revelation. It explained the swollen face, and inspecting her body a little more closely, small bruises suddenly seemed to appear that had previously gone unnoticed.

So much for keeping our opinions to ourselves, but we were not prepared to hear such nonsense, and certainly felt duty bound out of our love for her, to convince her she was wrong. Verbal abuse was bad enough, but physical abuse was just not acceptable, period.

At our gentle grumblings of protest toward Rich, however, she attempted, unsuccessfully, of course, to convince us the blame lay squarely on her shoulders.

"No, no, he's right," she said, "I just need to spend more time listening to him and work harder to try to understood his wants and needs better; he wouldn't get so angry and frustrated,"

Oh, how we wanted to tear into him, tell her what our true feelings were regarding Rich, but unless the abuse was what she wanted to tell us, and we were certain it wasn't, we still didn't know what we were dealing with, and any denigrating comments against Rich would only serve to shut her down, immediately.

"Juliet, honey," Lora softly pleaded, "I think he's man enough to choose his own behavior? Don't you? Or do you think he waits to see how you act before he decides how he'll respond?"

Lora's question made us all very nervous, but I have to admit she padded it very well. So well, as a matter of fact, Juliet seemed momentarily puzzled. So Lora went in for the kill, at least she hoped.

"Juliet, it's typical for…for some men to place blame on others for how they behave." Juliet remained quiet and we grabbed at it as a sign we were making progress.

"And," I added, gently, "You're actually encouraging him by allowing things to continue."

We were exhausting ourselves in the attempt to omit the words abuse and abuser. Meanwhile, Mel was softly massaging Juliet's shoulders, inquiring if she needed something for pain. Juliet, calmly accepting the gentle barrage of objections, suddenly shrugged defiantly, and straightening in her chair, stated she was fine, and continued as if she'd heard nothing. We were devastated.

"We have a wonderful life together, except for those times, and besides, who doesn't fight once in a while?"

Kiki's face was flaming. She jumped up violently, startling us, and placing a hand on either arm of the chair Juliet was occupying, she was barely restraining herself from screaming at her. "We all have squabbles Juliet, not physical fights, and no son of a bitch is ever going to be provoked enough to lay a hand on me, and I can't believe you actually hear what you're saying and believe it!"

Juliet, understandably startled by Kiki's outburst, pulled her head back to obtain some distance between their faces, but when Kiki finished, we were stupefied to hear Juliet continue as though Kiki hadn't uttered a word. She actually strained her head to look around her at the rest of us, excitedly supplying the details of their working partnership in one of the small gift shops for which Rich had been buying. They had dependable, trustworthy management, she continued, seemingly unruffled by Kiki's outburst. So they were free to travel all over the country on buying expeditions. If we just knew that side of Rich, we'd see why she loved him so. He really was a wonderful person. Kiki shaking her head in disbelief, plopped back down in her chair, resigned, she said later, that Juliet was a total idiot, a hopeless case. Though the rest of us weren't inclined to describe her in such harsh terms, or to give up on her just yet, we did view her suddenly as a total stranger.

She continued. "I think we'll be getting married sooner or later, although he never mentions it, and when I bring it up, he just laughs and says, 'no way baby, no ball and chain for me.'" As she spoke, the mystery deepened, but assuming we didn't interrupt this would, hopefully, be leading to the reason she'd called us here. Her voice suddenly weakened, with sadness replacing the excitement that shone in her eyes just moments before. It was difficult to relate to this madness. We'd never experienced such profound love, or what we believed, was a dysfunctional love. We were aware of Juliet's neediness, but never realized the depth of it. Her words reflected delusion and denial and we watched, aching for her, as she vacillated with inner anguish, evident by the swings from nervous behavior to giggles of giddiness. Obviously, her mental faculties were sparring, and we were witness to the battle tearing her apart. She paused, looking down at her lap where her cupped hands were writhing and twisting, one inside the other. She sobbed, "I know he doesn't mean what he says, I know he loves me, he tells me all the time."

We tried desperately to convince her that this wasn't love and, finally, throwing caution to the wind, he was not a man worthy of her. Now a spark of anger found its target as she looked at each of us, and stated boldly. "You don't know him like I do, and if you did, you'd understand what a wonderful man he really is." We looked at each other in amazement. How could something so obvious to us be seemingly nonexistent to Juliet? Or was she working hard to convince herself? At this juncture, we knew we had our work cut out for us if we cared, and, of course, we did. Was there more? I asked what I felt could be a potentially volatile question, but one that needed an answer. "What does he say about the baby?"

This sent Juliet into a new round of sobbing spasms as she mumbled almost inaudibly, that Rich didn't know. "I'm afraid to tell him since he's never mentioned marriage, and he's always been so careful with our lovemaking and is very adamant about me staying on the pill. I know…I know if I tell him, he'll leave." Moans of disgust and frustration were emitted from Kiki, who had removed herself to the other side of the room. She'd had it. Sherry, speaking in a whisper, filled with love and compassion, asked, "Juliet, you just told us what a wonderful man he is, now you say you're afraid he'll leave you if you tell him you're carrying his child. Juliet, please listen to what you're saying. And what do you mean, if you tell him? You have no choice… he's going to know before too long, anyway. How far along are you?" Juliet squirmed, looking extremely uncomfortable, and her tear filled eyes darted around the room, looking everywhere but at us, as she replied in a shaking voice, "I'm six weeks, I know, because I just had a doctor's visit yesterday. I wanted to be exact when I talked with all of you."

Really? Our minds were whirling…This is it!…What is it? The big "why we were here"! The mystery solved as she blurted the words out in rapid fire succession…"I want to have an abortion, and I need your help."

Oh God, no, not again. We were stunned into speechlessness, even Kiki, never expecting this from Juliet. And after what seemed an eternity, she continued. "Look, my life, with or without Rich, is going to be hell, and maybe you don't understand or agree, but it's my life."

We needed a few minutes for this disturbing news to sift and settle before we could proceed further, and in a little while, we began analyzing each option and scenario from every angle, desperately seeking another solution. But Juliet rationalized that even God wouldn't want her to have this child. Her reasoning being that she'd committed herself to being Rich's wife long ago, and her father, as a pastor, taught her it's the duty of a wife to obey her husband's wishes. And who held the authority? The law or God? Simple as that! We attempted in every fashion to expose the folly of her logic, but to no avail. But of course she couldn't see it; she wasn't rational at this point. She was trapped and could see no way out. She was haunted by the prospect of facing her father with news of a pregnancy. It couldn't happen. He was a pastor in a small town, and his own daughter would be the cause of his disgrace. And, of course, there was the disapproval of the rest of the family. Certainly she'd been taught the sin of abortion, but in her confused thinking, it paled in proportion to the disgrace and the prospect of losing Rich.

But abortion was no more a viable option now than it had been with Kiki. It was a murderous act, the taking of an innocent life. We knew the kind of "loose" women that had abortions, and God help us, as much as we loved her, Kiki was one of them. It was still morally incomprehensible, we had not been persuaded and if Juliet had consented to it, she would have spent the term of her pregnancy with one of us, adopted the baby out, and Rich would have been nothing more than a bad memory. Unfortunately, she couldn't see her life without him. After exhausting every option, and using what persuasive powers we had, we finally yielded to the night to begin again tomorrow, hoping that in sleep, or more likely, sleeplessness or dreams, a solution would miraculously surface or Juliet would come to her senses. Odds were on a miracle.

CHAPTER XXIII

Kiki, ignoring us and our "sappy sentiments," as she called our opinions regarding abortion, had been busily making phone calls, not only to her friend Ron but a few others she had met in Florida when she worked as a waitress. One young man, Smoky Givens, lived about forty-five minutes away and he called her that afternoon with a doctor's number his family knew, who sympathized with women who found themselves in situations such as this. And after a quick call, they agreed to meet that evening at eight thirty at a nearby bar. We attempted to dissuade Kiki from going. First of all, for the obvious reason she was getting involved with subterfuge, abortions were illegal, and God alone knew what kind of man this doctor might be. And secondly, we hoped if we stalled Juliet, we could convince her to explore other avenues. We pounded her relentlessly with the plan of housing her until the baby came and then give it up for adoption. But, with abortion arrangements being handed to her, there was no going back. Kiki's view was to get it done and over with and get the hell out of here. She didn't view abortion as wrong as the rest of us, and besides, she gave Juliet up for crazy, believing if we talked her into anything other than what she wanted, there was a good chance she'd end up doing herself in. We were in tears at the horror of the step she was about to undertake. We understood her dilemma, but abortion we couldn't grasp, now, or ever. Maybe the only way to comprehend it was to be wearing those desperate shoes.

Sherry was insisting on going with Kiki, but Kiki informed her, a condition made by the doctor, was she come alone. She was meeting him in a public place, and attempted to assure us she would be safe. To say we were unhappy with this arrangement was an extreme understatement, and the helplessness we felt, was frustrating.

The bar was nothing exceptional, tropical in its appearance both outside and inside. Teeming with vacationers, it seemed to be successfully fulfilling its mission: keeping its patrons laughing, drinking and oblivious to the world outside.

If the doctor was interested in deflecting attention from himself, he failed miserably. He'd been described to Kiki, and she spotted him without difficulty, sitting in a corner booth, alone. A thin, wrinkled rain jacket, swung open over baggy wrinkled jeans, and gleaming white sneakers, which looked as though they'd been plucked from the store shelf moments ago. His receding, sandy blonde hair looked clean, but was thin and tousled. Looking around furtively through narrow brown eyes, his hawk-like nose seemed to sniff the air around him as he watched Kiki approach. She walked over, seemingly fearless, but, oh the fear was there, tucked deep inside so no one would notice, including herself. Otherwise she would've easily turned, making a quick exit back to the safety of her friends.

"Dr. Morris?" she asked with a boldness she hardly felt. He stared menacingly as she forced a slight smile, bending her pretty lips noticeably.

"Sit," he said gruffly, sans kindness or courtesy. He wasn't much for small talk, asking straight away if she had the money. Kiki nodded. Even her extensive experience with unruly men in bars hadn't prepared her for Dr. Morris. She was extremely uncomfortable in his presence. Nevertheless, she forced herself to keep her mind clear as she asked for identification, proof he was, in fact, a doctor. He opened a well-used burgundy portfolio, begrudgingly so, and closed it up so quickly, Kiki barely saw it, but she did notice a golden seal on what could certainly pass for a degree. He explained, or rather grunted, that he had references if she wanted to see them.

Kiki was satisfied and, anyway, ultimately trusted the friend who had recommended him. She wasted no more time, wanting to escape his mangy presence as quickly as possible. "I'll call you with arrangements first thing in the morning…here's half now," Kiki said as she discreetly patted a flat bank bag under her hand to be left on the table when she left. "The other half when it's done."

Without a word, he stood swiftly, and with the deftness of a magician's sleight of hand, grabbed the bag and walked hastily, head bent low, to the door. Kiki plopped down, releasing the pent-up tension which was about to explode out of her as she watched him disappear out the door. She couldn't wait to scrub away the smell of him with a hot shower. She began walking slowly down the almost deserted, darkened beach, lit only by an assortment of party lanterns, swaying gently in the evening breeze on the decks and patios of the restaurants. The waves crashing in their eternal rhythm soothed Kiki's aching head, washing a little calmness over her. She couldn't remember when she needed a drink more. Tilting her face upwards to catch the cooling breeze, she began to run, running as best she could through the constricting sand, feeling it stinging her legs, filling her shoes, tipping her from side to side as she attempted to keep her balance. She began to sing, loudly, a song about rainbows which her mother had sang to her night after night at bedtime in hopes of preventing nightmares from sneaking into her sweet dreams. Now she sung in hopes of blocking out the torturous thoughts compelling her to sidle up to the nearest bar stool to drown herself in some mind-numbing concoction and wipe away her loneliness and despair for Juliet. She loved Juliet, in spite of their obvious torment of each other, and she wasn't without feelings as the rest thought. On the contrary, she was tormented by deep seated hurts and anger, most of which she couldn't discuss because she was unable to identify them herself, but was dealing with them the only way she knew...drinking. Drinking and fast living. They afforded her a respite, short-lived to be sure, but some relief, nevertheless. Her bluff and swagger were tools used to disarm herself and others, from finding the real reason for her behavior.

Melanie was distraught. She entered the medical field to save lives, and here she was volunteering to help destroy one. How would she ever forgive herself? But the facts were clear: she was here, and Juliet was going to go through with it, with or without them, so how could she not help her? What if she refused and Juliet died?

They were each struggling with their consciences, and each came to the same conclusion, right or wrong...Juliet's health and well being took top priority.

Dr. Morris, or "Dr. Joy," as Kiki facetiously called him, was expected at eight o'clock a.m., and wanted everything ready, per his instructions. The bedroom, the scene of the crime, resembled a beehive the next morning. A pall hung so thick in the house, we could feel and smell it. Juliet cried sporadically all morning, deepening the air of despair and sadness. Now, with the decision made, there was a permeating sense of urgency to get it done and forget it. Forget? We knew that would never happen.

Dr. Morris showed up promptly and without pleasantries, barely grunting a "where is she?"

Mel led him to the bedroom. He found Juliet cowering deep under the sheet, shaking and sobbing. Mel, offering the only consolation and compassion available in the room, held Juliet's hand while cooing words of comfort. The first order of business, the doctor said, was to sedate her immediately. "I don't need any sniveling and yelling to interfere with my job." A lousy bedside manner, but certainly not unexpected. With Juliet's safety uppermost on our minds, we liked the no nonsense attitude, as long as he did the job competently. Dr. Morris barked out orders, demanding we leave the room, and, of course, we objected vehemently. Melanie was in medical school and would stay close by to assist. He objected, but the prospect of unrelenting nagging by four nearly hysterical women, and being motivated by his own sense of urgency, he wasn't in a negotiating frame of mind.

We left the room praying, ironically, that Juliet was in good hands. That's all that was left. All the words had been spoken, the pleading, and begging. We were nervous and paranoid, and set about closing the window shutters, then filling our glasses with iced tea, intermittently, paced and sat. Within minutes, whimpers began to seep through the doorway, followed by increasingly louder moans and then, horrible, muffled screams. The fear and confusion tore sobs from us, and ignorant of what the procedure involved, we assumed what was taking place, and what we heard, was terrible, but normal. Besides, Melanie was there, at Juliet's bedside. Though in medical school, Abortion 101 was not part of the curriculum. Kiki rose from her seat looking as pale as, I'm certain, the rest of us looked, and claiming she needed a breather, left for a walk. The situation before her was a blatant reminder of her own abortion, although she breezed through hers by comparison. Yes, she'd experienced pain, but it was over in twenty minutes and she walked away actually smiling, thrilled her dilemma was resolved. So why was she having such a difficult time now with Juliet? Perhaps it was watching a loved one suffer. It seemed harder than going through it yourself, somehow. Or, perhaps, it was her conscience, deep in the recesses of her mind, nagging at her. Now, there were two deaths for which she'd be held accountable.

Melanie filled in the horrid details later. How the doctor pulled an ugly, hook-like device out of his black bag and, displaying a modicum of compassion, told Juliet to hang on, it might hurt a little. A little? Had Juliet known, she might have chosen to face her father and Rich rather than go through the unbearable pain. She writhed and squirmed as much as was possible in an attempt to alleviate the pain, but she endured and remained conscious to the end, and when Dr. Morris told her it was done, she then passed out. Melanie covered her with extra blankets, checked her breathing, and came out trembling, collapsing into a chair, crying unabashedly. Who was going to console whom? We were a mess. Kiki had had the right idea to escape. We never expected Juliet to experience such intense pain. We thought she'd be sedated and, at worst, wake up sore and uncomfortable with some residual bleeding. We weren't prepared for screams and torment.

Dr. Morris asked for the remainder of his money, which Kiki had left in Sherry's care, snatched it out of her hand, and made a quick exit. Later, much later, we realized he hadn't left us with prescriptions for painkillers or potential infection. Kiki would have to get back in touch with him. Juliet couldn't be expected to tolerate the pain without medication. There was nothing more to do than check Juliet constantly, and wait, wait, wait for her to awaken. Melanie recognized the sedative Dr. Morris had given Juliet...bless her, she demanded to see them. Dr. Morris was irritated, growling he didn't have time for such foolishness. Melanie wasn't in a mood to care, and brazenly grabbed the bottle out of his hand to get a look at it. Thanks to her, we could relax, at least knowing what she was taking and the dosage. Now we were getting concerned about Kiki. She'd lost the battle with the bottle on more than one occasion, and it was obvious she was having a difficult time coping. It was confusing to us. Kiki was tough...the toughest, we thought. Why was this sending her over the edge? When she hadn't returned by seven, we decided it was time for a search party. Sherry was the logical choice to go, and I joined her. Lora decided to stay behind, giving Melanie a much-needed break. Juliet had been sleeping most of the day... the stress and pain exhausting her, and we were grateful she was, at last, resting peacefully.

We decided it best to search the bars together, and started with the one closest. There were at least twenty or more, but we hoped, being in a hurry to drink, as we were certain she was, she'd settle on one close by. The first three turned up empty, but the bartender at the fourth recognized the picture we showed him, and said she'd left no more than an hour before, with a guy the bartender recognized as a regular.

We found them together, sitting in a back booth, and the two combined couldn't have created a sober breath. We approached them slowly, and when Kiki saw us, she smiled snidely, slurring, "Well, well, well, I guess you've come to arress me. I did it, I'm guildy, I confess to everythin." Her scraggly looking companion agreed wholeheartedly, nodding his head so violently I thought he might throw himself onto the floor. Obviously finding the situation humorous, they broke into riotous giggles, slapping the table, thoroughly enjoying themselves. Sherry moved gently and cautiously to Kiki's side, rubbing her arm, lovingly, encouraging her to come home. We reassured her we were not going to arrest her and she wasn't guilty of anything. We wondered just how much of the last twenty-four hours she'd revealed to this man or, perhaps, someone else. We plied her with soothing words of confirmation of our interest strictly in her well being. It worked, and Kiki began crying like a baby, jabbering almost incoherently that it was all her fault, she was a murderer, and how could we ever forgive her? She was a rotten person, and on and on she babbled, and thankfully so, as her weakness at that moment offered the opportunity to get her to her feet over the protests of her drinking buddy. He attempted to stand and make a grab for Kiki, but Sherry gave him barely a whisper of a shove, toppling him back to his seat with a thud. The bartender appeared, seemingly out of nowhere, and when the drunk rose a second time, threatening and swearing, he stepped between us, and strongly suggested the man sit down, behave or get out.

We heard him spitting and cursing as we ushered Kiki out as quickly as possible.

Between the difficulties created by her limp, uncooperative body and the heavy, uneven sand, we knew it was going to be a long and arduous trek back to the house. Kiki mumbled and cried all the way, expressing regret for her part in Juliet's present situation.

Upon our arrival, Mel quickly and accurately surveyed the situation, and immediately headed to the small kitchenette to prepare the first of many pots of strong coffee. Meanwhile, we struggled to get Kiki undressed and into the bathtub, whereupon Sherry activated the shower spray of cool water directly onto Kiki's face. She gasped and gurgled and thrashed about attempting to elude the needle pounding deluge soaking her alcohol-saturated body. She swore, using words I never heard spoken before, but was well aware they were part of the usual vocabulary used by Kiki and her motley friends. We dried her off brusquely, leading her to the couch where Mel waited, and adjusting Kiki's limp, uncooperative body into a modified upright position, she began plying her with the steaming liquid.

Even though, at the moment, we were physically occupied with Kiki, we were never totally distracted from Juliet. Melanie used every medical trick of her limited knowledge to comfort her, but she had awakened, tossing restlessly and was in a lot of pain. A constant, though small, trickle of blood was frightening, but Dr. Morris assured us it was to be expected.

What a mess! A house full of ignorant women involved in a life and death situation and illegal to boot. And, ironically, the only one with experience was useless, involved profoundly in her own crisis. My God! What happened to those innocent young girls who had big dreams of marrying their princes and living happily ever after? Nothing was manifesting around us that faintly resembled a fairy tale or the princess and her prince. So far we had a frog, one drunk and one interracial couple plagued by a bigoted society. Surely, the best was yet to come.

The more we plied coffee to Kiki, the more aware she became of what she'd been drinking to forget, and the more she cried. The consequence of her decision in this ongoing drama was obviously torturing her, and drinking was her coping mechanism. But not understanding the pressures or compulsions responsible for her addiction, we were angry and resentful towards her. The last thing we needed was more complications. And even though we were ignorant regarding therapies for the addicted, we proceeded correctly by gently but firmly reprimanding her for the problems she was creating for those who loved her. We reaffirmed our love again and again, but made it clear we would no longer accept excuses for her behavior. She just sat, head hanging dejectedly – and painfully, I'm sure – and continued to cry softly.

CHAPTER XXIV

Juliet suddenly cried out and it was a stampede to the bedroom. We found her sitting upright, crying almost hysterically, pointing to her lap in which a bright red pool was enlarging rapidly. Post-abortion complications may not be part of the curriculum in medical school, and yes we were ignorant of a lot of medical facts, but one thing was blatantly clear, losing so much blood so quickly was obviously too serious to ignore. Mel barked out commands to ready the car and get Juliet bundled. We were headed for the emergency room. How thankful we were, now, that on the way here, because of Melanie's medical interest, she excitedly pointed out the local hospital, casually commenting on the conventional, boxy, architecture, indicative of most institutions, and even with the landscaping of beautiful bougainvillea, banana trees and the "bottle brush" trees, as they were called by "lay" people, it was still, just that…an ugly institution. But it was only ten minutes away, and a beautiful thing to us now. Sherry's foot lay heavy on the gas pedal, speeding as she had never done before, but neither had she ever carried a passenger whose life was in jeopardy. We attempted to remain calm for Juliet's sake, soothing her with words of reassurance which we hoped afforded her more comfort than we were feeling. She was in enormous pain… her moans and whimpers growing more intense by the minute. It was difficult, to say the least, to concentrate on directions while ministering to Juliet. Those were the longest ten minutes of our lives. The vehicle had barely stopped in front of the emergency entrance, when Lora jumped from the car, running, arms flailing for attention, screaming for an attendant.

It was a horribly botched abortion, and the hemorrhaging and ensuing infections almost cost Juliet her life. She'd be calling the hospital "home" for the next two weeks until she was completely out of danger. The local police were notified and we were subjected to a multitude of questions in an attempt to discover the true identity of Dr. Morris. It was obvious he was a lousy doctor, but the question ultimately was…was he a doctor at all? We supplied the authorities with the information we had, which was skimpy at best. And as they viewed a group of frightened teens standing before them, we pleaded ignorance, deferring to the authority and education of what we presumed to be an MD. We were duly and thoroughly reprimanded, lectured and, thankfully, dismissed. Relieved and reassured that Juliet was, this time, under the care of a competent doctor and resting comfortably, we rushed back to the beach house, threw on our bathing suits, and hit the beach. I don't ever recall the sun and fresh air feeling so good. The weight of the world had suddenly been lifted from our small shoulders, and now our tension-filled bodies were craving, no, demanding relaxation. Yes, of course, we'd expected we might experience some unpleasantries on this trip, but the scenario which had just played out, even Sherry with her fertile imagination couldn't have produced.

The next two weeks were spent between visits to Juliet's bedside and the beach. She was deeply depressed and overcome with unexpected, residual guilt and fear, not only for the present, but fearful of the prognosis of her future childbearing capabilities. We attempted to keep our visits lighthearted and positive, but it was difficult under the circumstances. She was too busy wallowing in self pity and hatred, for herself and, yes, even Rich. Apparently, with so much time to think, a sliver of logic and solid reasoning and been able to find its way into her, otherwise, muddled thinking. Now if only it could sprout wings, and land at every synapse, to fully occupy the remainder of her brain.

She was adamant about not contacting her family, and we couldn't think of any reason at this point why we should. We were successful in convincing her to stay with one of us, or go to Maine with Ellen, until she'd fully recuperated. After weighing the advantages and disadvantages of each, she opted for Maine. Maine was more or less home. It was a great healing place for her, she said, and she would also reestablish her normal routine as quickly as possible. The following week, we helped her on a plane to Boston, where Ellen was waiting to carry her home. We'd had several discussions with Ellen, advising her of Juliet's delicate mental status and pleaded with her not to hesitate if she needed help.

Dr. Morris, as was revealed to us later, was, in fact, not a doctor, (surprise, surprise) but a medical school dropout by the name of Raymond Clinton who had managed one year of pre-med but couldn't muster the academic discipline necessary to finish. Kiki's "friend" who found him, was Raymond Clinton's nephew and partner in this sordid business, which they'd been profiting from the last few years. But it was over now and in the hands of the courts. But, unfortunately, not for Juliet, who would suffer the mental and medical consequences of her decision for years to come, and Kiki? Well, one more notch was added to her also overburdened psyche.

Now, it was time to get back to our own lives, which seemed to be simple and wonderful, by comparison.

I called Michael the minute I arrived home, and he seemed happy to hear from me. There'd been no communication with him the entire Florida trip. He was under the mistaken impression (*boy was it ever*) I was vacationing, and I elaborated, ad nauseam, on the beautiful scenery and climate. It was too early in our relationship for him to pry any deeper, thankfully. He invited me for coffee, and as tired as I was, I only needed the vision of his beautiful face floating before me to transform into a quick-change artist. My stomach filled with butterflies and I felt a silly smile spreading, dreamily, across my face. Was this falling in love? Or was it simply an infatuation? I didn't know or care. It was wonderful, and I hoped, without end. Michael looked as gorgeous as I remembered, and we hugged briefly and still a little awkwardly, but long enough to enjoy the masculine fragrance emanating from him…a combination of the outdoors and spice. His translucent, fair skin was burdened by a five o'clock shadow, adding to his appeal and was a compliment to his short, dark hair, which, with its natural body, lay just right with little wisps attempting to curl here and there. His full, square jaw was the perfect showcase for a beard, but I felt, staring at his handsome face, it would be a shame to cover it with anything but my kisses.

Only once that evening did my mind betray me with fleeting, guilty thoughts of Juliet. But I knew she was healing, physically at least, and was in good hands with Ellen. More than that, there was nothing I, or anyone else could do. I sighed deeply hoping to exhale the negativity into some dark, irretrievable recess of my mind, not to return, at least not tonight.

We talked and walked for hours, until, forced by exhaustion, I called it a night. Michael was gracious and gentlemanly, almost disappointingly so, seeing me to my door with the promise of a call tomorrow. The wonderful thoughts and feelings rushing through my brain and body normally would not have permitted much sleeping, but tonight, my body insisted on it. But one last thought before closing my eyes? I knew this man could easily help me discover exactly what the sexual revolution was all about.

I was aware that we didn't have a promise of tomorrow, but it was all I could think about: to hear Michael's voice, and to hopefully see him again. Conversely, I was feeling a little uneasy, realizing just how quickly and eagerly I could forego my independence, which I treasured, and totally give myself to another person. I suddenly felt extremely vulnerable, my defenses gone. And with so few experiences with love…none, to be exact, it was frightening, but I was also reveling in every wonderful second of it.

Fate soon proffered one of its cyclical respites from troubles, and we thankfully settled into a day-to-day routine. Juliet had resumed her business and, yes, disappointingly, but not surprisingly so, her love relationship. We discovered much to our dismay, her physical recovery was still ongoing, and, so we continued to worry. We kept in constant touch with her and knew Ellen was doing the best she could. But with Juliet's insistence on keeping Rich in her life, there was little, really, any of us could do. And other than Kiki's usual drinking, the months flew by in a happy flurry of love and activity for the rest of us. Mel was finishing her second year of medical school, and taking some accelerated, summer courses. She had decided to reach for the golden ring…to become a pediatrician. She knew it was a long, arduous road but was willing and eager to pursue the goal. Sherry and Almon became a "live-in" couple, moving to a small town in northeastern Pennsylvania and were planning a wedding in the fall. She got a great job, again, with a newspaper office, and picked up where she left off in Virginia. She was turning into a competent reporter, and ultimately wanted to write a book of her experiences. Almon was finishing his master's, still working as many jobs as possible, and looked forward to the day he held that hard earned and much sought after Doctorate in his hands. The only troubled spot on Sherry's horizon was Kiki. She was considering moving, creating ambivalence for Sherry. She and Almon had fought through a lot, and were looking forward to the anonymity and peace of new surroundings, but Kiki, by all accounts but blood, was Sherry's sister, and Sherry wanted her close by. Maybe being removed from old stomping grounds, a complete change of friends and surroundings would prove helpful. If not, we'd seek out the next option. We just hoped we wouldn't run out of options before she destroyed herself.

CHAPTER XXV

A classmate of Lora's who hailed from Los Angeles was visiting family at spring break and invited Lora to go along. She was beside herself with excitement, and pronounced it her final fling before graduation. She'd been irresponsible with her allowance, she'd admitted, spending money as though it were water, and was feeling a little guilty. Her grades came nowhere near her parent's monetary commitment, but she determined to give her all to the next, her last, year. So Los Angeles had to be good.

Michael and I settled into a wonderful dating pattern of two nights a week, and unaware of which nights, the spontaneity was exhilarating. He never pressured me about sex, or made me feel in any way guilty or awkward about abstaining, but with free love the motto of the day, I was applying plenty of my own. A nineteen-year-old virgin surely was a rarity in a culture of blatant permissiveness, and I have to admit that only my mother's ghostly presence jabbing sharply pointed moral spears at my conscience kept me from succumbing to Michael. But also, it was wonderful to enjoy each other outside the sexual arena with all its ensuing entanglements. I felt we were fully able to explore the outer layers of each other's personalities and as we slowly removed each layer, the attraction was sustaining, and so we continued comfortably, to the next level. Birth control pills were an available option, just in case I felt my moral life raft slipping away, but I knew me, they would be my ticket to ride. My mother's disgrace at having a pregnant daughter would become null and void and the ghostly voice would disappear into a wisp of sixties psychedelic smoke, along with my innocence.

Lora called one evening, bubbling over, which wasn't unusual for her, but this time she was exceptionally excited. Her friend, Stacey, had introduced her to her big brother Dana and they hit it off instantly. Lora said they were a perfect match, crazy for crazy, and she loved it. Promptly upon greeting him with a pleasant "hello" following their introduction, he responded in kind, of course, but speaking with his best "duck" voice. She was delighted and giggled with amazement at his lack of inhibitions. Laughing, he traded hats with her, removing her wide brimmed straw hat and placing his ball cap sideways on her bouncing curls and placed her wide-brimmed straw hat on his sandy blonde ones, announcing, "There, that's more like it." Then, having to slightly lower his six foot one inch frame to offer his arm to her, she linked hers in his, and asking, "shall we?" Off they strolled, unabashed and unrestrained for the remainder of the day. He bought ice cream cones for everyone and insisted they bite off the bottoms and suck out the delicious, cold contents. He constantly shot off one-liners and had a high pitched, goofy laugh which might have proved embarrassing to most, but Lora found it quite endearing. And, if she had any qualms at all because of their height difference or his blondeness, his comical antics wiped them away. She was totally enamored. After only one week, Lora claimed, again, she was in love, madly and unequivocally this time. We teased her unmercifully. A week didn't go by that she wasn't in love with someone new, and always, "this time," it was the real thing. Thankfully, she was well aware she did it, accepted it and laughed right along with us. But we sat up and took notice when she announced by mid-term, she'd made plans to relocate to Los Angeles immediately after graduation. Maybe this time it was the real thing, after all. Our first response was that it was impulsive, but hey, she was young, full of energy and free. Why not? Grab the gusto while you can. We found it very telling that Dana's looks were secondary in her description of him. We had to push for details of his appearance, and she didn't readily offer any, except to say he didn't fit her usual profile, and ordinarily wouldn't have given him a second look…her tastes running towards brunettes of shorter stature. She did admit, however, to feelings of vulnerability, having someone towering so far over her. But it was Dana's enthusiasm for her specifically and life in general, that attracted her, quickly replacing her initial reaction with feelings of profound security, although I would have thought they'd exhaust each other with their boundless energy. Each with a head full of blonde curls and bookend personalities, giggling and bouncing through life, demanding attention wherever they ventured, created a vivid picture of the pure, unadulterated joy witnessed mostly in children. Dana's sense of humor and innocent goofiness was infectious and a tremendous asset to his success in real estate. A man her brother Terry would have liked and admired, and ultimately that was all Lora needed.

Excited to share her happiness, I called Mel. We hadn't spoken for weeks and after discussing and exhausting the topic of Lora and Dana, I requested she catch me up on her progress, in love and life in general. I was interested, of course, in hearing about school, which she was still very enthusiastic about, but I was more interested in her love life. I worried about her. She spent too much studying and not finding time for relaxation and reveling in just being young. I was happy and relieved to hear she was actually dating, though strictly within the medical field because of time and convenience, and of course, the plethora of cute little potential doctors walking around everywhere. But now, I explained to her, a little birdie had informed me that she was dating one guy, exclusively, for the last couple of months. "Is there any truth to this, or is it a hopeful rumor?" Mel had certainly come out of her shell, as was evident in Florida, but moving back home with her parents to save tuition, certainly didn't allow for much exploration and expansion of one's self, not to mention being tough on her love life. "Yes, yes, and double yes." Mel exclaimed, full of the bubbly excitement manifested by women in love. "Rainey, I truly believe I've found, not only my soul mate, but my lifelong mate. He's everything I could ever hope for and more, he's—"

"Mel, Mel, hold up a sec., can you fill me in a little about him? Now, take a deep breathe, and let's just start with his name." We laughed.

"Sorry, I get a little goofy where he's concerned. He's just so wonderful, he even—"

"Mellllllll!"

"Sorry. Okay." I could hear her inhaling deeply to calm herself before she rattled off the basic facts of his life. James Shields was a student, her age, specializing in cardiology. Robert Shields, a renowned cardiologist at the Carstairs University Hospital, was his father. Apparently they were "old" money and steeped in the traditions of such. James actually played polo and went on "hunts" in Virginia. "Do you know anyone who plays polo, Rainey?"

"Not only do I not know anyone, I only vaguely know what it is, except that English Royalty plays a lot. What a kick! And hunts? That's where the dogs chase a fox until they catch it, and, I suppose, kill it. That one I'm not so fond of. I wonder if they eat the fox or foxes, or what? You'll have to ask your James Shields that question for me."

So far, so good. Then Mel described him to me: tall, dark and handsome. The description, I pointed out, reminded me of her brother…a perception she was quick to shoot down, "Oh no, I can assure you, he ain't nuthin' like my brother," she purred.

Unfortunately, their individual lives, set up as they were, didn't allow for much privacy, and they worked diligently to create ways to be alone, including friends lending them apartments a couple of times a month. And with the workload these two had ahead of them, it was going to be a long time before life consisted of fun and relaxation. When I mentioned this, she replied sadly, "Yeah, I know, believe me, we've been thinking about that; we've just about decided on making 'the' commitment to each other. Life's too short to put off five and six years down the road what you can have and enjoy now."

I was ecstatic for her, and told her to inform us as soon as a wedding date was set. With their school schedules, if and when it happened, it would be a quick trip to City Hall. My heart filled with sadness, as once again another dream wedding would dissolve into nothing more than a few quick words exchanged in a cold, impersonal courthouse. Reading my thoughts, she replied, "I know, Rainey, it's sad, but my dream wedding will just have to take place later, when we can enjoy it."

"I'm gonna hold you to that." In spite of the disappointment over her wedding plans, I was ecstatically happy for Mel, and would enjoy rehashing the details with the others.

CHAPTER XXVI

The joy we'd been experiencing at the exciting events of our lives unfortunately and inevitably was short-lived when word came from Ellen that Juliet was experiencing serious complications and had been in and out of the doctor's office for the last few weeks. Rich was in Florida and Juliet in Maine, but he was calling constantly, making noises about coming to get her. Juliet was still torn between her love for him and fear of him, and when he became abusive over the phone, Ellen threatened him with a restraining order, and the conflict was creating a chasm between the sisters. Finally, Juliet came up with an explanation to, hopefully forestall his arrival. The doctor had diagnosed serious female problems, which necessitated his continuing care and plenty of rest. He appeared sweetly sympathetic and promised to give her space. Juliet relaxed.... a little, but fear and apprehension never left her completely, aware of Rich's unpredictable behavior, and she wondered just how much time was actually bought. All too soon she would discover, not much. A few days later, Rich arrived, full of himself and demanding Juliet get packed. He was escorting her back to Florida. She was caught. She couldn't explain the extent of the problem without rousing more questions. If she underplayed it, he would insist on reinstating their sexual relationship, wanting her to leave with him. And if she overplayed it, he would press for more information, perhaps even wanting to consult with the doctor himself. Being caught in a predicament with Rich was nothing new; she was forever walking a tight rope with him, never knowing what might set him off, and an eruption eventually was inevitable. Juliet, at least, convinced him to stay a few days, hoping, stalling for time. She couldn't return, just yet. But the fact that she even wanted to, still remained a mystery to us.

Ellen, not caring a whit for Rich, and not wanting to be in his presence, spent those few days with friends, but demanded that Juliet call the second trouble started, as she was certain it would. Rich initially was sweet and considerate, romancing Juliet, telling her he wanted their first evening together to be a special one: an evening, he said, to undo the damage he'd done, to show her how much she really meant to him. And he set about doing the little things a woman appreciates in a man, attending her every need, waiting on her, bringing her water, placing and patting the pillows behind her as she sat and, the *piece de resistance*, removed her shoes and began massaging her feet, a relaxation technique he knew was Juliet's favorite. But filled with fear and trepidation as she was, her stiffened body would have needed a bottle of Valium, at the very least, she was certain, in order to relax. Eventually, Rich removed the phone from its cradle, smiling a beautiful smile, lighting his deceivingly handsome face and belying the evil that lay beneath the surface. He wanted absolutely no interruptions. It was, indeed starting off beautifully, but Juliet was torn emotionally. She still loved him, the sweet, wonderful Rich who treated her as an equal and showered her with attention as now, although it was rare, she'd admit, and she knew him well enough to know payment for services rendered was fully expected. Oh God, the thought of his sexual advances and his response to her refusal of them instilled her with such fear and anxiety that at times her teeth chattered audibly and sweat broke out on her upper lip and palms. If Rich had been truly sensitive and tuned in to her, he would have noticed these obvious signs of uneasiness and distress, early on. But he was, as usual, all about himself and his needs, wining and dining her, treating her like a china doll, all with the intent of seducing her. But, at some point, due to her obvious lack of participation and enthusiasm, he'd realize all his attentiveness was for naught, and the tension and pressure would seek an outlet. He finished off a second bottle of wine, and began making the inevitable advances toward her. She tried to dissuade him, pleading with him, that she wasn't physically well enough yet. Her pleas fell on deaf ears and she grew more panicky by the moment, as his ardor became more intense. She absolutely could not let him proceed. It was unthinkable, especially in his Neanderthal mood – she'd end up back in the ICU. And as she expected, when she began to aggressively deflect his advances, he exploded into a string of invectives, snarling and spitting, sending terror through her as she had never experienced before. But with the inevitable surge of adrenaline rushing through her system, aiding and abetting survival, a plan, literally, exploded in her brain. Albeit a temporary one, it was better than standing defenseless, allowing him full reign over her body to do…no she couldn't allow her mind to even venture there. She began screaming over him as best she could, backing away, explaining that he misunderstood her, that she only needed some time to prepare for him properly as befitted the evening. He calmed, momentarily, eyeing her suspiciously as she, trying to still her beating heart and shaking body, seductively sidled up closer, but not close enough for him to grab her, telling him with a pout that she had shopped for hours that day for some sexy undies with her sweet man in mind. She pleaded with him to please not spoil it as she had thought of nothing but the feel of him around and inside of her for the passed few weeks. At this, his snarl relaxed into a lascivious grin. And utilizing the deadly combination of coyness and sexiness oozing from her eyes and pouting lips, she begged him to please leave her for just a teensy weensy short little thirty minutes, with promises of eye-popping surprises when he returned. He hesitated and she thought her heart might stop. She was playing her trump card. If it didn't work, she was sunk, but adrenaline still pumping: she came up with a little extra persuasion. It had to work. With head bowed, eyes peeking up at him invitingly, she began raising her dress torturously slow, all the while whispering and cooing, "Pleeease?" Half hypnotized by the beauty and sexiness of her exposed thighs, and his mouth watering, he moved toward her, she dropped her dress and the suddenness of it stopped him instantly. Once again, she begged, "pleasssse?" But to her relief, he began backing, painfully slowly, out the door. "Okay," he said in a gruff voice smoldering with sexual desire and practically spitting at her, grinning, "that's more like my little Juliet." Stumbling back, the grin suddenly disappeared from his face, as he began shaking his finger, and speaking in a drunken slur, threatened, "I'll be back in thirty minutes exactly, and you better be ready." Then, the smarmy leer returning, he added, "mommy and daddy're gonna have some fun tonight."

Her heart was pounding much too hard for her fragile, thin body, and she thought she might drop dead any second, but she blew him a kiss, and gathering every ounce of oxygen she could pull up from her panting lungs, she purred sexily, "That's my big man." She didn't relax an eyelash or exhale, until she heard the car roar to life, and with tires spinning, he peeled out of the driveway. She collapsed into the nearest chair with relief, but the thought of escape had been formulating in her mind the entire evening, and mere seconds later she grabbed the phone and called a cab. While waiting, she threw the few things she had with her into a small suitcase and began pacing, willing the cab to arrive before Rich returned. Thirty minutes and counting.

CHAPTER XXVII

She stared expectantly at every passing car, deciding that if Rich appeared, she'd have no choice but to run out the back door. She could catch a cab somewhere, anywhere! She just couldn't be there when he returned. Before she could finish the thought, and with relief flooding over her, she spotted the lighted taxi sign pulling into the driveway. As she ran, she examined the approaching cars, praying none were Rich. Shaking uncontrollably and with small sobs escaping her throat, she threw herself into the backseat, slamming the door and locking it. The cabbie, acutely aware of her sense of urgency, wasted no time reaching the one-way street. After conveying to him the airport as her destination, she at last settled back with a sigh, into the wore-torn seat and relaxed for the first time in hours. She hated not being able to leave Ellen a note, but realized, fearfully, Rich would find it if Ellen could. She'd call her as soon as possible. Even though the nightmare was over, she couldn't help envisioning the scene back at Ellen's when Rich arrived and found her gone. Would he break down the door? Well, it didn't matter now, and she refused to let her mind give in to another horrible thought about it. She was feeling very proud of herself, reliving how she pulled out the stops of her emotional and mental arsenal, which until minutes ago, she thought was depleted, or at the very least, badly damaged. That aside, she was now, without a doubt, emotionally drained, and once situated on the plane, fell into a blessed, mind-numbing sleep and didn't awaken until the screeching of the airplanes tires, touching the runway, jolted her back to her sickening reality. She then contacted Rob, who arrived at the Tampa Airport three hours later to carry her back to his home. Rich, being only vaguely aware of Rob would have no idea where she had disappeared.

True to his nature, he'd never displayed an interest in Juliet's family, and paid no attention during discussions regarding them. Unless it benefited him someway, he didn't care. What a loser!

There we were again, monopolizing phone lines hoping to find out what was happening in Maine, and every call, frustratingly, ended with a busy signal. It was just the day before that Ellen had called and we assumed Rich and Juliet were keeping the line hot between Florida and Maine, and it made for another restless night. Oh, I was thankful I had Michael to distract me until there was news. Thankfully, I didn't have to wait long. Lora called the next day at work with the details of Juliet's escape. I was thrilled she was finally, hopefully, through with Rich. It was unthinkable she would ever return to him. But now she was depressed more than ever, her hopes smashed again that Rich would somehow transform into her prince. If ever there was a toad, he was it. We would have preferred him leave under other circumstances, of course, but he was, we hoped, out of her life permanently, and were ecstatic at the thought. But, of course, being sensitive to Juliet's feelings, we never bashed or trashed him again, after Florida. She was more than aware of our feelings, so we continued to cry with her.

I had no complaints about my workday after speaking with Lora, or anything else about my life for that matter. I felt very blessed, and I was looking forward to my date with Michael that evening. We were dining at a new restaurant and that was wonderful, but he was more excited about something exciting he wanted to share with me. Another surprise? He was constantly giving me sweet, unexpected gifts. Buying tickets to a play I had casually mentioned I would enjoy seeing, or surprising me with a day trip to a beautiful, historical town in Ohio. A town whose cobblestone streets he knew I loved to stroll, as I savored its history and old, enormous, lovely oil-boom homes. And later, after walking for what seemed like hours, enjoying all the small shops lining the waterfront, I'd navigate the river in a sternwheeler, and end the wonderful day with a scrumptious dinner aboard a paddleboat, docked for the benefit of the tourists.

Yes, Michael was special. I don't know which of us derived the most pleasure from the gifts. But I would've loved him just the same without the generosity. He passed the ultimate test of love for any mortal woman; he gave me his undivided attention when we were together, listening intently to what I had to say, proof being, he knew what I liked, hence the surprises. What was there not to love about this guy? Still he was not a "love god." He possessed some of the same irritating habits of any normal man. Some habits which drove women with unfair expectations to divorce. But I figured the good outweighed the bad, and besides, I had my share of personality quirks with which he had to cope. And one of the worst for Michael was my incessant need to share with him every thought, big or small, that floated through my brain. That made for more conversation than was necessary for anyone, and more information than he ever needed. It was especially bad on long drives. I would catch myself rambling on, and, eventually, seeing the glaze forming over his eyes would stop, laugh, and apologize. He would simply smile sweetly and say, "Honey, I love you." It worked for me, but maybe not for him, actually, in the long run. That was, after all, positive reinforcement. We were a mismatch in theory, but in practical terms, we complemented each other. I was impulsive and impatient and he was methodical and had the patience of Job. But in spite of, or because of our different personalities, we enjoyed each other's company, and laughed a lot. And one of our common interests was hiking in the beautiful mountains of Pennsylvania. But because we agreed that the romantic, isolated setting posed a real threat to my abstinence policy, we never lingered in such spots, especially after dark…except once, and as wonderful as it was, and why wouldn't it be? I didn't want to tempt fate again unless I was ready to follow through, and I wasn't. We planned a long weekend with friends of Michaels, Jack and Cynthia Carter. Jack and Cynthia married young and were living out part of their life's dream; owning a mountain lodge two hours north of Pittsburgh. Jack and Michael were high school buddies and Jack had done some climbing with Michael before realizing it wasn't for him. Cynthia was a cute little redhead, with a liberal sprinkling of freckles across her nose and cheeks, and she upheld the promise of redheads to provide spirit and spunk to the world. Jack was handsome with strong features and his strawberry blonde hair complemented Cynthia's red tresses perfectly. Cynthia was trim and toned, never giving a thought to the consequences of a calorie. And evidence of that was discovered as we sat relaxing the very evening we arrived. Cynthia appeared on the deck with an ever-present bag of candy bars…my weakness. She proceeded to consume two, poste haste, as I sat greedily lusting after them but enjoying only the memory of their taste. I was envious, as calories seemingly grew on me through visuals alone, and I probably gained a pound as I watched her devour them. That eliminated her as one to be counted among my circle of close friends. But, otherwise, it promised to be a great weekend. Once settled lakeside in the beautiful, rustic cabin, we rented a pontoon boat and headed out to play. The sun was hot, but we dove into the biting cold water often enough to stay comfortably cool, and the afternoon was spent lazily talking, eating, laughing and feeling more worthless as the day wore on. The gentle, constant rocking of the boat lulled us like the arms of a doting grandmother. It was wonderful! Soooo relaxing and very soon I felt the tension draining from my body. Juliet who? But, of course, it ended much too quickly. Jack and Cynthia had an appointment at seven to look at a piece of real estate and needed to get back. Michael and I weren't eager or willing to give up the day, and after returning the boat, we took a long walk to regain our land legs, enjoyed a delicious meal at the lodge and feeling like two overindulged slugs, found an open spot to watch the glorious, impending sunset. We tossed the blanket down haphazardly, and plopped down, feeling satiated not only with food, but sunshine and fresh mountain air. Again, I found myself thinking, *it doesn't get better than this*...but it did. We gave kudos to the sun as it presented, for our pleasure, a magnificent performance. The sky and a handful of clouds floating close by, changed from one glorious color to another in the blink of an eye, attempting to hang on to the last bits of the sun's rays as it made its descent, all too quickly, behind the majestic pines. The sudden coolness sent a shiver over my body. Or was it the sudden realization, that with the disappearance of the sun, my attention had been diverted back to us, and the sweet closeness of Michael's beautiful sun-drenched body? If I'd stood instantly, and headed in...but oh how was that possible? My body screamed to stay, while my mind was screaming to leave. The hesitation produced a silence between us as loud as a sonic boom; our bodies pleading with us to indulge in the pleasures inspired by the romantic setting and private surroundings. Looking at each other with raw, aching desire, I suddenly felt the heat of Michael's hand as it slowly moved to gently caress my exposed thigh; his touch, potent enough to spawn a deep sigh, broke the dam of aching need building in us since we began dating. His moves were slow, sweet and gentle. Touching my waiting lips tenderly, we moaned with the promise of sexual release. My hands busily explored the nakedness of his beautiful back, loving the feel of the powerful muscles, as his fingers lovingly explored my face, my shoulders, and hesitating briefly, then slowly and sensually moving to the tops of my breasts exposed by my flimsy tank top. I thought I would die from the pleasure of it. Our hungry mouths took on a life of their own, waiting so long for the final fulfillment... the payoff for all the previous tantalizing kisses. Michael's fingers slipped inside my top, and the ensuing gasp of delight, escaping from my lips, startled me, and shaking my head briskly to regain my senses, I instantly pulled away, visibly shaken. Michael mumbled, barely audible and gruffly, "Oh God, let's get out of here." We rejoined Jack and Cynthia back at the lodge. The deck overlooking the mountains was huge and inviting, and safe, and we sat until the wee hours sipping hot coffee and enjoying each other's company. But all good things, etc. etc.. We stayed until the last possible moment the next afternoon, extracting every last ounce from the incredible weekend. And still unwilling to give up, we lingered at my doorstep for another hour, talking and nuzzling, with promises of spending more time together. The insatiable hunger for each other was tormentingly delicious, but I was determined not to let sex sidetrack us. This relationship definitely had marriage potential, but we didn't know each other well enough to move to such a serious level, and if and when we decided we did, I wanted a commitment, not just sex. Those ingrained values were strong, and no matter how I tried to rationalize them away many nights before seeing Michael, and oh how I tried. They made too much sense to simply toss aside. So for now, the only lovemaking taking place in my life was in my fantasies, and if Michael lived up only partially to those, it was worth waiting for.

CHAPTER XXVIII

Corina's work day began later in the morning than mine, and she'd usually be sleeping when I left, but this morning she had an early appointment and coffee was ready when I arose. She informed me, casually, that Sherry had called the night before. My head snapped around instantly, anxious for any news. "What did she say? Is Juliet alright?"

Corina, in mid sip, nodded her head yes while motioning with her hand for me to calm down. Sherry told her to assure me it was a call with some exciting news as well as to inquire about anything new concerning Juliet. I was relieved and disappointed. Not knowing, on the one hand, was good, but on the other, it was tortuous. Good news, huh? Maybe Sherry's parents had relented and had finally accepted her and Almon's relationship. That would be a "dream come true" for her. But as anxious as I was to hear what it was all about, it would have to wait. It was another workday, and another wonderful opportunity to see Michael. I rarely saw him at the office; he was extremely busy and we agreed discretion was the best policy. The gossips would have a field day, and since office romances were discouraged, it could jeopardize our jobs.

That evening, after Michael and I had our daily phone conversation, filled with sweet cooing and, eventually, the perfunctory news of the day, I called Sherry. It was, as usual, delightful talking with her. In spite of the difficulties and pain resulting from the split with her parents, she remained optimistic and upbeat. She was brimming with exciting news of Almon's recent acceptance of a professorship at a local college. He was now, officially, "Professor" Moon. The pride and love evidenced in her voice was enviable. She calmed her excitement only momentarily by taking a deep breath, then, no longer able to contain herself, squealed "Rainey, we've set a date and I'm calling so you can make appropriate plans to be in Albrightsville September fifteenth."

"That's wonde—!" I started to exclaim, but Sherry interrupted.

"Let me explain. It's not gonna be a 'wedding' wedding…you know, bridesmaids and all. We don't have a penny to spend on such a luxury. We're going to be married at the courthouse. I know, I know. As much as I hate the idea, that's the way it has to be. But now," her voice rose in excitement, as she continued, "the reception is a different story, altogether. Almon has great connections at a resort in the Poconos. Actually he spent two summers working there, and they're arranging a dining room for us, and even donating a lot of food as a wedding gift. It's costing us next to nothing."

I'd never been to the Poconos, but had heard great things about the area and was excited at having the opportunity to not only spend some time there, but to spend it with friends and for such a wonderful reason. I was ecstatic for them.

"The plan is," she continued, "to leave right after the wedding and start partying. We've reserved three cabins. They're pretty big, but you'll still have to double up, but hey, we're all friends with no secrets, right?"

"Wait a minute…what's this 'we're' stuff. You and Almon aren't staying in the cabins with us, are you?"

"Well, actually I thought about it. It's not like we're really 'newlyweds,' you know? We've been living together now for six months. But, it is still our 'wedding night,' and at least that first night we'll celebrate, after that, who knows, maybe we'll all end up in one cabin. Wouldn't that be great?"

"I think it'd be great, but you better be checking with your man on that one, he may have a different plan."

"I honestly doubt it, Rainey, he's done nothing but work for the last three years, and he's exhausted. It'll probably take him the next three years to get unwound. It's been quite a run, a good one, and it's paying off, but it's been like living with a coiled spring, and I've noticed these last few weeks he's starting to relax a little. I think he's really looking forward to sitting around, doing absolutely nothing, no phones, no work, no nothing, just being worthless. Anyway, back to the cabins. The guys are going to share one and the girls the other. And If there's gonna be any switching around in the middle of the night, I don't wanna' know a thing about it." She laughed.

"Sherry, this is wonderful, not only do I get to see the Poconos, but witness one of my best friends beginning the happiest journey of her life. And no one I know deserves it more."

She hadn't been successful in contacting Juliet and still needed to call Mel, and requested that whichever one of us spoke with Juliet, to fill her in.

"You better try to catch Mel right away; she has such a crazy schedule, and we've all got to be there, it just wouldn't be right if even one of us couldn't make it."

Sherry agreed and planned on calling her next. But as happy and excited as Sherry was, I still detected an undertone of sadness as she spoke. It was going to be the happiest day of her life, and her parents weren't going to share it with her. "What about the rest of your family? Are they coming?"

"Oh, yeah. Even though Mom and Dad have tried their best to discourage any of them from participating in any way. They still believe that I'm going to come to my senses and stop this foolishness. They actually think I'm rebelling against them. You'd think, after all this time, they'd realize that there must be something more to it, but I think they're just in denial, afraid that once they accept it, all hope of it ever coming to an end will be gone. It's going to be the happiest day of my life, Rainey, and one of the saddest at the same time, isn't that ironic? Well," she continued, "it's their choice, the invitation is open, and I pray to God every day they'll change their minds. I just can't imagine my future without them involved in it, but I'll never give up Almon, Rainey. He's the most wonderful, kind, generous human being I have ever known. I want everyone to get to know him, and it will be clear why I love him so much."

We then reviewed the logistics and details of the wedding and reception, which didn't take much discussing. I inquired about Kiki, and Sherry filled me in on her progress. "She's doing great right now, not involved with anyone in particular and is excited about her new job. She had a lot of projects going on at work and thankfully, it's keeping her busy and out of trouble. But the best news is, I've lined up a therapist for her, and she actually promised me she'd go. Her first appointment with him is this week, and I'm real excited about it. His name is Gere Handel, a little older, thirty-five, and Almon says he's almost movie star handsome…not that that seems to matter much to Kiki. But it certainly won't hurt. You know? He's from Germany and only been here for two years but he's established quite a professional reputation for himself. But God help him, I'll bet with all the patients he's had, he's never met anyone like Kiki, and I know he's dealt with some lulus."

"She'll give him a good run for his money that's for sure. Probably by the time she's through with him, he'll need more schooling, or counseling for himself, or both. Well, look at the bright side; she'll probably never miss an appointment."

"Yes, that's very true, but after the first session, *he* may not show up again."

Sherry's voice suddenly took on a serious tone. "All kidding aside Rainey, I don't know how it's going to work out with the three of us, although so far so good. So pray a lot. As much as I love Kiki, I can't let her behavior in any way jeopardize my relationship with Almon. She's got to get her act together."

I agreed and commended her on her commitment to Kiki despite the problems she caused. We all loved her and cared about her so much, but she could stretch and test the patience of a saint, and I was glad to hear Sherry was so protective of her relationship with Almon.

CHAPTER XXIX

The next afternoon at work, Michael and I ran in to each other in the lunchroom. Not literally, this time. There were others present, so we were cool and cordial to one another, but it took all of my inner strength not to give those sweet lips a hello kiss. This was, after all, the honeymoon phase of our romance and it was difficult to keep our hands off each other. There were times when I thought surely the sexual heat generated by the proximity of our bodies could be detected by outsiders. We satisfied ourselves with winks and silent kisses discreetly thrown at each other before returning to work.

Shelley, a co-worker, interrupted my short walk back to the work area, informing me I had an urgent call. Instantly filled with trepidation, I hummed as I hurried to the office, attempting to occupy my mind in order to postpone "hearing" whatever it was, but a bad feeling was managing to wriggle its way around the humming, filling my every step with dread. I took the call in my supervisor's office; she was gone at the moment, and it afforded me privacy. It was Ellen. Finally, I thought, feeling relieved, she'd heard from Juliet. She said she'd tried Lora first, to no avail. I could have told her that. Lora was never home. She and Dana were living the high life, traveling and jet-setting all over the world. It was wonderful, and though we rarely spoke to her anymore, we were ecstatically happy for her. Suddenly I realized how upset Ellen sounded and was terrified to inquire why. My hesitation prompted her to quickly reassure me it was not Juliet. I exhaled deeply, blowing out the lungful of anxiety filled air I was holding, but remained terrified of the "but" I felt certain was coming. She said it was about Rich, and asked me if I knew about the situation between him and Juliet. "Yes, it wasn't successful and she's tucked safely away out of harm's way, right?" I asked, being cautiously optimistic. I still wasn't sure we were out of the woods with this thing. Ellen then snickered ironically. "Well, she may definitely and forever be out of harm's way where Rich is concerned. When he left her the other night, he was flying high, and never should have been driving. He didn't even make it a mile from the house before losing control of his car, leaving the road and crashing through the guard rails headlong into several trees. He's alive, but barely, from what I understand. Officers on the scene said he was probably going about seventy miles an hour." I sucked in my breath, the shock reverberated through my body, shaking my bones. *Oh Juliet! My God! Juliet!* "Ellen? I'm assuming Juliet knows?"

"I don't know if she knows this minute, Rainey, but I talked to Rob, and he's going to find the right time and circumstances to talk to her. I just talked to him this morning, and I asked him to call one of you or all of you when he talked with her. If he doesn't make it, she's going to need all the comfort and love you can give her. I know Juliet, and she's going to feel guilty and responsible for his accident and, maybe…death. As if she hadn't been emotionally burdened with enough already. Rainey, I almost hate myself for saying this, but my God, hopefully he's out of her life for good. He was destroying her and she seemed helpless to stop him. I mean, I certainly don't want him to die, but I honestly believe he was capable of hurting her or killing her, but when I voiced these concerns to her, she just told me I was being foolish. So, the way I feel, if it had to end in death, better him than her."

I agreed. "That's the sad part about the whole thing, Ellen…something like this was probably the only way she was ever going to be rid of him."

I thanked God Juliet was alright, physically, but emotionally, she was going to need all the help she could get to make it through this. "Ellen, you know we're going to be calling her constantly. Maybe we can talk her into coming to stay with one of us, or, maybe she'll want to come back up there with you?"

"Yeah, I thought about that, and she knows she's welcome. I'll certainly encourage her. Rob's a wonderful young man, but right now, I think she needs women around her for emotional support." We promised to keep each other abreast of anything new, and said our goodbyes.

It was extremely difficult concentrating the remainder of the afternoon. I needed to see Michael, have him hold me and comfort me, but I'd have to wait until tonight. Maybe he'd come over for a little while. Corina and Sheila would be there, and I was glad of it. With my defenses weakened, I would definitely need chaperoning. Well, had I been in my right frame of mind, I would have known better than to have Michael over, anyway. The telephone lines hummed with all the conversations taking place off and on until the wee hours of the morning. Michael stayed about an hour, but, in spite of the circumstance, it was a wonderful hour. I needed him, if only for his sheer presence, emanating love and comfort for a little while.

My focus after that was on Juliet. She was flying back to Maine tomorrow. We were glad but frightened for her. If Rich recovered, what then? Would he just start again? Pick up where he left off? Ellen spoke with the attending physician, confiding the circumstances of the accident. And considering such unsettling revelations, he adamantly advised against a visit from Juliet, just in case she'd even entertained such a crazy idea. Ellen discouraged calls to Juliet from Rich's family. Believing Juliet's frame of mind was too fragile to support the barrage of questions and perhaps accusations, they'd throw at her. What would she say? That she'd sent him away in a drunken stupor, knowing he was an accident waiting to happen? The emotional strain was too much for a mental state hanging in a delicate balance, anyway.

I called Rob, and as much as he loved and enjoyed her visit, he realized Ellen was definitely better equipped to cope with her emotions than he was. Juliet wasn't up to talking, but related to Rob to tell all of us not to worry, she really was going to be okay. Rob confirmed that she was holding up better than he expected. "When Ellen called her with the news, Rainey, she reacted very strangely. Well, *I* think, anyway. She was almost hysterical at first, and cried for a long time. I felt helpless to do anything but hold her and let her cry. But a little later, after a hot cup of tea, we were sitting, talking, and she told me if he died, she almost would be glad…then she started crying again, saying she was such a horrible person for feeling that way. I did my best to explain it was natural, or at least I believed it was, considering the way he treated her, but I don't know…this is way out of my league, I'm just anxious to get her back to Ellen."

I was stunned and thrilled at the same time. This attitude held promise. And surely a human being is designed to balk, to recoil and defend after so long, it's our nature. Wars have been initiated with classes of people rising up, rebelling against unjust and abusive treatment. *Come on Juliet, we're pulling for you!*

Rob reminded me, once again, of his offer of the beach house, anytime. Lord, that sounded wonderful. We could all use some lazy, worthless days lounging around a pool doing nothing but playing. But we were using vacation time for Sherry's reception, and it'd be a long while before we could plan another reunion, just for the pleasure of it.

CHAPTER XXX

Michael called to tell me he'd made reservations at one of the finest dining places in the city for Saturday night, if it was okay with me. "Uh, let me think about it?" There was silence on the other end. "I'm kidding, Michael. It's more than okay, it's heaven sent."

I'd heard nothing but raves from everyone in the office about a particular restaurant close by called Shades. It was too rich for my blood, but certainly not Michael's. "What's the occasion?" I asked.

"Well," Michael laughed mischievously, "I've been keeping a little secret from you only because it wasn't ready to be revealed until now. I don't know if I can wait until Saturday night, so I don't want to talk about it anymore until then."

"But what—"

"Uh, uh, uh," he interrupted, "I'm serious, honey. It wouldn't take but just a few 'pleeeeases' from those luscious lips of yours for me to confess all, and this is just tooooo good to tell you over the phone. So, how was your day today?"

He had to be kidding! "Michael, how could you do this to me? Why say anything, if you had no intention of telling me?"

"Because," he said excitedly, "I have to say something or I'm going to explode"

"Oh this is just great, It's killing you, but at least you know what it is!" I was nearly screaming at him.

"I'm sorry, sweetheart. I didn't realize how selfish that was." His remorsefulness fell way short of the mark, and now he attempted to backtrack. "But it's not that big a deal, really, I'm just making more out of it than it actually is, and, anyway, Saturday night is only two days away, we can make it."

Was that a snicker, I heard? As difficult as it was, I respected his wish to not question him any further. Of course I didn't want to spoil his surprise…it was like peeking at your gifts before Christmas. But, whatever it was, it certainly meant a lot to him, in spite of his protests after the fact that it didn't. I had never seen him this excited about anything. I needed to find a project to bury myself in for the next two days to survive the suspense.

Lora called the next morning with news that kept me mentally occupied for the next several days and beyond. I'm fond of the phrase, "timing is everything," and her telephone call only served to deepen that opinion.

Leave it to her to do something drastically impulsive but fun and silly. She and Dana had flown to Las Vegas the night before and gotten married, deliberately, in one of the tackiest chapels they could find. She had difficulty speaking, laughing as hard as she was, and never completed a sentence, but never seemed to notice or care as Dana jumped in, not only finishing for her, but beginning, immediately, with another silly anecdote. Then, it was her turn to interrupt. I was innocently involved in a verbal volley here, each constantly talking and laughing over the other, my ears were ringing, my mind racing in an attempt to keep up and untangle the barrage of words being hurled at me at mach speed. I got the gist of it, but I don't think their intent was to be certain I knew every detail. I was just another excuse, another avenue for them to enjoy each other; they were happy I answered the phone. They sounded crazy! They were crazy! But crazy in love with each other, and life.

Only momentarily, again, did I allow a little niggling of disappointment that another wedding would be taking place without the rest of us. But I didn't mention it, not wanting to dampen the joyful spirit exploding through the telephone wires; on second thought, that wouldn't be possible. The effervescent happiness percolating from these two was infectious and delightful. Lora, as if reading my mind, attempted solemnity, voicing regret, between giggles, that none of us were there, but never fear, a reception to beat all receptions was to be had, and the entire world was invited to celebrate their union. It was two weeks away, on Saturday, and "no" was not an option. *Be prepared for the party of our lives*, they enticed, or perhaps with these two it could be construed as a warning. I asked if we could bring a date and Dana said emphatically yes. "And maybe," he continued, "before the weekend is over, we'll fly back to Las Vegas, and everyone can be married."

The new eruption of laughter exploded in my ears. My God, after hanging up the phone, I realized I was drained. How in the world could I spend an entire weekend with those two, when thirty minutes took so much out of me? I'd have to find places to sneak away and hide every once in a while to get my next wind, I thought, amused.

I called Juliet the next night to check on her. She'd arrived at Ellen's just a few hours before and was exhausted. I didn't keep her, just reassured her of my love and concern, and if she needed me, call. Otherwise, I'd call again in a few days. She sounded somber, of course, but then she never was one bursting with exuberance. I guess I'd raised my expectations after the conversation with Rob. But shaking off the disappointment, I realized she could've sounded a whole lot worse…I'd take what I could get. She'd been through a lot, and I hoped it was over. I know we make our choices and have to live with the consequences, and she had some doozies to work through. The best we could do was be there for her. Tomorrow, fate might toss me something horrific with which to deal, and I could only hope my family and friends would be there for me.

Saturday night arrived finally, and I anxiously paced, waiting for Michael. He was always prompt: when he said seven, he'd arrive at a quarter till. I loved that aspect of his personality. I was punctual, and I'm certain it's because mother preached to us that it was disrespectful to show up late. Our reservations were for eight and at seven thirty I began to worry and pace. Rich's accident was still fresh in my mind, giving rise to moments of anxiety. Unnecessarily so, as it turned out, for seconds later he came bounding in, apologizing. "I'm so sorry honey, I hope you didn't worry, but I had to run this little errand or the surprise tonight would be that there was no surprise tonight. It was totally out of my control."

"Okay, okay, already," I said, laughing, feeling relieved he was okay, but, immediately, my anticipation returned, full force. "Let's not stand here torturing me, let's get to dinner before I snap." We'd agreed to have dinner first. Stupid, stupid, stupid idea! How was I to enjoy the meal with this mystery hanging over my head? And, of course, it was Michael's idea, wanting to drag out the suspense, for his enjoyment, as long as possible. Thank you very much. Oh, he owed me big time for this one. But I hoped the glamour and opulence of Shades would succeed in distracting me for the better part of the evening. It was just a short ride to the restaurant and Michael was being exceptionally chivalrous, I thought, attending to my needs, sometimes before I was aware of them. He wanted the evening to be perfect he said with a smile…and me, suffering the mystery every second.

CHAPTER XXXI

To say Shades didn't disappoint is an understatement. It was spectacular and I was enthralled by the splendor. And it was just a place to eat! We entered, what appeared to me, to be a winter wonderland complete with sparkling icicles everywhere. The décor was almost solid white. White damask tablecloths were embellished with embossed white rosebuds. A bough of white roses sat regally inside crystal vases which adorned the center of each round table with crystal chandeliers dazzling the eye with prisms of rainbow colors dancing across the room. The natural hardwood floors, contrasting beautifully, shone and glistened.

My first instinct upon entering the foyer, was to check the bottom of my shoes, or better yet, remove them. It was lovely beyond description. Michael spoke with the maitre 'd, and we were seated momentarily. Dining was secondary at this point. My dilemma was dividing my attention between the beauty of the room and the gorgeous man sitting across the table from me. And dressed in black, he was a direct contrast to the surroundings. But what sent earthquake size spasms through my body, looking at him, was the way he was looking at me.

"You look beautiful, my sweet Rainey." And taking my hand in his, keeping his smoldering eyes on mine, he gently kissed each finger, and turning my hand over, kissed the center of my palm tenderly. I began a slow, sizzling meltdown. Just the lightest touch of his lips sent shivers up my spine, my body screamed for more. I loved him so.

We were totally absorbed with each other when the waiter appeared, discreetly, not wanting to interrupt an obvious romantic moment. Feeling, more than seeing him, I tore my eyes away from Michael, breaking the magic. I turned to the waiter. His face jolted me momentarily. Everything about it was French: a strong, distinct nose, dark eyes, and his mouth had taken on a specific shape carved by speaking the lovely romance language for so many years. *He even smiles with a French accent,* I thought amused, and he looked so elegant and distinguished standing there, his back board-straight. When he greeted "good evening," he ever so slightly bowed his head and I listened, intently, expecting to hear the clicking of his heels. The entire scene was straight out of a movie, and I loved every extravagant second of it. I wondered what the evening would cost; my menu was sans prices. Well, I wasn't going to think about it, just enjoy the decadence. I asked Michael to order for me. When I was with him, food was the last thing on my mind, with the exception of ruling out any quirky ocean delicacies. The word "delicacy" threw up a red flag, inducing fear, since my first experience with it had sent raw squid to my table. No, I wasn't into delicacies, no matter from what exotic country the chef hailed. But if the extravagant décor was indicative of the food. Our palates were about to experience the gastronomical treat of a lifetime. Again, we weren't disappointed. Michael ordered the house specialty, Chateau Briand for two, made with venison and a pink peppercorn cognac sauce, accompanied by a scrumptious array of roasted vegetables. The recommended wine by the sommelier was "El Gran Vino Tinto." And though I knew zilch about wines, I knew enough that it matched the taste of the entrée to perfection. Dessert was out of the question, but we lingered over a delicious light dessert coffee. I didn't want the romance of the evening to end, but looking into Michael's eyes, I realized his eyes were glistening not just with lust, but with the excitement of his surprise. The romantic mood broken irretrievably, I asked impatiently, "Now will you tell me?" I think I'd been extremely patient, but that virtue was quickly dissolving into something very ugly. His smile, as he suddenly felt the air temperature around our table drop thirty degrees, changed from sweet contentment to a contorted mixture of apprehension and delight. He sighed deeply as if preparing to plunge into unfamiliar waters, leaned forward in his seat, and took my right hand in his.

Michael's news was more surprising than anything I could possibly have conjured up. The most I could imagine was a surprise weekend, again, or something, at least, on the same planet. Surprise didn't quite get it. He'd applied for, and was granted a sponsorship from his favorite magazine, *Ultimate Climb.* They generously offered him a year of traveling to countries and mountains he had heretofore only read and dreamed of. Now, he was to not only climb, but photograph and write of his exploits with the promise of publication in said magazine, contingent, of course, upon approval of his work. "Michael, I'm…I don't know even what to say, where to begin, that's fantastic."

He continued exuberantly. "Honey, do you realize what this means to me? This affords me the opportunity to climb in Washington, Alaska, Africa, and I…this'll prepare me, probably in two years, for my ultimate dream, Mt. Everest."

His face was alive, his eyes dancing. I didn't want to put a damper on it, but I was helpless to erase what I knew was a look of devastation and confusion on mine, and though it should have dimmed his enthusiasm, he was still smiling, obviously oblivious; I was glad. We could discuss my feelings later. Right now, it was his night. I knew this was an opportunity of a lifetime for him, a dream come true, and I did my best to stretch a smile, weak as it may be, across my face. Absorbed in my own thoughts, it took a moment to register that Michael had suddenly risen from his chair, the smile, yet lingering on his face, and was coming around the table. The look of confusion I worked so hard to remove moments before, not only returned but intensified as he knelt before me, taking my hands in his. *"He's lost it,"* I thought, as I frantically looked around at the other diners. "Michael," I said softly, with a nervous giggle, what are you doing? people are staring."

"Let 'em stare, sweetheart," he said in his best Bogart voice, which was horrible. "I don't care if the whole world hears what I have to say, Rainey, but it's only for your ears and heart." I was about to continue my protest, but he quickly placed his fingers to my lips to quiet me. "Rainey, you know you've stolen my heart completely."

My heart softened, momentarily.

"Do you really think I want or could spend the next year away from you? It's killing me to be away from you a day and every night," he leered. And with that, titters of laughter came from around the room, confirming my suspicion that we had an audience. Michael enjoyed the attention and continued. "Mountain climbing is my hobby…yes, I'll readily admit, an obsessive one, but it's still second to my love for you. This opportunity being handed to me, I can't imagine turning it down – but neither can I, nor do I, imagine being separated from you, so I've found the perfect solution if I can just convince you to agree."

My mind raced, trying to catch up, there was too much information thrown at me too fast. My face was flushed with embarrassment, realizing that we had the attention of the entire room. But I was loving and enjoying Michael, and the moment, at the same time. It was surreal. And as discreet as the diners were trying to be, a cursory glance revealed many heads tilted in our direction, straining to catch every word as they were caught up in this romantic drama being played out to their delight. It was difficult to focus. "Michael, please," I whispered pleadingly, "everyone is listening."

He laughed, ignoring my pleas and continued, "Rainey, do you love me?"

"Michael, yes, yes, of course, you know I love you." I replied softly, feeling frustrated at this tacky display and pulling at his hands in an attempt to get him off his knees. After this spectacle, there would be no doubt we'd not be allowed to return to this restaurant. Although, to dine here often, I'd imagine we'd have to resort to bank robbery, anyway. My thoughts wandered.

"Do you love me enough to marry me?"

"What?!!!! Mar—? Michael!" The audience gasped along with me, at his request, then, quieted just as quickly to hear my answer. But suddenly, and instantaneously, for me, our audience disappeared. I was caught up in the magic of the moment, and no one existed except Michael and me. I threw my arms around him so enthusiastically he lost his balance…Rainey up to her old tricks. Michael being quick and agile, threw his powerful arms behind him, breaking his total collapse.

"Michael, I'm sorry for being so dense, I thought you'd lost your mind, I was not expecting this. You said you're leaving and, you—" was all I managed as the diners returned, and by now, feeling more like family, I enjoyed the waves of laughter flooding over us.

"Rainey, you can't refuse me in front of all these people, I'll never live it down."

I looked through tear-filled eyes at his lovely face reflecting hope and anticipation. "Yes, yes, yes, oh yes, Michael, I love you so much." Our "family" broke into applause, followed by quiet, dignified shouts of congratulations. Michael stood and bowed slightly to the delighted audience, then finally took his seat. He retrieved a tiny box from his pocket, opening it slowly and turned it toward me. There sitting upon royal blue silk padding, was a one carat solitaire of yellow gold winking at me, brilliantly in spite of the subdued lighting. I sucked in my breath at its beauty. "Oh Michael, it's gorgeous."

He gently removed it, took my left hand in his, and slipped it on my finger. And speaking *sotto voce*, he continued, "I searched hard for one to match your beauty, Rainey, but realized I would never succeed, so I had to settle."

I laughed, tears of tender love and joy springing to my eyes, and feeling more contented than I ever remember feeling in my entire life. How could I not love this man? After a few minutes of savoring this romantic interlude, reality hit me square between the eyes. "But Michael! What are we thinking? You're leaving. We don't even know when we'll be seeing each other again! How can we be talking about marr—?"

"Yes, Rainey," he interrupted, laughing. "Actually I have thought of nothing else for weeks, but I won't be going for two months." And pausing, he looked questioningly into my eyes, as if waiting to see the solution explode in my brain and come flying off my tongue. It didn't, and the pause lasted interminably long, as I sat there mulling over the options in my mind, and not liking any of them. A hasty wedding? No, I didn't want to be cheated out of the anticipation, shopping and even the nervousness that was involved in preparing for a wedding. Another option? Waiting for his return? A year away? Maybe… then he mentioned climbing Mt. Everest. How much longer would that be? "Please Michael! What have you been thinking? I don't understand. What am I missing here?"

"Rainey, now don't say anything until you hear me out, totally. I've been stashing money into savings and investments since I started working and I've accumulated a sizable amount. I was thinking," he began slowly, and then finished the sentence in machine gun fashion. "Why don't we get married now, and you go with me."

That option never entered my mind for obvious reasons: it was ludicrous. "Go with you? Michael, I have a job, you'd be climbing, traveling all over—"

"Yes, I would be spending a lot of time away from you, but we're going to be apart anyway, and we'd certainly see more of each other if you went with me. And yes, we would be traveling the world, and isn't that another reason to go? You won't be bored. Rainey, don't answer me now, I know this is a monumental decision, one that you shouldn't answer without a lot of thought. I'll understand if you say no, I'll have no choice but to accept your decision, but this next year will be hell for both of us if you do. If you say yes, you're right, maybe you'd experience some hell once in a while, but we could have a liberal sprinkling of heaven too, huh?" Desperation and love intermingled in his eyes. I wanted to scream, "yes!" of course I'd go. But the thought of dropping my entire life to cavort around the world, alone most of the time— "Michael, you're right, I have to have some time."

The tone of the remainder of the dinner was changed dramatically. Our minds were totally preoccupied with the burden of my decision. If I chose to wait for his return, our relationship would definitely be put to the test. We would see each other only a couple of times during the course of the remainder of this year. It seemed unthinkable, but to be married so hastily in a civil ceremony? No friends, family? That was equally unthinkable. What to do? Time was not on my side, but I decided to attempt to relax and enjoy the remainder of the evening, anyway. A solution would come, of course, so why not take advantage of the, otherwise, wonderful evening. I had it all planned out in my mind…I'd read myself to sleep tonight to keep my mind occupied, and within ten minutes after waking in the morning, my instincts would gently present the answer to me. All that was necessary for me to do was be still and listen to my heart. Over the years it had stood me in good stead, and I didn't see it deserting me now. It was amazing out it worked for me, reminding me of the Eight Ball after shaking it around a bit, the answer slowly appeared. But forgetting about it for the rest of the evening was easier said than done. Gazing at the beautiful ring on my finger, I was relishing Michael's proposal. The dream of every little girl of my generation, and it sent my heart soaring. Then, the thought of an impending year long separation, slammed me mercilessly back to terra firma.

Michael walked me to the door as usual. Corina and Sheila were asleep. We lingered over sweet kisses and Michael teased me about never experiencing torment again when saying goodnight: "*Au contrare*, our night would just begin."

I lovingly reprimanded him, reminding me he was not to use any type of persuasion to influence my decision. He laughed, but as he moved closer to kiss me, his eyes turned smoky and sexy, and he kissed me so tenderly and lovingly I almost succumbed…almost. I pushed him gently away, scolding him for resorting to such unfair tactics. He loved it, whispering in my ear that that was just a small sample of what was waiting for me, if I just said yes. That sweet sexual tingling sensation raced through my body, and it took all my control to shove him away again. He snickered smugly, his ego swelling to the bursting point at his obvious sexual effect on me. I unlocked the door quickly to deter further sabotage and peeking safely out from inside of the door, said good night. His smile broadened like he was the cock of the walk and he blew me a kiss as he sauntered away. I stood there watching his broad back disappear down the walk and could hear him whistling. He was very sure of himself, this Michael Dreason.

CHAPTER XXXII

We were committed, happily so, to flying to Los Angeles for Dana and Lora's reception, the party of the century, as Dana said, and I never doubted it. I could surely find the time and space for discussions, to analyze the details of my decision, whatever it was going to be.

The next morning when I awoke, a rush of disappointment washed over me. My mind was blank and a feeling of dread had settled in my heart from whence, I thought the answer would spring. I felt sick with disappointment. My only option left was to focus on every aspect of my life until I came to a decision. Patience is not one of my virtues. I like everything done promptly, correctly, and a neat bow tied around it. When it isn't, I get no rest until it is. It's like waiting for the other shoe to drop. Unfortunately, fate doesn't play by my rules. So back and forth I went, mentally dissecting the advantages and disadvantages all morning while packing and waiting for Michael. That was weighing on me heavily too. I knew he'd expect an answer when he arrived, and I envisioned the look of disappointment on his face. I was feeling pressured, after all, with guilt. He felt the answer was simple, and so I was the stinker here. Maybe he'd doubt the depth of my love for him if I said no. Oh, if ever I needed to consult with my cohorts, it was now. Thank God I would be seeing them in a few hours. That, too, produced a little guilt. I didn't tell Michael I was going to discuss our personal lives with my friends, and I hated the thought that it might upset him. But these people were special, family, whose counsel we had each depended on, and trusted. We had grown up together, had been through a lot over the years and still were going through some pretty rough times. I'd only known Michael for a year. Or maybe I didn't love him as much as I thought, or maybe it wasn't the love necessary for a successful life together, or, or, or—. All I did know for certain, was I was driving myself crazy thinking about it.

Just as I expected, Michael practically exploded through the door, looking at me expectantly. And also as I expected, the look on his face was devastating when I told him I didn't have an answer. I didn't pull any punches. I didn't want to extend his misery, and besides, we had a plane to catch. Then, suddenly feeling a little defensive, I thought, *you know? It's my life here we're talking about changing and disrupting, totally! He'll have to get over it.* But, unfortunately, that blustering resolve didn't get me to the airport; my feelings of inadequacy summoned guilt back into full swing.

The flight was uneventful, with the exception of the complete silence exhibited by both Michael and me, and the turbulence inside me made up for any atmospheric lack. I had enough to rent out. Oh, the blissfulness at the thought of a frenetic two days with Dana and Lora. I laughed to myself thinking, that up until last night, I was becoming expert in deception, plotting, planning and praying for ways in which to find refuge from them. Now I ached for the distraction. Not that it mattered, they wouldn't be permitting spare moments of privacy for anyone, anyway, let alone meditation. But it was their day, and I wouldn't dream of detracting from it.

A limo was waiting at LAX to escort us the short distance to the small hotel they called home. My eyes began the exercise of bugging out as we approached the massive black iron gates, atop of which regally sat two huge lions. The driver promptly announced our arrival by phone, which, to our enjoyment, proved to be the formula for opening the gates. A quarter-mile long driveway, beautifully lined with gorgeous palms, led, eventually, to a circled drive, in the midst of which, stood an impressive, gurgling fountain filled with cherubs and, of course, Dana's favorites, clowns. The driver insisted on our staying put until he arrived at each door, whereupon he helped us from the car. He then removed our luggage from the trunk and led us to the massive, mahogany, double doors. We rang a huge red clown's nose, passing for a doorbell. I hadn't even seen Lora and Dana, yet, and already, they'd succeeded in wiping away some of my overriding gloom.

Maybe I couldn't shake off the burden of guilt of failing to come to a decision quickly. Maybe I was being consumed with turmoil and confusion, and I was certainly having a difficult time weighing my options with any credibility, let alone thinking straight the last twenty four hours, But here, in this atmosphere, filled to overflowing with love, peacefulness and tranquility emanating from the childlike surroundings, hope suddenly took root in my heart. Perhaps my psyche would be forced to release the grip of anxiety, to laugh, enjoy, be ridiculous, and while its guard was down, maybe, just maybe, the answer would sneak in, totally unsuspected, announcing itself like the proverbial light bulb. Oh, if only it could be.

Dana and Lora appeared, giggling and yelling, arms outstretched, as they bounded down a long, hallway. Lora's large bosom, half bared in a tank top, which struggled to restrain its contents, were bouncing up and down causing me to wince in pain at the sight. A wide, yellow tie hung to her knees and partially hid a white skirt covered with huge red and blue polka dots. Large blue ladies' clown shoes with large red buckles covered her small feet. Dana and Lora both wore large, red clown noses and Dana's was accompanied by a gigantic, red bow tie that covered a large portion of an, otherwise, bare chest. Bright orange suspenders held up white, ballooning pants at the bottom of which, peeked out silly, oversized shoes of different colors. I was amused to see that neither needed the curly wigs to complete the outfits. Dana's blonde curls came over his ears and were flying loose in every direction. Their smiles, though left unpainted, were as big as any circus clowns. How could any depression or sadness survive? Lora and I squealed and hugged as was our usual greeting after being away from each other, even the shortest length of time. Introductions were made all around, and Lora, catching my eye, pulled me aside, and shaking her hand at the wrist exclaimed, "Vah–Vah–Vah–voom! He's adorable!"

Michael appeared suddenly, to take my arm, but Dana was quicker, grabbing my hands and kissing me quickly on both cheeks. "Well, well well," sounding a lot like W.C. fields, he continued, "It's about time I'm meeting the rest of this here outlaw gang! Are you by any chance the head moll? The top banana? The big cheese? The he—"

"Okay, okay Dana." Lora grabbed his arm, tugging at him to stop. "Once he gets started he doesn't know when to stop."

"The head honch—" He attempted again, leaning in toward us, the side of his hand at his mouth, and eyes furtively looking around.

"Dana!!!" squealed Lora, swatting him lovingly. "Stop, already."

And as if we'd conspired against Lora, the rest of us proclaimed in unison, "the head honcho!"

"Oh no! God help us all, that's all we need is a bunch of Danas running around loose. I told you he was infectious," and looking at her watch, she asked, "and how long have you been in his presence?"

Their gaiety was, indeed, infectious and within minutes, Michael and Dana were exchanging slaps on the back as they walked away, deep in conversation. I was thinking how well they hit it off, but then, I realized, Dana didn't know a stranger and wouldn't accept any awkwardness from anyone.

I took advantage of the moment alone with Lora. "Lora, I need advice. I know this is not a good time for anything serious, but then if I waited for a serious mood around here, I'd never get to it. Anyway, I need to talk with everyone. It doesn't have to be long and involved. I just need to throw something out to all of you, have you mull it over in your minds and tell me what you think, but, well I just need an answer by the time I have to leave. I have to have an answer by then."

"An answer?" Her already broad smile grew even bigger. "Is there something we should know?"

"That's what I need to discuss. Is Juliet going to make it? When are they all coming in? I've got to do this as soon as possible."

"Hey, hey, hey," said Lora, displaying one of the few times you'd see a smile leave her face. She sensed the seriousness and urgency of my tone. "They're all due just anytime, but Rainey, please don't give me bad news now, I know this might sound selfish, but this is my honeymoon time and I can help you, anything you want, but can it wait for just these two days? I mean, I can see you standing here looking okay, so obviously, it's not your health, but—"

"No, no, it's not anything like that. I'm sorry sweetie, I didn't mean to upset you, but no, it's a very tough, actually, life-changing decision I want…no, I need to make by the time I fly back. I wouldn't jeopardize this special time for you, not in a million years. I'm so happy for you. You're glowing, by the way. But tell me Lora, please, you two don't carry on nonstop like this, do you?"

Lora giggled. "Well, to be honest with you, it is most of the time. We do have plenty of down time, but really, even those times are positive and uplifting. He's always planning something, Rainey. He's the stereotypical salesman, always looking for something to sell, but more than that, he's an entrepreneur and as you can see, a very successful one. It seems like anything he touches turns to gold, just like Midas. As a matter of fact, a lot of our friends call him that, and he loves it. He knows he's been blessed with a gift and appreciates it. Rainey, he's everything you see plus he's generous to everyone who needs anything and, he agrees with me on wanting a large family. Lots and lots of goofy kids, as he says, running around under foot causing all kinds of ruckus. You want goofy? I told him he didn't have a thing to worry about, with his contribution to the gene pool, the kids will have no choice."

"Well, excuse me for saying so, Lora, but in a roomful of kids, it would be difficult to pick out either of you." We laughed as we turned toward the stairs leading to our rooms. The chauffeur had taken our bags up already, and Lora apologized for keeping me. I told her no need for that, I was thrilled to be here to share this wonderful time with her, but I was anxious to get changed so she could give me the grand tour. She led me to my room while Dana was escorting Michael to his. And what a room it was…at least three times the size of mine at home, with a fireplace, sitting area and a bathtub big enough to swim in, but it was decorated simply and elegantly. I'd seen houses like this, but only in movie magazines. And I'd heard rumors that people actually lived in them, now I knew it for a fact. A giant sized basket filled with fruits and cheeses sat on the coffee table, along with a bottle of, I'm sure, delicious, expensive wine. I wouldn't know. I was completely ignorant when it came to wines, only aware of red and white, or domestic and foreign. That was it. But it was on my list of interests to be studied in my goal setting book. In the meantime, I'd just drink and enjoy. What a kick. I turned to open my luggage and there on the bedside table lay pictures of the whole gang, from our earliest days together, to our recent trip to Florida. How like these two to be so thoughtful. I was delighted, and sat reminiscing until a masculine voice somewhere close by interrupted my reveries. Michael? Sudden warmth flushed through my system as a delicious smile made its way across my mouth. Ooooh, I had to hurry, but once I stepped into the room-size shower, rushing was the last thing I wanted to do, after all. A showerhead was anchored on two walls and a large built in bench provided comfort if one cared to linger, and the lavishness of it all definitely lent itself to luxuriating. I turned both showers on, positioning them out, spraying my front and backsides at the same time. I took full advantage of the opulence. Yes, I was anxious to get back to Michael and Lora and Dana, but the pulsating spray of hot water peppered my body, unwinding the kinks, and releasing the pent up tension. I had to force myself to quickly dry off with a huge, fluffy Egyptian cotton towel, big enough, actually, to wrap me and Michael in at the same time. Whoa, now there was a pleasant thought that helped get me moving. I'd only been away from him for an hour and was missing him terribly, already. Now, how was I going to be away from him for three or six months at a time? That thought produced a deep sigh. I threw on a cool, white sun back dress, tan sandals, ran a comb through my hair, swished a dab of blush on my cheeks, a little eye shadow and I was ready for a big glass of iced tea, piña colada, margarita, mai tai, etc. etc., and a chaise lounge by the pool. It didn't get any better than this.

CHAPTER XXXIII

It was an incredible stroll to the pool area. I lingered, enjoying the grandeur of the palatial residence. The light danced off the crystal chandeliers, which dangled exquisitely from the huge foyer and dining area. Thick Persian and Oriental carpets were strategically placed on the tile, marbled and hardwood floors. The color motif was neutral. Lora and Dana, both loving bright colors, showcased their individual tastes without appearing gauche. The halls were covered with exquisite paintings intermingled with whimsical ones. Dana wanted a visitor's heart to be lifted no matter where they were. He had succeeded. Life-size clowns were everywhere. Each dressed colorfully and delicately created to appear realistic. Dana's dream, as a child was to literally run away with the circus. His parents had taken him to his first one in an attempt to assuage his grief over the recent loss of his beloved dog. The clowns brought much needed laughter to his overly saddened heart, then, and have continued to do so through the years. Not only were Dana and Lora one of the first through the gates when the circus came to town, but on some occasions, there'd been as many as twenty children tagging along.

My eyes began to ache from staring, and dizziness resulted from spinning my head in an attempt to catch every detail. It was gorgeous, and I was thrilled for Lora. I guess you could say she married well.

Suddenly, squeals appeared on my left and turning quickly, my heart swelled at the sight of Melanie and Sherry being ushered in my direction by Lora, arms outstretched. I ran to them, enjoying their warm embraces. Sherry looked youthful and healthy. She said that's what love had done for her and with a sly, and hopeful smile, added, "You don't look so bad yourself, huh?"

"Okay, enough of this," quipped Melanie, and they both leaned conspiratorially toward me. "Where's Michael?"

I laughed. I couldn't believe it, but I actually hadn't thought of him for the last ten minutes or so, being preoccupied with the grandeur of the surroundings. As I turned to locate him, he was starting toward me with that beautiful smile lighting his face. "Wow," said Mel. "When you get through with him, can I have him?"

"You're telling me," whispered Sherry. Michael was extending his hands to both ladies, as I made the introductions.

"Now," Michael began, "let me see if I have this straight. Melanie, you're the shy one, right?"

"Used to be the shy one…not anymore, I'm all grown up now," she replied boldly to emphasize the misconception.

"And I believe you," Michael said in mock offense, with eyebrows raised. "And," he continued, "Sherry, you're the sweet one, or," Michael threw a glance at Melanie before adding, "have you grown up and are now the Wicked Witch of the West?" Sherry was delighted with the description and started to thank him, but Michael, seeing Lora feigning a frown, and realizing how that sounded, backtracked.

"I don't mean that none of the rest of you are sweet, but, well—"

We laughed to let him off the hook. Michael took my hand and pulled me tightly to his side gazing lovingly into my eyes, "None are as sweet as my Rainey."

"Ooohhhhh." They gagged, laughing, but were duly impressed by his loving attentiveness to me.

"Where are your guys by the way?" I asked.

"They're upstairs showering and changing," Mel responded. "They decided to look around first. James and Almon hit it off right away and talked nonstop from the time they were introduced."

Mel and James flew to Kennedy, connected with Sherry and Almon and flew out together on a twelve passenger commuter. Melanie, splaying her hands out around her, said, "Can you believe this place? I think we should all just pack up and move in here, and there'd still be room for more, whaddya think, Lora?"

Lora laughed. "I can't think of anything I'd like better."

"Can you really die from too much happy? I wonder," asked Sherry.

"Well, do I look dead?" asked Lora.

"No. As a matter of fact," I responded, "and, true enough, you and Dana would certainly have died already."

Melanie, still craning her neck to take in her surroundings, said, "James' family comes from money, but when he saw this place, he said forget about all this school and doctor stuff, he wants Dana to teach him what he knows. He's kidding, of course. In his heart, he's a doctor already, but this does give one pause. I mean I'm talking eight years of school and working day and night and not even coming close to this kind of lifestyle."

"I know, that's what Almon and James talked about on the way here, but when they saw this place, they realized that they'd had no idea what real wealth really looked like."

Sherry turned to Michael, "Michael, what do you think of all this?"

Michael laughed. "This is way out of my league. We each have our dreams, and my palatial mansion is in the sky, Mt. Everest, you know. The thought of dealing with people every day and sitting around a pool making deals is definitely not for me. Rainey agrees, don't you, honey?"

"It's overwhelming, that's for sure, but, I don't know, I think I could easily settle for at least half of this."

Melanie and Sherry laughed in agreement.

"Well, who knows, Miss ssmartie," replied Michael, that just may be in your future. I think money would look a whole lot better wrapped around you."

"Ohhhhh Lord!" said Mel, "you two are disgustingly in love, and it's making me miss James, and speaking of, what in the world is taking them so long?"

I was looking forward to meeting James. I knew if Melanie loved him, he had to be a great guy.

Dana suddenly appeared, announcing that Kiki had arrived and was taken to her room. "She said to have the drinks ready, she's on her way." As we exchanged horrified looks, Dana threw his arms in the air, a hopelessly guilty look on his face and said, "I'm sorry, I thought that was in poor taste, but Kiki wanted me to tell you, after I received the expressions you just gave me, that she was just kidding. And you know if I think it's in poor taste, man, it's got to be bad." He laughed.

Sherry sighed with obvious relief. "I'm gonna kill her. My sense of humor is as good as the next, but not when it involves her drinking." They left then, with promises after locating their lost men, of getting together later at poolside, with Juliet, too, if she would just get here.

Michael and I located some comfortable, lounge chairs partially shaded by palms, and plopped down to partake of some delicious, tropical drinks served to us almost before our butts hit the chairs. What a life, I could get used to this.

The pool was surrounded with lush foliage and palm trees swaying gently in the balmy breeze. A huge white cabana sat near the entrance to the house filled with bathing suits, bath towels, lotion and anything else one needed, to enjoy a day, poolside. The late afternoon sun seeped into my skin, warming me to my bones and forcing contented sighs from deep within. The soothing buzzing of voices, the birds singing their sweet melodies and the sound of the breeze playing gently in the trees transported me within minutes into a euphoric state. But my semi-comatose moment was abruptly interrupted by the excruciating sprinkle of cold water on my overheated, exposed tummy. I gasped, sucking in a deep breath, rising quickly to see who was going to be murdered by my bare hands. I should've known. There stood Dana, hands on either hip, legs splayed, proud as a peacock. No shame, and grinning from ear to ear. Michael was snoozing. I never knew it was possible for a human being to not only go to sleep so quickly, but to sleep so soundly. "I'm going to kill you, Dana, that water was frigid, where'd you get it, from the fridge?"

"Yeah," he laughed, "how'd you know." And he held up a bottle of drinking water for me to see. "Lora hates it when I do that, but usually, if I know the person a little better, and they're wearing a bathing suit, I throw them in the pool, so you got off easy. It's a nasty habit she's helping me break. I'm sorry. You okay?"

But laughing and enjoying the moment as he was, the apology didn't ring quite sincere. "Hey, you get me next time." And eyeing Michael, he said, "He's next…you wanna help?"

"No, I don't, and don't you dare!" He winced at my outburst, but stood there looking so remorseful and pathetic, I couldn't have stayed angry if I tried. Besides it was impossible to do anything but smile seeing a grown man standing before me wearing a large red nose. Lora came strolling up, smiling. "Is he tormenting you Rainey?"

"How'd you guess?"

"Oh no, Dana, you didn't do the water thing? Did he Rainey? Did you Dana?" Lora was quickly looking from one of us to the other and Dana, clasping his hands in front of him, head bowed dejectedly, simpered in a voice filled with mock remorse. "I did it, I'm guilty." He held out his hands for Lora to put on the cuffs.

"Rainey, I'm sorry, he's insufferable. You have to understand he's a little boy inside."

"Yep, that's me," Dana retorted with a prideful smile lighting his already cheerful face. We all laughed, while Michael slept on. We sat lazily talking and were joined shortly by the others, freshly showered and in their newly purchased swimsuits. Almon and James headed straight for the pool. Dana joined them with a cannonball jump. He had changed into swimming trunks, but left his bow tie and nose on, and after his jump, his nose could be seen bobbing around in the water and, at the moment, he was feigning panic, looking about, frantically screaming, "My nose, my nose, help me please, somebody, I've lost my nose." His laughter reverberated around the entire pool area. Thank God for his craziness. He kept us laughing.

Michael stirred, raised his head, and looked around groggily trying to get oriented. I leaned over and kissed his forehead. "Time to get up sleepyhead, you're missing the fun." He said the quickest way to wake up was to get in the pool and off he went. While the guys displayed their repertoire of dives in a male game of one-up-man-ship, we sat back and enjoyed the moment.

We were discussing Juliet's imminent arrival when Anna the housekeeper brought the phone to Lora. "Juliet, where are you? Great!!! Stay put. Someone will be there shortly." We could scarcely believe what we were hearing. Juliet actually came. Our shocked and loud responses of disbelief obviously had not escaped Juliet's ears, which quickly prompted her disclosure to Lora that Rich was alive and the prognosis looked good. And with that "wonderful?" news for her, anyway, she felt a few days relaxing in the sun would be restorative as well as enjoyable. Well, being around people who love and cherish you, laughing and acting like carefree children once again, certainly wouldn't hurt. Shrieks of pleasure were for the possibility of seeing Juliet, but not, God help us, necessarily for Rich. Deep down, we didn't want him to die, but the thought running rampant through all our minds, I'm certain, at that moment, was, oh God, no, he's back. Juliet felt it might be a sign, a positive turning point for their relationship. She was of the belief that Rich, because of his close call, could have experienced an epiphany, and come back a new man. *Lord help us all.* Was all I could think. Was this optimism born out of remorse? Was her ignorance that profound? Or, was she that, mentally, far gone? I realized, resignedly, that kidnapping and brainwashing her might be our only recourse. But in spite of Juliet's elevated spirits, Lora still detected an edginess. But of course, all she'd been through, it was to be expected. Otherwise, we were excited and anxious to see her, to tuck her under our collective wing, so to speak, to give her succor and healing for the next few days.

CHAPTER XXXIV

Juliet arrived on schedule and was escorted to poolside by Anna. Our first instinct was, of course, to squeal with delight at seeing her, but those instincts came to an abrupt halt the instant her appearance registered. She looked like a bedraggled, skinny version of our old Juliet. I felt as though I was back in Florida. Tears sprung to my eyes, as my heart filled with pity. But we were thrilled she was here, nevertheless, as she presented us with a huge smile and we closed the distance between us, enclosing her gently in a group hug. It was going to take more than just a few days of healing to bring this body back to its former self. But what better place than this? After freshening up, she rejoined us wearing a skimpy sun back dress revealing bones barely covered with flesh. She had dropped more weight from a body that already couldn't afford it.

The afternoon passed all too quickly as we sat eating and chatting. The sun continued its relentless journey across the blue sky, preparing for its nightly descent, and we were confronted with a decision to stay put or hit the beach. The latter won and we walked, seemingly, for miles in the moonlight and returning, energized, refreshed ourselves in the pool. Mexican food, and plenty of it, was served and we made certain Juliet had her share. We were as a bunch of clucking hens, but as it turned out, it wasn't necessary. She seemed to be holding her demons at bay, or, hopefully, left them back in Maine, altogether. But with the workout we'd just had, she ate with the best of us. We couldn't have been happier.

Sun-soaked, lazy and stomachs full, we practically had to roll ourselves to our respective rooms. It was going to be a big day tomorrow, with people milling about like ants, but Lora assured us everything was taken care of, and it was easy enough to believe, watching her. Anyone who could relax as she did, when hosting that kind of shindig, had to know it to be so.

Exhausted, I must've fallen asleep as soon as my head hit the pillow, and somewhere in the early morning hours, I began a lovely dream. Michael and I were sitting, relaxing and talking, but as strange as dreams can be, we were surrounded by a prevailing aura of sensuality, as though we had just made love. Of course, I knew that from hearsay, not personal experience, but it was lovely. Then suddenly, Michael began floating away from me, anguish appearing on his face as he was whisked away, arms outstretched, calling to me, pleadingly. He was moving gracefully and quickly alongside a beautiful lake, and I was running as fast as I could to catch up with him. Without warning, he stopped and began hovering directly over a soft blanket spread out beneath him, and the look of distress on his face intensified. Huge snowflakes fell around him only, and a bundle of soft, white clouds rolled in and about the lower half of his body. He continued to call my name, and as I attempted but failed to near the blanket, the clouds rolled away, revealing to my horror, the missing half of Michael's body. I bolted upright, screaming. I immediately left the bed, and began pacing for relief of the tension and fear already consuming me. Thankful for Dana and Lora's thoughtfulness in supplying our rooms with a wide variety of books and magazines, I grabbed an arm full from the bedside table, and with the voraciousness comparable only to a wild, hungry animal, I sought distraction. A couple of hours later, I was thrilled to hear outrageous squeals and splashing...sounds of people enjoying themselves, rising up from poolside, enticing and inviting me to join them.

I quickly headed for a welcoming, hot shower, hopefully to wash away the ugliness of the horrid nightmare. Contemplating it, momentarily, I reasoned that with the exhaustion, excitement and an abundance of caffeine and drinks, plus the burden of the decision I was troubling over, could certainly explain a body's desire to scream out in pain, in the form of a nightmare, in the early morning hours.

On my way down the stairs, I noticed people in every nook and cranny: caterers, entertainers, etc. were busily preparing for the big day. The reception was scheduled to officially begin at one. Dana wanted an early start so the party would last longer. It seemed, so far to me, that life was one long party where he was concerned. We decided the best thing for all of us was to stay out of the way, and what better place to lounge, than around the pool. Michael found an available phone and would be occupied for thirty minutes or so, contacting his friends, shoring up details, etc., etc., for the upcoming climb.

Lora and Dana were even sillier and giddier than usual. Dana donned his clown outfit for the day but Lora had opted for some fun, normal duds. At eleven thirty, before the expected guests started pouring in, we decided to stroll around and enjoy the results of the efforts being made all morning. Gorgeous flowers were arranged at every possible space. There was no particular flower theme, unless no theme was considered a theme. At any rate, there were flowers of every color and variety, imaginable. Several small pyramid "fountains" of champagne were set up offering up the delectable bubbles. Live peacocks were brought in to roam the property at will. Their tail feathers fanned out, rivaled the beauty of the multi-colored flowers they strutted around. A rock and roll band was set up in one area, and when the raucous music began promptly at one, Juliet amazed us all by displaying her nimble and awesome dancing talents. We wouldn't have believed the transformation before us, if not for seeing it with our own eyes. And If a dance partner wasn't immediately available, she pulled one from the cluster of people standing near the dance area. She danced until perspiration was obvious and dripping from her face. I marveled at, but worried about her withered body's ability to withstand such a workout. But I wouldn't have attempted to stop her for the world. We hadn't seen her enjoy herself like this for a long time.

A big band group was set up in another area for those not so enamored of rock and roll. And the *piece de resistance* was a spectacular fireworks display on the beach at midnight for those who could hang on. It lived up to our expectations and more, with hundreds of beautiful colors exploding and filling the night sky, not only for our viewing pleasure, but for those, yet awake, along that particular stretch of beach. It had been a glorious evening, and morning, and we finally said our goodnights at three a.m.

It had been a successful weekend for more than just the obvious reason of pulling off a fantastic reception. We watched in awe as Juliet, not only nibbled at food constantly, but we laughed right along with her, as she contributed to conversations taking place around her. It was analogous to watching a movie on fast speed, accelerating a beautiful flower's opening, gloriously, from a seed in the ground, to its full potential in a matter of seconds. And as ridiculous as it sounded, Juliet looked as though she'd gained weight, although, it was more than likely that the consumption of a little food had simply returned a spark of life to her, otherwise, drawn face. Lounging so much poolside, the sun had kissed her gently but firmly on her full cheeks and a beautiful smile seemed to have been permanently planted on her pretty mouth. It was refreshing and wonderful to see her like this. Maybe Rich had been good for her, comparatively speaking…all the misery she'd been through with him served to give her a new perspective and appreciation for everything good. Whatever the reason, we simply enjoyed it, and prayed, somehow, some way, it was a new beginning for her.

CHAPTER XXXV

Dana and Lora were leaving for Disneyland the next day, which would officially begin their honeymoon. Then it was off to Switzerland and wherever their fancy led them, for two weeks. Lora mentioned once to Dana, that after seeing Heidi as a child, she longed to see those magnificent Alps and, of course, that's all she had to say. Her requests to Dana were like a magic wand...voicing them made them magically happen. He'd arranged a helicopter tour not only through the Alps but included a flight around the Matterhorn itself to get a closer look. Oh they'd be full of wild and naturally funny stories when they returned, and would have an appreciative audience looking forward to hearing them.

It was only a few hours later, that we all began to stumble out into the hallways, staggering to the kitchen for an injection of caffeine, the lot of us resembling a congregation of zombies. Dana and Lora were not their usual giddy selves, but still had the rest of us beat for enthusiasm. They grabbed coffee, along with hugs and kisses and promises to call as soon as they returned. Dana placed a ridiculously oversized pair of sunglasses on his, finally, normal nose, conjured up his goofiest grin, and out the door they went taking with them what modicum of life there was in the room. We were suffering, but it was a small price to pay for the joy we received, participating in a small but happy part of Dana and Lora's life.

Our flights were scheduled for late afternoon, and that was no accident. We planned ahead for plenty of time to rest before returning to work on Monday morning.

It was an interminably long ride to the airport. First because we were so miserably tired, and secondly, I wasn't talking, which meant I didn't have an answer, and Michael didn't ask questions. I was disappointed I hadn't had the opportunity for a discussion with the rest of the group, but there just wasn't an opening. Well, I would make the right decision, I was sure of it. Basically, I felt if I had to scrutinize, ponder and weigh so much, it probably wasn't right. And I also realized I could second-guess it to death.

We both napped, mercifully, on the flight home. But we were forced to endure another thick silence on the ride to my apartment. Michael walked me to the door, and I knew by the pleading look in his eyes, he was hoping I'd say something. I simply whispered. "Tomorrow?"

I called him the next day and asked him to join me for dinner that night. He knew I had reached a decision. The silence which accompanied us the night before joined us again for the ride to the restaurant. Thankfully we were seated right away and Michael opened the conversation. "Rainey, just spill it out, I can't wait any longer, the suspense is killing me." There was such love and hope in his beautiful eyes, I almost conceded, but I couldn't. "Michael, I can't," I just blurted it out simply and firmly. He started to raise his objections, but I stopped him and continued. "But tell me why we can't work something out? Why, for example, can't I fly wherever you are for a weekend? That would be the only way I'd see you anyway, right? I mean I'm not going to be mountain climbing with you."

"Yes, Rainey, but the difference is I wanted us to be married." Running his fingers through his hair and sighing, he continued. "I don't know, I just had this romantic dream of you waiting for me when I returned from the 'hunt,' so to speak. Just knowing my wife was there. It's going to be a lonely time without you. You're not going to be able to get in and out of a lot of the places I'll be because of the time frame with your job. Rainey, give me the bottom line here. What is the real reason? Have you come to the conclusion you don't love me enough, after all, and don't ever plan to marry me?"

"No, Michael, I'm–I'm sure that's not it. Actually, I don't know any reason, other than it's just so scary to drop my life like this and as I said before, to go gallivanting to I don't know where, and most of the time alone. Why can't I think about it just a while longer? If I decide to join you, it won't matter where you are, because I will have given up my job at that point and I'll eventually reach you. It's just all too sudden for me. Can you try to understand? Please?"

"Yeah, I guess I have no choice. It's just that I've dreamed about this opportunity for so many years, long before you came into the picture. And realizing how much I love you and want you with me…well, anyway, we still have some time, and hopefully," he said smiling, "I can use my manly wiles to change your mind. He took my hands in his, kissing one then the other, looking soulfully into my eyes. "All I can do, Rainey, is assure you of my love, regardless of your decision."

I don't know what we had for dinner or what it tasted like. What was supposed to be a celebratory episode in Michael's life was mixed with disappointment and sadness. I felt some guilt about this, of course. But this was too monumental a change in my life to be taken lightly. The remainder of the evening was somber and the only conversation that took place was that which was necessary because of his departure.

He had given notice at work and was leaving immediately for some God-forsaken mountain in the state of Washington. He'd never done any climbing there, and I'd never seen him so excited, and I was very happy for him. But our parting was torturous, so we made it quick, with promises from him, to call me at every opportunity.

Thankfully, I had plenty to do to keep myself busy. Michael's absence left a large gap of time to fill, but, thankfully Sherry's wedding was just a month away. Michael promised he'd be back to attend with me and I hadn't finished planning for that yet.

We wanted to get in touch with Juliet, to hear, hopefully, her voice still filled with the laughter and excitement we experienced in Los Angeles. And was she ready to come to Sherry's wedding? It seemed we were in a constant state of worry where she was concerned. And it was difficult to maintain excitement over her display of happiness at the reception: we'd been there before. Her mood swings, ranging from giddiness and happiness as witnessed in Los Angeles to the depths of despair we'd experienced in Florida could manifest within the same hour. And, we needed a physical update as well. Well aware she'd been plagued with complications since the abortion, we were hoping to hear news of a clean bill of health for her, finally.

Michael called right away to let me know he'd arrived, and excitedly filled me in on all the arrangements in the works for his first climb. He wouldn't be alone. There were seven other wives and/or girlfriends without their men tonight. No women, he assured me, teasing. Our phone calls lasted forever, since we never knew when we'd talk again. He was heading for base camp the next day, but even that was quite a trip in itself, up treacherous, unyielding mountains. I just didn't get it, to deliberately place oneself in such extreme life and death situations and love it. I never allowed myself to visualize his climbs or I'd never make it through a day.

I didn't hear from him again until he was ready to return home. His entire three and a half weeks had been spent climbing or learning the ropes, literally, at base camp. The training was intense, and he was exhausted and actually looking forward to returning home. As it turned out, he didn't have much time to recoup as our plane to Pittsburgh was two days after his arrival, so it was a hectic turnaround of unpacking, sleeping fast and off to the Poconos. When I met him at the terminal, my heart flipped over at the sight of him, and I hugged him so close, he winced with the force of it. God, how I missed him! Again I wondered, *how, am I going to stand it for months at a time?*

Settled back on the plane, Michael mused that being thrust almost instantly back into the frenzy of the upcoming week was going to take some adjusting. He'd spent three weeks eating out of cans and pooping on the mountainside. But as he said, "it's a whole lot easier adjusting up than down." I certainly intended to do my part to help him adjust up.

It was definitely going to be another exciting and fun-filled week. But even so, I yearned for the time when we could set around relaxing with nothing to do but chat and enjoy. Florida certainly didn't fit that criteria and even as much as we all enjoyed Dana and Lora's reception, it was quick and filled with frenetic activity. Would we ever again? We were going our separate ways, and it looked doubtful it would happen anytime soon. Thanks to Alexander Graham Bell, at least, for the telephone.

We didn't arrive until one in the morning and Mel, and Lora, who had just barely returned from her own honeymoon, had shooed Sherry and Almon off to bed promising to take good care of late arriving, travel weary guests, including Juliet. Yes, Juliet had made it. It was hard to say what her frame of mind was at this time, and we were so exhausted we didn't care at the moment, and with hasty hugs and kisses all around we crashed. We'd catch up tomorrow.

We must have been quite a sight the next morning, the horde of us straggling in, sleepy-eyed, groping for the coffee pot.

"Wait a minute," I said, looking around, "did I dream? Or did I really see Juliet last night?" I barely finished the question when she entered the kitchen wearing a little, flowered gown, looking frail as a china doll, but even though she looked as though a few pounds had been added, my heart sank. What was done in LA looked to be undone when she returned home. The glow, so prevalent in her eyes just not so long ago, had been doused and the roses in her cheeks had definitely wilted. I don't know why I'd felt optimistic. I suppose, because her transformation at Lora's reception seemed magical, I was instilled with hope that it had remained. Rich was obviously back in her life. Juliet was an addict…growing to hate the drug, but helpless to resist it, as it continued to fill an indescribable, deep-seated need. Well, I hoped, at least because she was here, and putting the distance between her and her misery, Rich, she'd be different. But I knew I was only deluding myself. I'd spoken with her right before we left and I was responsible for holding up the conversation, even feigning cheeriness in an attempt to lift her spirits a little. It didn't work, and I hung up emotionally crushed. Our hopes of her continuing high spirits, smashed to pieces. And she was still under her doctor's care. Ellen was failing at her attempts to persuade Juliet to seek counseling. Juliet believed she was making progress, and insisted more time was all that was necessary to claim hold to her life. Ellen was fearful, believing Rich had already laid claim to Juliet's life, and until she herself decided it to be otherwise, nothing would or could change. Juliet claimed he was remorseful for all the suffering he had caused her, and he forgave her! *He* forgave *her*!!!! My God! Just how deep was this man's psychosis? Then, calming, I realized, sadly, as deep as Juliet's. Well, we could at least be thrilled that Juliet was hanging on to a slender thread of reality, actualized by her determination to own her own shop and continuing her business classes at night. The little coffee shop she had frequented before had become her regular hangout and she'd made some new friends. That sounded promising… at least she wasn't cutting herself off totally, from the rest of the world. But there was, always, that underlying sadness betraying the optimism she was attempting to communicate, and it was confusing trying to understand who the real Juliet was. I believe, in the light of day, she knew she was deluding herself where Rich was concerned. She readily admitted she was, ultimately, extremely afraid of him. Maybe she hoped it'd run its course: he'd soon tire of her and move on. Who cared why he left, I thought, as long as he was gone. In the meantime, we'd do what we'd always done…rally around her again, and hope the week could work its magic once more.

CHAPTER XXXVI

Kiki looked fabulous as usual. She had been dry for four months, her longest dry spell ever. But she was also glowing, an excitement shining in her eyes I'd never seen before. I hugged her. "Okay, Kiki," I said suspiciously, "What's going on? You're positively radiating all over the place, and the only thing I know that makes a woman glow like this is a man, a real man. Who is he?"

She laughed. "Hot damn, you are right on, Rainey, and he is a real man this time, not like one of those dirt balls I used to hang out with."

"Well, c'mon, I'm dying here, who is he?"

"Well, you know I've been seeing a therapist since I moved here. Sherry was going to hang me out to dry if I didn't do something about my drinking. But I knew after one visit, he was gonna end up with more problems than I had because damned if I didn't fall in love with him." She slapped her leg, laughing heartily. Sherry came in on the tail end of her comment. "Isn't that great, guys? I mean this time I believe Kiki is really hooked. I've been around her and her men all these years, and I've never seen her affected by any of them like this. But you'll see why when you meet him today. He's just a great guy. He's originally from Germany and has only been living in the United States for the past four years, and wow! has an incredibly sexy accent. But I think he probably doesn't understand half of what Kiki says to him, otherwise, he'd probably run for his life. There isn't any other logical explanation for his sticking around." Sherry laughed as she threw a quick glance at Kiki.

"Yeah, but Sherry just knows him socially, he's the greatest in be—"

"Whoa, whoa, wait a minute," we interrupted her. "We don't need to hear sexual details, thank you very much. We won't be able to look at the man with a straight face when we meet him today. Besides," I said, "We know you've taught him everything he knows, so he's got to be good."

Jumping up and feigning pride, she puffed out her chest, "Damn straight," and began singing one of her favorite little ditties, "When you got it, don't lose it, show others how to use it."

"Kiki?" Lora asked seriously, "do you think you'll ever change?"

"Hell no, why should I, my life's too damn good the way I am." And with a swift glance at Sherry, she added, "Now that I'm done with drinking."

"I personally don't understand what he sees in her, except an incredible challenge. I suppose, being a psychiatrist, she's great to study under a microscope. And you all need to be glad she doesn't live close to you, I'll be thrilled if she and Gere get married. Maybe she'll finally settle down, and…move." Sherry joked.

"Never settle down," said Kiki shaking her head briskly. "My energy will just be transferred to other activities, besides hunting for sex. I'll probably join the Junior League and—"

"Ohhhhhhh No!" we howled at that. "You in the Junior League?" giggled Lora "I can just see it now, they'd pitch you out on your ear probably after the first meeting with you. Kiki, they play for keeps, those ladies. That's their life, and honey they take it verrrrry seriously."

"Well, how do you know?" retorted Kiki, defiantly. "Maybe they're just a bunch of tight asses who've never been shown by anyone how to have a good time? By God, I'm just the one to do it." We exchanged amusing glances, visualizing the picture she was painting. "But," she suddenly turned serious. "I don't know if Sherry's brought you up to date on the kind of crap that's been happening in my life. I mean heeavvvy stuff, stuff that there for a while, turned my whole world upside down, but then, uprighted it better than it's ever been before."

Sherry was shaking her head. "No, I wanted it to come from you, Kiki, it's your life and your story."

What now? I thought, as I quickly began flipping through the repertoire of life's calamities, but Kiki interrupted the process.

"Well, you all know that Gere has been my therapist for the last year. When Sherry arranged my first appointment, I was madder than hell at her. I knew I had a drinking problem, and I had joined AA, what else did she want from me? But if I didn't go, she was going to forget we were ever friends. I didn't believe her, on the one hand, but I sure's in hell didn't want to take that chance. As a, supposedly, grown up adult person, that shouldn't have scared me, but it did. And I agreed that the drinking was causing the challenges in my life, giving me "stinkin' thinking,' as they say in AA. But after a few sessions with Gere, I began to find out I had it backwards, I drank because of things in my past that were buried deep in my psyche," and she paused, smiling, "like that word, Mel? I'm starting to feel like a psychiatrist myself, learning all these educated psychological terms. But anyway, all that buried stuff was what was causing all the pain and anger that I couldn't put a finger on... scary crap about my childhood, began to surface. Things I hadn't thought of for years. And the more he dug, the angrier I got and the more afraid I got. I didn't understand why, but I just knew I didn't want any more sessions. Between Gere and Sherry, they convinced me that maybe there was something in my past that was really frightening to me, something I didn't want to face, and so I buried it deep inside. When he told me that, I said, well, hell, Gere, why would I want to find out about something like that? Let's let sleeping dogs lie, for goodness' sake. But he helped me understand that even though it was buried, it was still there, and it was affecting my choices and the way I behaved. He explained to me very patiently, that when problems are brought out, faced and dealt with in a healthy manner, they'd go away, permanently. Yeah, I may never forget them, but they no longer have control over my life. I was still leery about the whole thing, and besides, I couldn't and hadn't remembered anything anyway, so what did it matter? Then Gere talked to me about hypnotism. That really bummed me. I'd only seen magicians do that on television and thought it was just a trick. But by this time, I was falling hard for him; he was kind, sweet and gentle, unlike any of those bums I'd ever dated, so I decided to trust him. Turns out, I was an easy mark for hypnosis. Zap," she clicked her fingers, "just like that, I was gone. The next thing I knew, my eyes were opening, and Gere was asking me how I felt. I felt weird, strange, because I knew I had just done something, been somewhere else, but didn't know what, when or where. Then it got bad. He taped the whole thing and talked to me about it first to prepare me for what I was about to hear. Turns out it wasn't much, if just anybody was sitting there hearing it, but for me, it was a terrifying experience. I was talking about a cousin of mine, Rolley, who was six years older than I was and how he used to babysit me when I was just seven years old. I hadn't given him a thought for years. And when I heard myself talking about him, I started crying and fear shot right through me. And this was just the first session; I hadn't even gotten into the nasty stuff. But Gere wanted to draw it out slowly so we could discuss it, and maybe it would come out on its own. "I don't want to go into all the gory details, but suffice it to say, Rolley molested me on a regular basis until I was ten years old. And I don't mean just touching here and there, I mean intercourse!" We gasped in horror at this revelation, and sympathetic comments abounded as we assumed our mother hen mode, clucking over her, crying, and telling her she didn't need to go on if she didn't want to.

"No, no, it's okay, I feel better every time I talk it out." And she continued with the horrific tale. "One time, when I told him I would tell, he knocked me around and told me to tell mom and dad I'd wrecked on my bike. They believed me, of course. There was no reason to believe anything else. And I believed him after that, that he'd really hurt me, or maybe even kill me and hide my body somewhere where I'd never be found, as he said. My best friend at the time… this is right before we moved where Sherry lived, was Litty Owens. She was my age and we told each other everything, and one time after Rolley had just finished with me, I ran to her house crying. I didn't plan on telling her, I just said that Rolley made me mad and I hated him. I was pounding on her bed and screaming into her pillows. I can now see her face, clearly, when I sat up on the edge of that bed. I was wiping my eyes with the backs of my hands, and I felt her standing in front of me, real close, and she reached her tiny, sweet hand to mine, patting very gently, and said, 'Kiki, he's bad isn't he?' When I looked up, she was crying, and I knew, oh my God, I knew. 'Litty, what are we gonna do?'

"'Nothing! Kiki, nothing! Ever! I don't want to die!'"

Kiki paused, took a deep breath and began again. "This will never be easy to talk about, but Gere says every time I think about it, I should feel everything I can about every aspect of it. That way, I can deal with it. It took three more sessions and we'd discuss what we'd just heard, thoroughly, and he'd have me yelling and screaming at Rolley and, my God, it felt good to get rid of all that, to tell someone about it. I felt like I'd been reborn. Except I was disappointed I didn't get to kill the son-of-a-bitch. But the burden of that's gone now. Yeah, it's horrible, and there's not been a day that, at some point, I haven't thought about it, but it's getting easier to think about. And the best part is, I don't run for the bottle or some man for comfort and security anymore, except to Gere, of course. I had to stop using him as my therapist as soon as he realized there was a serious chemical reaction taking place between us. It's unethical, you know. Now, he just counsels me in bed." She laughed.

"Lord, Kiki," I said, amazed. "I can't believe you can sit there and joke after telling us that story, but I'm sure glad you can."

Melanie joined in. "Kiki, this is incredible, have you talked to your parents about this?"

"Yeah, and the terrible part about that is, they found out about it years ago because Rolley was caught messing with Litty, and it all came out. The police were called, but while they were waiting for the police to get there, he took off, and they still haven't found him. I asked Mom and Dad why they never talked to me about it, and then I realized they just didn't know how or what to say, and honest to God thought if they just never brought it up again, it would all go away, like it was a bad dream. My mother cried and cried, it broke my heart. I told her I forgave her, of course. I wasn't mad at her or Dad. They thought they were doing the right thing. But it sure explains why my parents were so attentive and extra nice to me all those years."

"Now that Gere has straightened you out," laughed Lora, attempting to bring some levity into the situation, "when's he planning on making an honest woman of you?"

"That's gonna take a few more private sessions, I think," said Kiki. "I'm the one holding that up. After divorcing, I'm scared to death to do it again, even though I know why I married that bum." Anyway, we don't have to rush into anything. And besides, now don't anyone faint, but I'm actually thinking about going back to school, with Gere's blessing and, believe it or not, I'm thinking I'd like to be a shrink…not a psychiatrist, I don't have the brains or desire to go to medical school, but maybe just a counselor," she said the latter with a nod toward Melanie.

"Thanks for the compliment, but I think you're underestimating yourself," said Mel. "Although I do believe it's something you know you really want to do, or it'd be difficult to get through it. It's tough."

With all topics finally exhausted, we then enjoyed a delicious breakfast and prepared to help Sherry, wherever we could, with her big day.

CHAPTER XXXVII

No matter how much planning takes place, or how small the wedding, it seems everyone ends up rushing at the last hour. But we attempted to keep the pace slow and the rooms filled with calm and peace. We, lovingly, helped Sherry into a beautiful, cream, filmy concoction appropriate for an informal courthouse wedding, but with just a twist of whimsy to suit the occasion. She looked gorgeous. She borrowed a miniature, ancient bible from Melanie, since we decided years ago, when we were young and idealistic, that each of us would carry that same bible on our wedding day. Kiki carried it at hers and liked to tell us, that if it was meant to bring good luck, it was worthless. I politely informed her that opening it and reading it would definitely prove to be more helpful. Sherry's sister, whom she called Sissie, gave her a tiny angel pin with delicate translucent, blue wings, and Sherry pinned it at the very edge of her open necked gown high on her shoulder. She said it would watch over the ceremony. Of course her wedding dress was new, and she borrowed Kiki's garter belt, so she had more than fulfilled that particular, traditional ritual. Kiki applied her makeup and the rest of us supervised, restraining her to keep it light. We arrived at the courthouse thirty minutes early, which was great. It gave us a chance for a breather. Sherry had invited a few family members and a few friends from her work as well as friends of Almon's, and us. Her Mom and Dad sent a card at least, telling her they loved her, period. Nothing else, but Sherry was thrilled with that small morsel. It was a start, perhaps. That was the only emotional dip, in an otherwise, perfect day. The ceremony was quick and dry, as we expected, but Sherry and Almon were now, officially and ecstatically, man and wife.

Now, let the partying begin! The wedding party, so to speak, scrunched into three rental cars with Almon and Sherry in the lead. In the fourth, Sherry's family, who were returning home immediately after the reception, followed in their own vehicles. It was a long caravan to the Poconos. We arranged for Juliet to ride with Lora and Dana. Lora shot me a dispirited look when I mentioned it in front of Juliet. I did it purposely, so she couldn't refuse. I figured if anyone could bring light to Juliet, it would be those two. It worked, but it could just as easily have backfired; she could have sunk further into her depression, witnessing such joy around them, and Lora may never have spoken to me again. Well the risk was worth it, and by the time we arrived at the lodge, we watched the three of them tumble out of the car, singing and laughing. Dana and Lora had indomitable spirits that dared anyone to attempt to desecrate them. Everyone should have such a couple in their lives.

We divvied up the cabins as designated by Almon, and immediately changed to head for the main dining room for the festivities. The food was plentiful and looked beautiful as well as appetizing. Out of common decency only, we waited for the guests of honor to appear before digging in. Thankfully, they didn't keep us waiting long, and the DJ announced their arrival by immediately switching to "Here comes the Bride," and, of course, we all sang along. They looked the perfect couple, with enough love and happiness emanating from them to light the room. The rock and roll hits playing were enthusiastic and motivating. And with our heightened party mood, it took no encouragement to hit the dance floor. And much to our pleasant surprise, Juliet, once again, was one of the first. She hadn't done much talking since yesterday, as was usual, but then, we realized, neither had she been moping or complaining. But we were so preoccupied with Sherry that it really hadn't registered until she arrived at the reception, bright eyed and smiling. We didn't know what had transformed her, but we sighed with relief. Maybe it was, again, just escaping her own miserable thoughts through the distraction of so much joy surrounding her. But whatever the reason, she entertained us for hours once more with her fancy footwork. We saw her whispering to the DJ, and of course, Dana was her natural choice for a dance partner. He let the music carry him away just as Juliet did, except in Dana's case, it was difficult to view his body with one fell swoop at any given moment. Arms and legs flew in every direction. He couldn't dance worth a flip, but neither did he care, he moved as the music moved him. But our eyes only stayed on him long enough to realize we'd get nauseous if we lingered, and because Juliet, the unmotivated, morose drag she was most of the time, allowed the rhythm to work its magic, changing her, in an instant, into a high spirited, race horse. As we were to see, the dance moves she displayed at Lora's reception were only the warm-up, preparing her for the Olympics. She danced with all the razzle dazzle, bells and whistles of a broadway belle. And as was usual, when Juliet began to dance, we either left the dance floor, or at the very least, danced around the perimeter, giving her full reign, allowing her, her shining moment. And as usual, we looked on, amazed, pondering the human psyche. The energy and life we witnessed being displayed before us only surfaced with music. Life's everyday burdens and annoyances were, obviously too repressive, weighing her down, preventing her from pulling her spirits up through the mire. That's what made these moments so extra special, they were rare, and we watched as the roses climbed back into her cheeks, and perspiration, not the usual buckets of tears, poured from her face. Tears also fell from the eyes of those who loved her most. We applauded and squealed until we were hoarse and the songs ended. Dana deferred to her obvious talent, and being the ham he was, produced an exaggerated bow and kissed her hand, much to her delight. We gathered around her like proud parents after a successful recital, congratulating and hugging her. She was beaming, and I thought, as I allowed myself to gaze upon her glowing face at that moment, I'll forever hold close, this moment, this moment of pure happiness for her. To our delight, she danced, albeit not as extravagantly, or energetically, the remainder of the evening.

Dana, of course, was a crazy man, dancing by himself, and wearing Sherry's garter on his head as a garland of love, as he called it. He had a great time wherever he was, if no one else did, but Lora was able to restrain him from upstaging the "couple," totally.

The two-tiered cake was cut, with Sherry and Almon feeding each other, and Dana, impatiently waiting for them to finish, only out of common courtesy, began a "cake fight." We all joined in, with bodies slipping and falling, harmlessly, on bits and pieces of cake. And when Juliet slipped, landing hard on her bony backside, we watched nervously, but as she began laughing, we laughed right along with her. We partied until around ten, when exhaustion began setting in. It had been a long day and as enjoyable as it had been, we were ready to unwind, sleep fast and start again tomorrow. But first, we had to bring a proper end to their wedding day, and as Sherry and Almon proceeded to leave, we surprised them with the cornball tradition of throwing rice. The ludicrousness of it struck. They were going only a few hundred feet to their cabin, and that thought combined with the overindulgence of booze, induced another round of laughter. We walked, laughing and stumbling to our cabins and doing so without incident was nothing short of miraculous.

There were pamphlets in the cabins describing the pleasures awaiting us, nature trails, fishing spots, picnic areas, and golfing, for starters, for the outdoor types. For the shut-ins, there was the spa, and that's all I needed to know. We ladies spent our time steaming, getting massaged or lying around the pool. It was heaven. The guys played golf. We got together as couples only for meals and a few beautiful walks around the cabins to enjoy the mountain views. And they were breathtaking. Each of us felt a little uncomfortable and sad as we enjoyed our fabulous meals as couples, only to glance at Juliet, alone. We continued to pray for her full recovery. She had never healed completely from the complications of the abortion, and still had to be kept under a doctor's watchful eye. Dr. Morris had done a number on her. Kiki had committed some time to attempt to persuade Juliet to speak with Gere, and seeing the evidence of his abilities and results in Kiki's life, inspired hope in our hearts for Juliet.

CHAPTER XXXVIII

The week was turning into one long, glorious party. We'd never laughed so much in our lives, at least not since Lora and Dana's reception. Both couples had set a precedent with their receptions, a standard which, the rest of us could only hope to live up to.

We gave up the pace for one evening, slowing only to catch up on everyone's lives. And Melanie's inspired the most curiosity. Due to her hectic schedule, we rarely even spoke with her by phone, therefore, she was our first, natural target. She looked exhausted, and when we mentioned it, she confirmed it. The studies were tough and she was staying up every night, burning the candle at both ends. But, nevertheless, her fervor and passion for medicine still burned brightly and she felt it worth anything she had to do to achieve her goal. If she felt it was worth it, who was I to question it, I was happy for her. But I wondered when and how she had time to meet James. He was very attractive and seemed a perfect match for Melanie. He was quiet and calm but assertive enough to speak his opinion and we participated in some controversial and stimulating conversations. Melanie confirmed the relationship was as serious as possible, considering the little time they had together. There was a long pause, and she realized Lora and I were anticipating a confession. "What?" Melanie said smiling knowingly. "You guys are so obvious. Can't I keep anything to myself?"

"No," Lora and I both stated emphatically. "Of course not, you know better than that," I said. "Since when have we ever been able to keep anything from each other?"

"Well," Melanie sighed. "I know what you reeaallly want to know, and I wish I could tell you that something exciting and wonderful happened, but we were so tired and it happened so fast, I'm still not sure I wasn't dreaming." She giggled from the confession, but half out of sadness at the thought of it. She continued. "We had gone to James' friend Zeke's apartment, as usual, and I told him I was exhausted and looked forward to a hot bath and bed, which unfortunately, was also the usual. Have you ever been so tired that you almost fall asleep in the tub? I swear I was lying there and…"

"Melllll," we interrupted, motioning for her to get on with it.

"Alright, alright," she said, enjoying teasing us. "I told you there's really not much to tell. Anyway, I was wrapped in my robe and was heading down the hall for a drink of water. Oh, man," she said, licking her lips, "I soaked for so long, Lord I don't know when I was ever that thir—"

"Melanie!" I said, rolling my eyes, as she laughed again. "Oh, you just wait until it's my turn." I said. "You're killing us."

"Okay, okay. Well, like I said, I was heading to the kitchen for a drink, just as James was coming down the hall, going to bed. We rounded the corner at the same time and smacked into each other. It wouldn't have been a big deal any other time; we would have laughed, given each other a peck on the cheek goodnight, and moved on. But this time, my robe flew open and the look on James face was so filled with awe and lust, I just stood there, startled, and I don't know why, just enjoying it myself, I guess, because I sure didn't hurry to close my robe, and he slowly reached his hand to touch my breast, and that was it." She stopped, looked at us as if she was finished.

"What? What was it? What was what?" Lora asked. We realized we were leaning halfway into Mel's face, in anticipation of her next words.

"God, back off. Don't you all ever read any dirty books? Give me a break, here…I don't want to tell everrrrything, you know. Besides, I hardly remember anything after that except we did it right there on the hallway floor, well, actually, he did it, I just happened to be under him at the time, so there's nothing to tell except I'm no longer a virgin. James apologized afterwards and practically cried explaining that that wasn't making love. I told him I hoped not, I'd seen dogs take longer than that."

"Oh no!!!" exclaimed Lora, "you didn't."

"No, no, of course not," she laughed, "but it certainly was the truth. Look, I would feel ashamed and guilty telling you this, but I know that that's not the way it's supposed to be. James hasn't been with a woman for a year now and the pressure we've been under has been incredible. I look at it this way; now I know what the mechanics are all about, and the little bit of pain I experienced is done and over with, and so honey, it's going to be fantastic next time," she sighed, "maybe two years from now. We haven't done it since, and he's driving me crazy apologizing, and telling me over and over again that that wasn't lovemaking at all, but just plain old neanderthal sex and on and on and on he goes. I tried to tell him it's okay, I understood, but he's so anxious to show me how much he loves me."

"Oh Melanie," cried Lora. "That's so sweet and so sad at the same time. He must love you very much, and I can personally tell you that what he says is true. Are you going to give him another chance anytime soon? Or are you serious when you say two years?

"I'd love to, but it might be two years. We need time and energy to do it right, and both are extremely rare for us right now. But the excitement I did experience, sure gives me something to look forward to. The only real downer about the whole experience was that because it was done so impulsively, you know, no protection, I'm scared to death I might be pregnant. Wouldn't that be a riot? It was a slam, bam thank you mam' type thing and I'd end up pregnant. That would certainly put my career on hold for a while. I know that might sound cold, and not that I don't want children, but we haven't even talked marriage yet. Heck we barely have time to talk about anything. So keep your fingers crossed because I didn't keep my legs crossed." She laughed, resignedly. "It's going to be tough concentrating on my studies until I'm looking at negative pregnancy results. But enough about me, Rainey," said Melanie, "Speaking about marriage…when are you going to join Michael?" They already knew the sad news of Michael's departure and my decision to stay behind. They also let me know in no uncertain terms that they thought I was nuts. "Thanks for the belated opinion," I said. "That's what I had hoped for in Los Angeles, and it would have taken all of three seconds to get it."

"Well, for goodness' sake," said Melanie, "I can't believe you need input from anyone anyway, why is there a question? You're a fool if you don't grab him right up."

"You better believe it," agreed Lora. "He's so adorable, Rainey. What in the world's standing in your way? As cute as he is, some little sexy mountain mama's gonna invite him to go 'climbing' with her, if you don't."

"I don't know," I said. "I just get scared at the thought of being alone in some strange place, many strange places, as a matter of fact. Maybe I just have to have a little time for the whole thing to settle in my mind. Believe me, the thought of being with him, I mean intimately being with him, keeps me awake and perspiring some nights, but spending nights alone in strange, remote countries, terrifies me. I guess my adventurous spirit has its limitations. We'll see."

Once we were caught up on all the latest news, we sat back rehashing old times and spoke of our dreams of the future, just as we had always done and It was as inspiring and enjoyable as ever. Even though there was no request for the latest details of Juliet's life, and it was an obvious omission, it was also obvious she didn't volunteer to give them. And we certainly didn't want to encourage her. It would've killed our festive spirits instantly. But she was exhausted; she'd given herself quite the workout, dancing all day, but we'd noticed that tonight, she'd quietly slipped away from us for a little while, and suspected she was calling Rich, otherwise, she would have mentioned it. We never let on. What was the use? We were determined not to let her situation undermine this joyous occasion, as long as it was possible, anyway.

The guys came in and Dana – and Lora, when she could get a word in – entertained us for another hour with anecdotes of their travels to several European countries. It was a wonderful way to spend an evening, and we finally gave it up, when there was more yawning and drooping eyes, than talking and listening.

The next night was to be our last night together before we, sadly, each began departing, once again, to our own individual corners of the world. And we females made a decision, earlier in the week, to stay in that evening since the guys, starting a golf game late in the afternoon, wouldn't be finished until late, anyway. The refrigerator was filled with a variety of nasty goodies and all manner of drink was plentiful. Life was good!

The day began, we enjoyed winding in and out of several quaint little shops, laughing and picking up a souvenir or whatnot of some kind at every one, finally stopping at a small sidewalk café for a light breakfast. We realized that Juliet still vacillated between happy and sad at any given moment. But when we were seated, it was difficult not to notice a distinct nervousness about her. She kept fidgeting, until finally, Lora, seated next to her, asked if she was okay. Juliet, not meeting Lora's gaze, or not lifting her head up at all, for that matter, began biting her bottom lip. Oh no! We knew something was in the works, and I for one, didn't want to postpone or prolong the agony. "Juliet," I said, as calmly as possible, "try to break it to us gently. We're grown-ups, we can handle it." And terrified to ask, but necessary, "Does it have anything to do with your health? Please, are you okay?"

Juliet's shoulders dropped with a long sigh emitted deep from within, as she slowly met our gaze. "Please, please, don't be mad at me. I know how you all feel about Rich—"

Disheartened glances ricocheted from one face to the other around the table, and with sinking hearts, and an "Ah, craaaap! I don't think I even want to hear this!" muttered from an already exasperated Kiki, we asked her to continue, terrified she was about to reveal something horrendously upsetting, and we couldn't, didn't want to imagine what.

"I…I… I've been talking with him the last few weeks. He really is very sorry about everything, you know. I believe him. I know, you don't have to say it. I'm stupid, I guess, but I love him. You just have never given him a chance."

Kiki couldn't contain her anger and frustration and practically screamed, "Give him a chance? What the hell are you talking about, Juliet? Why do we want to give him a chance? A chance to do what? Kill you? What the hell is wrong with you?" Sherry grabbed Kiki's arm, begging her to be calm. Thankfully, we'd stopped for a late breakfast and only a few patrons remained to register looks of shock and surprise at Kiki's explosive behavior. My lord, I thought, here we go again. We realized, then, there would never be an end to this relationship. There couldn't be with two such emotionally dysfunctional people involved. It was a sick, symbiotic coupling, having a feeding frenzy off each other. There was nothing left to say. It had been said many, many times in every way possible.

Juliet continued. "See what I mean, Kiki? Look how you're acting…that's exactly why I've done what I've done. Because you don't know him. I…I've invited him here for tonight."

Before the rest of us could utter our protestations, Kiki screamed. "What? No, no, no! Hell no!" as she hurriedly walked away from the table for restraint, and mumbling expletives to herself that I'm glad we couldn't hear. God knows, she had quite a repertoire and shared it liberally, for any reason. But with this, I knew how difficult it was for her, with her temper, not to lunge at Juliet and strangle her.

"It's just for a couple of hours. I want him to sit with us and be a part of our group. I know you'll see the sweet side of him that I've seen."

"Hahaaa!" exclaimed Kiki, still keeping her distance. "It must be his ass, 'cause you've described in great detail every other side of him, and none of it was sweet. Damn, Juliet, I can't believe you!"

But Juliet continued as though Kiki hadn't spoken, and looking at the rest of us, pleaded. "Please, please do this for me. If you say no, then I…I'll…just have to leave, because I won't call him back now and tell him you don't want him here. Just this one time, please?"

It took every ounce of will power not to refuse her. As repulsive as we found him to be, it was, after all, only a couple of hours out of our lives, and it was so important to Juliet. But how in god's world were we to endure sitting with this creep even for five minutes, let alone an hour or two. We'd suck it up and do it, of course, for Juliet. Thank goodness we had plenty of disinfectant and bug sprays for the cabin after he left. We were filled with such repugnance for this man.

CHAPTER XXXVIX

Even though Juliet's shocking news left a pall hanging over us, we determined to enjoy the remainder of the day, and most of us did. It took Kiki a little longer, and we could hear her shooting out invectives under her breath every once in a while, but eventually, she began enjoying herself again. We met the guys for a quick, late lunch as they were leaving for their golf game, and it was agreed not to mention Rich's impending visit. We'd spare them the horror, and they might be fortunate enough to miss him altogether.

Then it was on to more shopping and sight seeing. Juliet wanted to find a special outfit for Rich's visit and we reluctantly indulged her, without a word, positive or negative. The day was fading and though we'd made arrangements to stay in after an exhausting day out, with Juliet's revelation, we decided to eat in the lodge's restaurant instead. We were in no hurry to congregate at the designated "crime scene." Juliet declined dinner, returning to the cabin instead, to prepare for Rich's visit. Maybe it was a sick love, but she glowed when she spoke of him. Some things in life, for certain, only God himself could understand, for it was definitely beyond our human, mental capacities. We managed to continue to enjoy ourselves in spite of, or perhaps because of Rich's involvement in our lives. Maybe, somehow, Juliet was serving as, if nothing else, a bad example; our lives, by comparison, were great, and our blessings were mentally calculated. As the hateful hour neared, we had to force our butts from the dining chairs. And as we began the dreaded trek to the lodge, I felt I was participating in a funeral procession. It was somber, quiet and filled with heaviness. We thought, finally, at one point, Juliet was over the hump, only to have the beast, Rich, of which nightmares are made, rise again, and when we least expected it. Quickly, before entering the cabin, we attempted to inject ourselves with a better attitude and replace the grimace on our faces with something warmer. My facial muscles began to ache within seconds from the force being used to hold, at best, a half smile in place.

We could hear Juliet humming, actually humming. I hadn't heard her sing since we were children, and for just an instant, my little friend, Juliet was back. She flounced into the room reminiscent of Loretta Young on her TV show, smiling broadly and eyes dancing with excitement. All was, for the present, anyway, right with her world. She took over, preparing drinks, alcoholic and otherwise, setting out cute, tasty hors d'oeuvre and choosing some lighthearted music, mellow and soothing. We commented on her "Betty Crockerness," and left her happily milling about, as we retreated to the bedroom to change. Rich should be arriving soon, too soon!

We lounged on the bed, gabbing, delaying the inevitable, until Juliet knocked, alerting us to Rich's arrival. Oh, how were we going to get through this?

"I think she's asking a hell of a lot of us, especially since all I want to do is go out there and rip his—"

"Hold on, Kiki," interrupted Sherry, "first of all, I'm sure I know what you're going to say, and just think about that visual for a second, yahhhh! Secondly, we promised Juliet." Sherry pulled herself up, fist high in the air as preparing to face a mighty foe, and mustering as much gusto as possible, said. "Let's…hell, let's take this hill. Ready troops? If he starts something, we'll…we'll spit in his eye."

Kiki smiled at that, in spite of the hideous situation. "Spit?" Yeah, that was as nasty as Sherry would get, and she looked so ridiculous standing there all puffed up feigning ferociousness.

But when we threw the door open, we came face to face with a dejected, crying Juliet. And the minute we entered the room and saw Rich, we understood why, fear exploded inside us. He was at least, three sheets to the wind, already, and we wondered how he had driven here. But we discovered later he'd spent the afternoon visiting a few bars down the road, and if a bartender refused him drinks, he'd head to the next bar, until he ran out of bars, then he'd retrieve one from the stash in his car, one of many places he kept bottles hidden. Juliet whispered to us desperately that part of his condition was due to the medication he was taking. Heaven help us, could she possibly believe that? And did she think we would? It was obvious to us it was booze, and we could tell from the smell of him, which reeked of alcohol, not Demerol. This, then, was our official introduction to Rich, and what an introduction it was. Standing…or attempting to stand before us, he lived up to the total package delivered to us by Ellen: gorgeous, even as drunk as he was, and vile. He swayed and halted, eventually finding his way to the sofa. His eyes attempted to stay focused on one thing, anything, for just a second or two. It was a very awkward, uncomfortable experience for all of us, except Rich, of course. I don't think he realized where he was, and he certainly didn't know who we were, nor was he interested in knowing at the moment, let alone being aware of the heightened emotional climate of the room. What we found most amazing was the fact that Juliet had apparently climbed at least halfway back into her delusional world. I guess not knowing what else to do, she zipped around offering her plates of canapés and dainty sandwiches, attempting to forestall any outbursts and hopefully add some normalcy to the evening. Rich made a feeble attempt to grab at one, hit the plate, and only Juliet's quickness saved it from crashing to the floor. Rich never noticed.

But he noticed when Juliet followed with a tray of drinks. His eyes widened at the sight in an attempt to direct his feet to the same spot. His tongue shot out to lick the slaver forming at the sight, and he made a lunge forward, falling on one knee, hands outstretched, to catch himself. Too bad, it would have lightened the mood to watch him fall on his stupid face.

"Don't get so damned excited, it's only iced tea…you boob!" Kiki imparted snidely.

Juliet shot her a look filled with anguish. "Please, Kiki?"

"Hmmpphh," snorted Kiki. "Please what? Juliet. What in the hell do you want us to do? He's literally falling-down drunk, and you want us to do what, exactly? Sit here and pretend he's not? Maybe entertain him? Aaahh," and throwing her hands in the air, and rolling her eyes, added in exasperation, "this is so damn ridiculous, it's a joke, and I'm through. When the rest of you come to your senses, you'll find me at your cabin, Sherry."

As Kiki headed for the door, Rich turned as quickly as he could, reached out and grabbed her arm. Kiki stiffened, "I suggest you remove that filthy claw from me now, unless you want to pull back a stump."

Rich moved his hand, swaying and swirling it through the air while mocking her. "Whewwww, I'm scared shidless. Whadda ya gonna do bich? Pleeeease doan' let'er hid me," he teasingly sobbed and gave his body a quick shake…not being difficult in his condition, and he lost his balance, momentarily, catching himself again on the back of a chair. Juliet quickly intervened, placing her small hands gently on Rich's broad chest, smiling nervously and pleading with him to please sit down. He immediately focused his full attention on Juliet, turning to mush and began petting her hair. "My swee' lil' Juliet." He leaned forward to impart a secretive whisper to her, but stumbled past her, instead. "Less go somewhere, less go." He began tugging at Juliet's arm, but at this point, Juliet no longer could deny what was abundantly clear: his present condition had nothing to do with medication. But when she refused, his gushing of love immediately turned sharply to anger. "Ohhhh, you gonna pull that same ole' shid? Not this time, ole' gerl. Oh, no, do it to me onse, bu' not agin." And without warning, he hit her solidly across the face with the back of his hand. The force knocked her across the sofa and Rich backwards, barely missing the andirons sitting beside the beautiful stone fireplace. We ran quickly to Juliet. Blood had begun oozing from her mouth and nose. Kiki was making a bee-line for Rich, full bore. Sherry caught her arm just as she was about to apply a martial arts move or two on him, as a farewell gift.

"Don't Kiki, I want to get rid of him, but let's think of another way."

"Fine, but let's get him the hell out of here; he's stunk up this place enough already." Rich was having a difficult time rising even to a sitting position, and totally oblivious that Kiki's foot was on his left hand. Melanie, with Lora's and my assistance, was tending to Juliet, who kept the apologies flowing. It was hard to discern who was doing the most moaning, Juliet or Rich.

"Just get him out of here," yelled Lora, as we helped Juliet to the couch. Sherry and Kiki grabbed Rich's arms, as we headed toward them for reinforcement. I opened the door as the others pulled and tugged his limp, but still struggling body through it. "She's nuthin' bu' a dam tese, always has been, I'll kill her one a' these days. She ruined me, yu' know, I almos' died, she'll pay, she'll pay." His words echoed in Juliet's ears as we finally got him outside. Now what? The air had a slight chill to it, even being early evening in late July, but Rich was wearing a long sleeved shirt and we believed with a body full of booze, he'd be fine. We decided against putting him in his car; we didn't see the keys in the ignition or anywhere on the seats, and any attempt to retrieve them from his pocket, produced a wild, flailing reaction from him. We certainly didn't want him back on the highway, assuming he could make it that far without killing himself or someone else.

"C'mon, let's take him over there," said Kiki, pointing to a hillside close by. "One little push and over he'll go."

"What? Kiki, what're you saying?" We asked, momentarily dumbstruck, thinking she must be joking. But as she pulled, we used every ounce of our strength to pull him back, instigating a human tug of war as we attempted to stop her.

"Damn you guys! Don't fight me on this, we don't have any choice."

"Le' me go, I'm gonna kill 'er," Rich hissed. His attempts to free himself were for naught, as each arm was being pulled straight out; his legs dragging behind. He couldn't get the leverage he needed, and we didn't intend for him to, but his mouth was free and he kept the filthy invectives flowing.

"Kiki," Sherry yelled, panic rising in her voice. "You're not serious, Kiki!...listen to me, stop!"

"Help me, damnit!" responded Kiki. "And hell yes, I'm serious, we can't let go of him, he's gonna go right back in the cabin, and we can't put him in the car, so unless someone has a better idea, and they better speak up quick, his skinny, drunken ass is going over, with or without your help."

We couldn't possibly let her do this. We pulled harder, stalling for seconds even, to think. God help us. Think, think think.

"Stop fighting me, damnit; get him over there. My arms are getting tired and we can't stay out here all night."

Kiki's fury showed in her voice, and realizing, suddenly, how maniacal she sounded, she realized she wasn't going to win without displaying a little calm and logic. She relaxed, giving a few inches, but still held Rich in a death grip, as she pled her case softly. "Look, I don't want to kill him, if that's what you're thinking. The idea is to shove him down the hillside, okay? He's so damn drunk, he'll either pass out when he hits the bottom, which is only a ten foot or so tumble, and it's a damn soft landing for his sorry ass, but if he doesn't pass out and tries to climb back up, his body's so tired and weak, he won't be able to make it, so he'll just sleep it off. We'll come back out and check on him later. Okay?! Satisfied?! Now c'mon, let's do it!" Though her final arguments convinced us she didn't have murder on her mind, it was with almost overwhelming fear and reluctance that we released the tension in our arms, responsible for pulling Rich's body in the opposing direction. Although we couldn't see much through the dusky light sifting through the thick trees, we'd seen the area in daylight and knew what Kiki said was true. Besides, try as we might, we couldn't come up with a better plan so it was on that fateful night, we stood side by side when Kiki gave the word, "heavo!" with more enthusiasm than we felt necessary. We did no more than release him and, feeling his limp-hanging body drop from our grip, we stood motionless as we listened to the sounds of his body tumbling down, swooshing the grass and twigs as it tumbled over and over. It seemed it would never stop, and I wondered for an instant if we had erred in choosing the spot and his body was literally for him this night falling into eternity. Suddenly we heard a faint thudding and then, stillness. A deathly stillness, which can only be appreciated high on a mountain range on a virtually moonless night. We stayed our posts long enough to be satisfied he wasn't attempting a climb back up the hill, and the assumption following that he'd in fact passed out. Then, we started for the cabin, to face Juliet.

She was sitting exactly where we left her. Though we'd cleaned her face with a damp cloth, a few spots of dried blood remained on her lower lip and chin. She sat slumped back against the chair, eyes closed and hands, palm side up, on either side of her thighs…a posture signifying total resignation. Would this be a watershed moment in her life? In ours?

CHAPTER XL

"Juliet?" Lora whispered sweetly, while soothing one of Juliet's arms. "Honey? You okay? Rich is not going to hurt you anymore...we can promise you that." Those innocent words were meant to assure her we were committed to never letting him near her again. Juliet slowly opened her eyes, looking at each of us with a look pregnant with questions.

"We led him to the back of the cabin and he pulled away, stumbling, and fell. He was vicious and still swearing at us telling us to leave him alone," volunteered Melanie. "We waited a few minutes, and he didn't move, so we assume he's passed out."

Well, there was a lot of truth to it, but right now, all we could do was breathe a deep sigh of pure relief that he was gone, no matter how ugly the process was. A stream of tears began the short descent down Juliet's cheeks, dripping onto the special dress chosen for this special night; a night she anticipated would be a turning point in her relationship with Rich, and her best friends as well. Well it certainly turned out to be special, alright, but unforgettable was a better word for it. We suggested she go to bed. She acquiesced instantly, and without a word. We led her to the bedroom, helped her into her nightclothes and tucked her in. But the thought of leaving her alone never crossed our minds. We climbed onto the bed with her, a formidable force, but one designed to convey a sense of security and warmth. Something we could all use tons of right now, that and a stiff drink. Instead, we chatted about the receptions, Lora's and Sherry's, and anything we could interject that was uplifting and positive. Kiki chose several crude, but funny jokes from her humongous repertoire, and within minutes, we were rolling and howling with laughter...all of us except Juliet, of course. At least she wasn't sobbing. But always there, close to the surface of our minds, was the nightmare, and we fought it back with great determination, in an attempt to keep smiling.

Of course, as with any decent sleepover, it was natural for a pillow fight to ensue. Juliet rallied a little; you'd have to be comatose not to, but only to watch. Her pitiful face was now swollen, and we tried to ignore it for the moment, concentrating, instead, on anything positive we could find. She got smacked with a pillow a few times, and wincing with pain, gently tossed it back. After a few minutes, we calmed and began talking again, discussing future plans. I, naturally, wanted to talk about Michael, but under the circumstances, thought better of it. So we rambled on about our jobs and general complaints, and other people's aggravating habits, which opened the door for funny anecdotes from each of us. But the evening had taken its toll and within thirty minutes Juliet had slipped, mercifully into welcoming sleep. Her facial expression, the normal fragment of it, at least, signified an absence of tension and satisfied us she might make it through this, at least for now. We'd worry about tomorrow, tomorrow.

A rustling in the living room alerted us the men had returned. How in the world were we to explain Rich? They couldn't miss his car parked out front and would certainly want to know where he was. And even if we explained Rich's abhorrent condition, and the ensuing problems, explaining our solution was out of the question. I should have known that with Kiki's devious mind and years of experience, she'd save the day. As we entered the room with shouts and hugs all around, we noticed their eyes scanning the room. "Whose car?" asked Almon. We quickly described Rich's condition, but wisely chose to omit the abuse, for obvious reasons.

"Well, where is he?" asked Michael. Thank God for Kiki.

"He called us a bunch of shithead squares and stumbled out the door, said he'd go find a real party, and that, hopefully, is the last we'll see of him."

Well, I thought, *that was simple enough*. But for those of us whose minds are not conditioned to lying and deceit, it didn't sit well. Satisfied with the answer, the guys hit the showers and we settled back comfortably to finally enjoy the remainder of the evening. Oh, it was so good to relax in the warmth and strength of Michael's body. He smelled wonderful and looked fresh and beautiful in spite of not having shaved since early morning, but when stubble is attached to a face like that, who cares!

But even then, with the casual, relaxed atmosphere enveloping us, the knowledge of Rich potentially lurking around outside, was unnerving and our ears were tuned for every little sound, picturing him climbing back up the hill. We didn't feel threatened that he'd reveal how he arrived at the bottom of it; we were sure he wouldn't remember, but we didn't want another confrontation, especially involving the guys. After another hour of chitchat and the guys harassing each other about the golf match, it was time to hit the sack. We were going to walk the men back to their cabin, and not having seen much of them that day, hated having them go. As I stepped out into the cool night air, the thought of the warmth of our cabins quickly eclipsed any desire to linger there. Michael detected my distraction, but chalked it up to the nasty confrontation with Rich. If they only knew. And it was thoughts of Rich which were quickly filling my mind, and the hair stood on the back of my neck, knowing it was possible for him to pop up at any second. It was a quick kiss goodnight, and it was the first and hopefully the last time we'd dismiss each other so casually and quickly. But I was anxious to check on Rich. What more we hoped to know just by walking to the hillside, I'm not certain, but I suppose it was to see if he'd made it back up and, perhaps, was lying around close by, even near the cabin. If that was the case, we'd drag his liquor-sodden body into the back seat of his car where, hopefully, he'd sleep till we were gone. Oh wouldn't that be wonderful? right! Well, at least until late morning. The walk back was a somber and anxious one, with not a word spoken among us until we arrived at the door of our cabin.

"I just hope he's still asleep and not wandered off the side of the mountain," whispered Mel.

"As much booze as he had inside him, he wasn't going anywhere," said Kiki. Well, she was the expert when it came to alcohol, and we were reassured by her words.

We lumbered slowly back to the cabin, eyes constantly scanning and hearts heavy with the events of the evening. Did I really have a normal existence somewhere out there? It seemed so far away, and oh how I looked forward to returning to that world again, with all my old, normal problems. Poor Sherry! What a frightful end to an otherwise perfect reception. One thing for sure, she'd never forget it. None of us would.

In spite of the stimulating events of the evening we slept, though fitfully, and throughout the night we ran into one another, in the living room contemplating space, or in the kitchen, rummaging through the refrigerator or cabinet for a snack that would be, ultimately, left uneaten.

It seemed to be an endless night, but, finally morning came bursting through the tiny openings of the window blinds, splashing bright yellow sunlight over the walls and penetrating our sleep-dulled eyes. I sat up with a jerk, jumped out of bed, threw open the door and screamed, startled by Kiki, who had gotten up moments before, gotten the coffee started and was returning to get dressed. She was as anxious as I to see what, if any, changes had developed through the night. And within minutes, everyone else began stumbling out into the kitchen, looking for coffee. Juliet appeared, looking remorseful and embarrassed, surrounded by puffy black and blue. Thank God it wasn't as bad as we thought, and with some good makeup, it'd barely be noticed, if at all.

"What do I say? What can I say? Besides I'm sorry, sorry sorry! I believed him again. Kiki? You're so right in calling me stupid. I guess I just want to believe him so much, I see what I want to see, but I didn't miss anything last night. And it's funny. I know you know this is not the first time Rich has hit me, but it is the first time he did it in front of someone. And as strange as it seems, that's what I needed. I can't explain it, except that it was like, suddenly, I was standing outside myself and seeing the whole horrible scene through someone else's eyes. I can't believe how I've allowed him to abuse me."

"Well, hot damn," shrieked Kiki. "If you're serious, it was worth all of us getting abused by that bastard!"

"You're looking much better, how's your lip?" asked Melanie, forever being the doctor.

"It'll be fine; I've had much worse, believe me."

Lora brought her a steaming cup of coffee and we felt compelled to listen to Juliet expound on her ill-fated relationship, but I'm surprised she didn't detect our impatience. All we wanted to do, was go check on "the body." Was he still sleeping? Did he make his way back up and wander off? Apparently he didn't do the latter, or surely he would have taken the car, assuming he wasn't in a mind to stir things up again. I should think he'd be too hung over to start trouble, but then again, knowing him, he seemed to thrive on it. Aside from that, I knew he'd be in sore need of a hot shower and a gallon or two of coffee. Of course, I'm talking about the normal hang-over. Rich's drinking problem had progressed to the point that Kiki believed he'd wake up in almost unbearable pain with his body screaming for another drink.

Juliet, still verbally analyzing everything, eventually made it to the window. "His car's still here! Where is he? Does anyone know? Has anyone looked for him this morning? Oh God, what am I saying? I'm sorry. That sounded like you even care. Besides, it's certainly not your problem, I'm the idiot that brought him up here, oh I still can't believe I…I'll go check."

"Whoa, wait a minute, Juliet. Maybe it's not our problem, but we're human beings first…then Rich haters. Just kidding, bad joke," said Lora. Sherry shot

Lora a dirty look. Lora shrugged and said, "I'm sorry Juliet, that was uncalled for, but anyway, we were just heading for the door to do just that when you came in."

We turned,heading for the door, when it flew open and our smiling, hungry men lunged toward us, sweeping us up in great bear hugs. Juliet did a disappearing act.

"I'm hungry as the proverbial bear," announced Michael loudly. But nuzzling my neck, he moaned and whispered for my ears only, "and I could easily settle for you, Rainey." And pulling away to look into my eyes, I thought I'd melt into a small puddle of love. The wedding and jokes of the wedding night had inspired a new wave of horniness for Michael. He truly accepted my policy of abstinence, but was forever hopeful I'd weaken. I'd come close so many times, but was determined to see it through till our wedding night. I needed every ounce of strength my body could muster at lust-filled moments such as this. Thankfully, with a room full of people, it was easy to be distracted.

Looking around the room, Almon inquired, "Did Rich come back? Where's Juliet?"

"No, to the first part, and still in bed to the second part, but we were just going to check around the cabin to see if there were any signs of him," Sherry said. And with that, we headed out, anxious to see what we would see. I felt my heart might pound out of my chest, the closer we got to the edge. We attempted a quickly scanned search of the area, while steering the group nonchalantly to the hillside. "My God," said James, when the thought materialized that Rich could have fallen over the hillside. We never uttered a word, but expressed horror at such a thing. Almon, Michael, James and Dana rushed to the edge, as we hung back, wanting desperately to know, but fearful at the same time, of what might be reported. I don't know what we expected. Either he'd be there, or he wouldn't. As it turned out, he wouldn't. We discreetly passed glances to each other filled with indescribable anxiety. But the obvious conclusion was that he'd awakened, and justifiably disoriented, wandered off through the woods. God only knew where he'd turn up. But I was in no hurry to find out, as long as it wasn't back at the cabin. It could be days or weeks before we'd know, as our checkout time was noon and we'd be long gone.

CHAPTER XLI

Needless to say, as relieved as we were that he was gone, Juliet was terribly distressed. As much as we detested the man, Juliet still loved him, and needed the assurance he was okay. She was planning to stay until he returned for his car. We begged her not to…if he returned and was drunk, he might pick up right where he left off. But it was to no avail. Yes, we could relax, she said. She was definitely through with him, but she was responsible for his being there in the first place, and if she left him, and found out later he was lost or injured, she would feel guilty. Well, at this point in her life, she was comfortable in that mental state, and we were helpless to change it, but one step at a time.

Once settled on the plane, with the miles rapidly separating me from the horror of last nights events, they began fading, as if it had all, in fact, just been a dream, and leaving Rich's disappearance only a residue of niggling in the back of my mind. I had no problem falling into a deep sleep almost the instant I snuggled against Michael. What was to be a fun-filled, relaxing week, ended in an unexpected and unbelievable nightmare, leaving in its wake, a trail of headaches, exhaustion and fear. No, I had no problem escaping into a peaceful, healing sleep.

Sherry and Kiki were sitting close behind and I floated off, listening to their whispered voices, undoubtedly rehashing last night, as we'd done a hundred times since, it seemed.

James and Melanie were taking a later flight. I was thrilled. If Rich showed up, maybe Juliet would luck out and Melanie and James would be nearby. They decided at the last minute to leave later since they rarely got away and had planned hiking some of the nature trails close by. As great as these weekends were, there never seemed to be enough time to spend with each friend, individually. I barely talked with Mel or Sherry, and made a mental note to call them next week.

I was suddenly jolted awake, arms flailing about, and a scream clawing at my throat for escape. Michael grabbed me, shushing and consoling me. For what? He didn't know, except I was in the midst of a nightmare. It was, indeed, a nightmare. I dreamt I was falling down, down, into infinite blackness. Perspiration dotted my forehead and I instantly felt a little silly. But Michael, being Michael, was sweet, and proceeded within seconds and a few delicious kisses, to erase the horror. Hadn't he ever heard of negative reinforcement? Anyway, there was no doubt why my mind twisted out such a terrifying scenario. No matter what the situation, until those small fragments regarding Rich's whereabouts and physical condition were pulled together, I'd probably experience more of the same. Needless to say, the desire to go back to sleep was gone. Besides, I wanted to be fully awake and aware of Michael's strong arms around me, pulling me as tightly against him as he could. Enjoying him as I was, though, served to pull my present dilemma to the surface and so once again my mind tumbled into "ifs," "ands," "buts" and "what ifs." I was miserably torn, and suddenly realized the need to talk to Vicki. We had, at last, reached that age in our adult lives where the emotional and intellectual distance closed, but only to a certain degree, of course. Intellectually, she was light years ahead of me, but we now had more in common than not. It was pure joy to rediscover a sister, and we'd started a telephone campaign months back, after her return from California. We'd spent several weekends together getting reacquainted, and it was wonderful. Oh, I needed her now, but she and Gordie had left town for the weekend, and wouldn't be back until late Sunday night. She still wasn't home when I made my last call at ten. The next night, I took her to dinner. She looked extra beautiful these days. If love did this for you, then she was definitely in love. I'd decided not to mention Rich and Juliet, no need to spoil a perfectly lovely evening. And besides, I couldn't tell her how it ended, yet, as I didn't know. But she was bubbling over with news. *Uh, oh, Gordie's given her a ring*, I thought, but didn't mention it, not wanting to spoil it for her. What else could get a young female so excited? We were barely seated at our table; I don't think she ever really sat, but was practically bouncing out of her seat. "Vicki, for heaven's sake, what's your news? I don't remember ever seeing you so excited."

"I haven't ever been this excited, Rainey. I start school next week! I finally got everything worked out, isn't that great?" Her face was glowing and eyes flashing with excitement. "That's it?" I asked. Feeling suddenly deflated. I didn't mean to sound so disappointed, but never being academically inclined, I couldn't instantly, muster up the enthusiasm she was expecting. Plus, I was so certain her news was going to be an engagement announcement, I was completely caught off guard.

"Rainey, I can't believe you, you know what this means to me, this has been my dream for years, and now, it's finally happening for me."

"I'm sorry, I know it has, and I really am very happy for you, I just thought it was news about you and Gordie, that you two had—"

"Oh, no," Vicki said, laughing, "we're not even close to that stage, yet. You know he's still in law school, so we're both thinking of our careers right now. And don't get me wrong, we're still enjoying each other, and at least, for my part, I'm not thinking of anyone else. And he hasn't given me reasons to think he is either. But we're still busy working through that, "just who in the hell are you, stage. You know, the little differences and irritations in each other we have to learn to adjust to, or not. We're now learning to give and take, or break. But anyway, back to school. I've already investigated the field of genetic research, and statistics show the field is wide open."

"Wow," I said, my eyes widening, feigning awe. I couldn't help having a little fun with her. "Please, Vicki, do you think there's a space for me?"

Thank God, she had a sense of humor and was used to my sarcasm.

"Rainey, you know this is what I've dreamed of. And I mean, just for me, personally. I'm not doing this to win Mom and Dad's approval any longer. I want this because I get excited about the future of genetics. Someday, in the not too distant future, I suspect DNA will be a household word, you can bet on it. It'll be used like fingerprints, to identify the heretofore unidentifiable." Vicki actually spoke like that sometimes. She continued passionately. "Innocent people will be freed from prison because of it and guilty persons walking around will be imprisoned because of it. Paternity will be easily proven and, God forbid, Rainey, cloning will be possible. I told Jason, at work, that when they get down to the DNA, they're going to see something written on the chain, and upon close inspection, it'll read, 'Made in Heaven.'" We laughed. I wouldn't have believed someone could get so excited over school, but I was a witness to it, right there in front of me. And oh, I was so happy for her. Between grants, loans and working as much as possible during the week, she was going to begin living her dream. It was going to be a long haul, and it would take her longer than the usual four years, but Vicki was an academic addict anyway. And when people commented on how long it was going to take her to finish, she responded with, "Well, if I'm alive during those five years, I might as well be doing what I want to do."

We enjoyed a great dinner. It had been too long since we just sat and enjoyed each other's company. We talked about Mom and Dad, whom we visited and played cards with at least once a month. They seemed content now in their lives and even happy sometimes. Who is happy all the time? Happiness is measured in moments or minutes, anyway. Few are privileged to measure it by years. At any rate, It was so good to reconnect with her, and we promised to do it more often.

CHAPTER XLII

I was feeling ambivalent about being back home. It was indeed wonderful, but then I was that much closer to Michael's leaving again, which he did, two days later. Although he was anxious and excited at the prospect of conquering another mountain, he left with a heavy heart, disappointed I wasn't leaving with him. Between thinking of Rich and missing Michael, I had a very difficult time concentrating on work.

In spite of that, the hours flew by. I was given a couple of detailed projects, forcing me to stay later than usual and actually was thrilled about it. Otherwise, I would have been moping. Now by the time I arrived home, it was time for dinner, bath and bed. No time to think, to be miserable.

I finished my assignments late the next day, disappointedly so: time would be hanging heavy. And Rich? I'd made calls, and no one had heard anything. And we weren't able to reach Melanie, why hadn't she called? What was going on? Those questions almost obliterated my thoughts of Michael...almost. No matter how hard I tried, I couldn't shake the bad vibes I got every time I thought about accepting his offer, and the thought automatically popped into my head several times a day.

I was gathering my things, getting ready to leave work, when my supervisor, Cindy, came racing down the hallway directing me to her office for an emergency phone call. Again, I couldn't yield to fear. There were too many potential tragedies to think about, I wouldn't make it to the phone. Grabbing it up, I took a deep breath, and forcing calmness across my tongue, hesitantly whispered. "Hello?" I didn't recognize the voice or name of the caller, and was trying to make sense of it, as he quickly began explaining details of an accident. "Wait a second!

Please!" I yelled, about to panic. "You're going too fast, I don't know who you are or even who you're talking about."

"Aren't you Rainey Perelli?"

"Yes," I replied, terror gripping my heart.

"Okay, okay, I'm sorry, I'll go a little slower. I'm calling about Michael." Oh my God, no, no, no! It took every ounce of control in my body to hold on to the phone, and in a desperate whisper I asked, "Please, tell me he's okay."

"Well," the man said haltingly, "I don't want to give you false hope, but I think he has a fighting chance. He was injured in a car accident...he's in intensive care, and keeps mumbling your name. We found your number among his things. I think you need to come immediately."

I didn't need any details other than he needed me. Wasn't that ironic? He's involved in one of the most dangerous sports around, and he ends up getting hurt in a car crash. The logistics of reaching him, physically, were complicated, a nightmare and I know I used every type of transportation known to man, even a donkey, to get to a makeshift emergency area where he was waiting to be airlifted to the nearest hospital. But eleven hours after I started the hateful journey, I was finally there.

As I neared his room I feared my heart might pound out of my chest. I was anxious to get to him, tell him I loved him and to hold on. Oh dear God, He couldn't die! it just wasn't possible!

The nurses were very sweet and sympathetic and led me directly to his room, reminding me of the ICU fifteen minute visiting rule. And as much as I needed to be with Michael, and I believed, Michael needed me, I certainly didn't want to compromise his delicate condition by overtaxing him mentally or physically. My heart swelled with pain and love upon gazing at his beautiful face. He looked rested and peaceful, as though he were sleeping. There wasn't a mark or bruise on his face except for a small cut on his bottom lip.

Specific activities of the next two days are foggy, except for the details of the crash being revealed to me as related to Michael's doctor.

Evidently, the driver of the van used to carry Michael and his crew to base camp was distracted by an overly excited passenger pointing and screaming at a bald eagle soaring just above their vehicle. He lost control, running off the mountain road, descending wildly, twenty yards or so, into thick trees which thankfully stopped them from continuing into the steep, rocky canyon below. They had been seriously tossed about, but all survived with different physical injuries, and hopefully would make full recoveries. Michael's head had taken serious trauma and was being monitored for brain swelling which could lead to complications, and even death. His spleen had been ruptured and there was evidence of internal bleeding, which the doctors were confident was under control. But the most frightening injuries were to his legs. Thrown and trapped under the van, both legs were crushed and broken in several places. It would be days before the extent of the injuries could be determined. His legs? My God. How would Michael face that kind of news? Just as that thought left my mind; it rewound to the nightmare I had of Michael hovering over the blanket with no legs. ESP? Or simply a silly dream? How were we going to get through this crisis? I was relieved and gave thanks he was alive, certainly, but if he could never climb again, he'd probably prefer being dead. I attempted to shake off the negativity, at least in his presence. And, for the most part, I succeeded. The doctor assured me Michael was being monitored closely, and if his vital signs were stable for the next twenty-four hours, he would be released to recovery. The room was intensive care quiet, nothing but the screaming stillness of injury and pain and thankfully the unceasing beeping of the heart monitor. By its very nature, it was anxiety producing. The constant, rhythm was reassuring, but the fear was almost palpable that it would suddenly stop, to beep no more. I sat in a chair provided for me close to Michael's sweet face, and tenderly touched and soothed his right hand resting on top of his chest. I gently called his name and whispered my love for him. I daydreamed on the flight here, of this moment, and when I called his name, telling him I loved him, his eyes would open miraculously, he would turn his head ever so slowly with love and tears in his eyes, and smile, and everything would be okay. It was a lovely daydream, but the reality of the situation was it might be a long wait before he stabilized. Three times in the course of that afternoon, x-rays were taken of his legs; a difficult procedure to implement under the circumstances. Each time I pleaded for results, the answer was the same: *tomorrow, we'll know more.* He had been given several blood transfusions, and the only thing to do now was wait. It was heartbreaking to leave his side. The family waiting room was close by and I purchased books, puzzles and magazines in an attempt to occupy my mind and time until the next hour when I would greedily seize my next fifteen minutes.

I made use of my intermissions. I called everyone, letting them know what had happened. I wanted to wait until he was in recovery, but – and I hated having this thought even for a second – but what if the worst possible scenario materialized? The shock would be horrible. No, it was best to prepare them, just in case. And still no news of Rich!!! It had been a week and a half, now! But thoughts of him only touched the surface of my mind at this time. I could only handle one crisis at a time.

Michael was air-lifted to the nearest city hospital that evening, with me by his side. The x-rays were inconclusive due to the extensive damage. I thought my heart would break at the news. Michael's physician, Dr. Swain and two specialist were forced to do exploratory surgery to ascertain what and where, if any, nerve damage was done, and it would be the next afternoon before I knew anything more. I didn't dare leave the hospital for a minute, and I lived out of my suitcase, showering and changing in any available room. After surgery, Michael weaved in and out of consciousness. The doctors moved him to recovery as soon as he stirred and was stable. I was there, and with Michael in such a weakened state, I had no desire to leave him, but fear and anxiety nearly catapulted me from my chair as Dr. Swain appeared at Michael's door. He motioned me to the hallway. His disclosure that Michael's legs had not suffered nerve damage sent my heart soaring, and my head dropping to my chest with relief. It was only the fear of disturbing Michael that I was able to contain the emotional outburst ready to erupt at the news, and I thought I might explode from the pressure of it. Smiling broadly through my tears, I constantly massaged his arms and face gently, showering him with hundreds of kisses, whispering my love to him. I, at times, felt like the prince in *Sleeping Beauty*, hoping a kiss would rally him. Talking to him seemed futile, but Doctor Swain encouraged it and now allowed me to stay with him as long as I liked. He was taking liquid and nourishment intravenously and was given an excellent chance for a full recovery. But it would be a long time before he walked again, let alone climbed. With the stress and tension released finally, I felt I might collapse. A nurse was summoned, who kindly escorted me to an empty room, gave me a light sleeping pill and bade me goodnight. I was too weak to object aggressively and the morning sun coming through the opened drapes beckoned my fuzzy brain to full awareness of my surroundings. Frantic thoughts, suddenly, seemed to have taken on a life of their own, and were springing into my head in rapid fire sequence. Later, I realized my mind was incapable of focusing on anything but Michael's recovery since I had arrived, but that didn't stop it from storing every thought that had formulated since, and at the first opportune moment, when the coast was clear, it bombarded me. The most frightening one of all…the thought of losing Michael, and what if he's not so lucky next time? Am I really willing to give up any time we may have together right now? No one is promised tomorrow. That was made very clear. He could be gone from my life right now forever, and because of some stupid fears. Did I really want to give up even one, glorious moment of sharing our love? How ridiculous my reasons seemed suddenly in retrospect, so senseless. It was like I was viewing them from another person's perspective, and I felt embarrassed and ashamed. No more time would be wasted. I was up, dressed and into Michael's room before breakfast, and I was starved. Entering the room, I saw Michael propped up on pillows, looking a little dazed but aware, watching intently as the nurse ministered to him. Hearing the door, he turned, and the look of surprise and pleasure lighting his face, filled my heart with warmth and love for him. I realized that in his tenuous condition, I shouldn't overly excite him, so I stuffed everything, snugly in the back of my heart ready to spill out as soon as he was able to hear it.

"Rainey?" he whispered, disbelieving, "I…I…I don't know how to voice this, but…this is so strange. I've felt, or maybe I really saw you sometimes, but I've felt you here with me, touching me, and kissing me? Have you been here? Or was I just dreaming?"

I walked swiftly to his bedside, leaning down kissing him gently on the lips. "You mean like that?" I said smiling.

"You've been here then. Oh God, Rainey I'm so sorry to have put you through this. Can you believe it? A car accident! And here we all were, sitting on the bus discussing our individual strengths and weaknesses and planning our climb around them to insure none of us would fall off the mountain. I'd laugh at the irony of it if I could. Remind me later, Rainey, will you? It's just too funny to forget about. Ohhhh, I'm talking too much. But just one more thing, I love you." He sank back, deep into the pillow, sighing and closing his eyes for a moment.

"Michael, don't talk anymore, please. There's plenty of time for that later. Did Doctor Swain talk to you?" I didn't want to mention his lengthy recovery time unless he had. "Just yes or no. Please."

"Yeah, unfortunately he did. I—"

"Shhh," I placed my fingers on his lips and then replaced them with my lips. The nurse says you have to rest now. You haven't done this much talking in a week. I'll be right here Michael. I've taken a leave of absence so I'm not leaving until you do. You need a proper escort home."

"But Rainy,"

"Michael, whatever you're going to say, it can wait, just know that you're going to be fine and we're going back home together. I'm going to go out for awhile cause I can see as long as I'm here you'll want to talk." I gave him another kiss, a little longer and lingering one this time.

CHAPTER XLIII

Our flight back to Pittsburgh was not unusual except for the medical paraphernalia accompanying us, and it was wonderful to be taking Michael home where I could look after him. In spite of pain pills, he hurt, and every move consequently was slow and deliberate. *One down and one to go*, I thought as soon as Michael was settled. Thoughts of Rich and what had transpired while I was away resurfaced and loomed large and dark in my mind, and as soon as Michael fell asleep that evening, I placed a call to Sherry. I was such a coward. Hopefully someone else had spoken with Juliet, and I could get the news secondhand.

"Rainey?" Sherry practically screamed, with desperation and relief filling her voice. "God, I'm so glad you're back."

"Whaattt?" I asked with trepidation, recognizing what could only be identified as really bad news.

"We didn't want to tell you anything until we knew you and Michael were back home safe and sound. You were dealing with enough already."

"Sherry, you're scaring me. Is Juliet okay?"

"As well as can be expected, for her…anyway…let me tell you. You know Mel and James stayed over so they could do some hiking?"

"Yes, yes," I answered quickly, impatience bursting through. "What? Please don't tell me they're hurt."

"No.. no! It's not them, they're fine. They went hiking that very day we all left. And remember? Juliet was going to hang around the rest of the day at the lodge, hoping Rich would show up? "Well," she continued, "he didn't show up, exactly, but he did show up, sorta. Mel and James ran into him, literally, in the woods. Rainey, honey, they found him lying face down on a rock pile, he was dead!"

My voice was stilled. I couldn't seem to move anything through my vocal chords. And as every ugly detail of that fateful evening at the lodge flashed through my mind, I realized Rich's dying was never a thought entertained by any of us.

"Rainey? You there?"

"Yes," I responded softly, "I'm here, Sherry…what? How? Oh my God. Juliet?"

Thankfully, when Mel and James discovered Rich, they notified the police first and persuaded Juliet to leave without telling her anything. The pain in her face had intensified to such a degree that she surrendered quickly to their appeals. But she extracted a promise from management to notify her immediately of his return.

"She's back in Maine, and Ellen says she's not doing well. She doesn't want to speak to any of us. I don't even like to think how this is going to play out, Rainey; I'm so afraid for her. Mel and James, of course, stayed to answer questions, and Rainey, they want to question you too. We told them of your situation, but be expecting them to be contacting you any minute now that you're back."

"The police?! What're you saying? What happened? Does anyone know for sure? Are you saying it was what we did? Oh God, Sherry. Did we…did we? I can't bring myself to say it. Were we responsible for this?" The pause was interminable, and I realized when the breath exploded from my lungs, that I'd been holding it, awaiting her answer.

"Rainey, we'll never know exactly how that evening would have ended had we not done what we did. The most important thing you have to remember is that we certainly didn't have any intentions of it ending this way. Unfortunately, what we didn't know, or see, was another twenty foot drop directly behind where Rich lay. Evidently, he got up during the night and stumbled on over, apparently, to his death."

I could say nothing, my thoughts swirling in an attempt to comprehend the horror of it…letting it seep and settle in my brain. I was numb.

"Rainey? Listen. I've had a little more time to think about this than you have, and all I can say is this. We did what we felt was the only thing to do that evening."

"Sherry, we could've forced him in the car and driven him somewhere."

"Where, Rainey? Where would we've taken him?"

"I don't know, down the road, somewhere, anywhere, but not over the side of a mountain. My God, what were we thinking?"

"Rainey, don't do this. Look, we can concoct a million different scenarios and 'what ifs' for the rest of our lives, and I'm sure we will, but...but no matter what, Rich will still be dead. We've got to accept we did what we did with the best intentions and let it go. You hear? Let it go!"

I hung up, with every emotion available to a normal or disturbed mind, roiling in my brain and every muscle in my body tight enough to be snapped at the slightest touch.

Thinking and functioning normally, over the next few days, proved to be an exercise in futility. I couldn't even use Michael's shoulder for a cathartic cry. God knows he didn't need a burden like this right in the middle of his own healing. And though I didn't add to his misery, the police, ultimately, would want to speak with him, and as much as I hoped and prayed they would forget, or not find it necessary to contact us, it was just so much wasted thought. They contacted us by the end of the week, questioning us closely enough to be considered an interrogation. I let Michael do as much answering as possible. He had no idea what had taken place that night, was privy to nothing and, at that moment, I'd never been happier at keeping a secret in my life. At least he didn't have to be evasive and deceptive. Our story was simple and mostly truthful. Rich came in drunk, disgusted we didn't have more booze for him, and stumbled out to find some. We never saw him again. The missing details would forever after be our cross to bear. Apparently, the police, and the investigation they'd undertaken, discovered nothing to contradict our statements and within a week, we were notified that the case was closed. Unfortunately, no matter how we attempted to rationalize our decisions and consequent actions, they haunted us. And the deception prevented closure and the comfort it would bring. Oh Juliet, forgive us...what have we done?

Ironically, I was almost glad for Michael's accident for the distraction it created over the next months. After three weeks, he moved back to his own apartment...his decision, not mine. He didn't want to burden me anymore than necessary, and besides, he had a lot of work to do to prepare for his next climb. I visited him every evening checking on his progress and reviewing his plans for the next day to be sure he wasn't overdoing it. He was looking like his old self and his energy level was soaring. The mountain climbing training he had been involved in for the past few years had paid off. His body was strong and could withstand more than the average abuse, whether from a car accident or sickness. He rebounded quickly, and was getting very antsy sitting around.

He was ready to get his stuff together and head out after four months, but only loving persuasion and threats of leaving him had convinced him to hold out for at least one more. He felt a great sense of responsibility to the magazine, and that was admirable. He didn't want to disappoint them, but besides that, he was anxious to climb.

The time passed quickly, in spite of my tortured mind. But I had Michael, after all, and we comforted each other, though my wounds, being of the deep, emotional kind, were going to take a lot longer to heal, if they ever did. He never questioned the change in my personality, chalking it up to residual stress from his accident.

Plans for his next venture were finally arranged and he was leaving the upcoming Thursday. On Tuesday after work, I surprised him with a picnic dinner at our favorite park. He was beside himself with joy, racing passed me to the car, holding the door for me, and delighting me with the captivating smile of a little boy. "After you, Madam," he said, bowing low with a sweep of his hands toward the car. "Wait, Madam," he said, his face appearing serious suddenly. "I've forgotten something." I stopped, waiting for him to go back to the apartment, but instead, he grabbed me around the waist pulling me so close I could hardly breathe and whispered huskily in my ear. "I haven't told you since last night, that I love you."

"Me too. Oh Michael. Me too." The kiss held the kind of excitement I felt the first time I kissed him and I hoped he was feeling the same. When we finally came up for air, the look of lust and love in his eyes was all the answer I needed. "Are you sure we have to go to the park?" he asked, hopeful and pitiful.

"Get in," I said, giggling, "I'm hungry."

"Ohhhhhhohhh," Michael joked, leering at me. "I'm hungry too, as a matter of fact, I'd say I'm a starved man, Rainey. What do you intend to do about it? Hummmmm?"

"Michael, stop it or we'll never get to the park." I knew that was the wrong thing to say the second it came out of my mouth. "I mean, you're getting me flustered. So this is what a few weeks of rest does for you. I've never seen you so rambunctious. We're going to miss the sunset, and you know what effect that has on me," I said with a leering smile right back. I didn't want to encourage him, but we were never going to get there otherwise.

I packed the traditional lover's picnic of cheeses, wine and fruit. But I also added some cold chicken for a little extra sustenance. The sunset was perfection as usual, and I felt the usual chill skim lightly across my skin as the sun made its final descent. I had thought of nothing but telling Michael I would return with him. With Rich's death still so prevalent in my mind, what I thought of before as hardships suddenly seemed like a vacation by comparison. But I couldn't seem to release the words from my lips, and I actually staged this picnic in the hope that I would be overcome with such passion and love for him, they would tumble, effortlessly, from my lips. I know it was dangerous and unfair to Michael if I didn't succeed. All I would have accomplished was the all too familiar sweating and panting of two, horny, sexually frustrated people leaving the park, unfulfilled and sullen. Michael's playfulness hadn't dimmed, and he immediately tackled me to the blanket, growling and nuzzling my neck. "Rainey, Rainey, you're driving me crazy!" He turned serious, sat up, looked at me and stated firmly but softly, "You know? I guess in a way, it will be a relief to be away from you. This is just too painful for me, more painful than the cuts and bruises and busted up legs from the accident. This is an ache so deep down in my body, it's an 'in my bones' kinda ache. Tell me please you know what I mean, Rainey. This wasn't a good idea to come here, you know that. Why did we do it? I'm drowning, Rainey, help me out here, throw me a lifeline or turn me loose to drown once and for all…whadda you say?"

I had sat there quietly, letting him ramble on, feeling guilty for tonight. It hit me what a sweet man he was. Not many would have the patience and love that Michael had displayed. How could I ever doubt his love for me?

"Rainey? Are you okay? I didn't hurt your feelings did I or offend you? Rainey, say something, anything." He moved in closer, taking me in his arms tenderly, and overcome with emotions, and love for him, I began to cry. Michael pressed his forehead against mine, entwining his hands in my hair and began apologizing for upsetting me. I couldn't stand his misery anymore. "Oh Michael, I'm the one who should be apologizing." I spilled out my miserable plan then, and told him that now, as it turned out, I didn't need to go through with it to come to a decision. His hands stopped instantly and he pulled away from me slowly but stayed close enough to see me in the darkness encompassing us. "Michael, nothing has changed about the way I feel at the thought of being off somewhere, alone, in some strange place." I felt him slump slightly with disappointment and he started to say something, but I interjected. "Let me finish. When I was in the hospital with you, after knowing you were going to be okay, I sat stunned on my bed that morning, realizing how easily you could have died, been gone, just like that." I clicked my thumb and forefinger together for emphasis. "What was I waiting for? I didn't like the idea of the kind of life I'd be living for the next year, but then it dawned on me, that without you, I would have no life at all, and—"

"Yes! Yes?!" Michael yelled out, grabbing me and throwing me to the blanket. We rolled over and over in the cool grass, laughing. He untangled himself from me so quickly, I fell to the ground face down, and barely escaped gulping a mouthful of dirt. He jumped to his feet, reached down and pulled me up to him, excitedly. "Rainey, I've got it, I've got the answer. Don't you dare tell me no, Rainey, uh huh! Don't even think it."

"What in the world are you talking about, Michael?" I thought for a moment he was manifesting symptoms from his head trauma.

"Rainey, you want to go with me…right? I mean you are going to return with me, isn't that what you just said, or did I misinterpret?"

"No, no, Michael, you understood perfectly, I jus—"

"Yahoo!" He yelled loud enough for every person in the picnic area, and beyond, to hear. "Rainey, let's do this right, well I mean, not all right, but mostly right—"

"Michael, for goodness' sake, what are you trying to say?"

"Rainey, let's get married, now, right here, right now, or…or tomorrow, right here in this hateful spot that's been a constant witness to my tortured groin."

"Tortured groin!?"

"Okay, whatever, but I don't want to take you with me as my girlfriend; I want to take you back as my wife."

A hundred thoughts raced through my head simultaneously. Yes, of course I wanted to marry him, right now, this very minute if it was possible. But my family, my friends, my beautiful white billowing wedding dress, the music and dancing and laughter. Oh, how could I just run off when I just scolded Lora and Dana for doing the very same thing? Why and how did life become so difficult? "You know Michael, my limited life experiences so far have taught me an extremely valuable lesson—"

He looked perplexed. "I hope this has something to do with our present discussion, Rainey."

I continued. "It does, in a strange way…I'm serious. You know, when we were all growing up, Lora and Melanie and the rest, we made such plans, oh, we had it all mapped out perfectly, It's funny and kinda sad how naïve and idealistic youth is. It kind of reminds me of the card game we played as children, you know, where you build a house with as many cards as you can? It seems life is like that, you build and build and plan, but a card here and there falls and you have to regroup and start again. That's life, isn't it? We really can never count on things working out the way we intended…life happens to you, and you gotta bend and sway and go with the flow or you'll break." I came out of my reverie to see Michael gazing at me stupefied.

"Rainey, I love you, but what in the hell are you talking about?" I grabbed his handsome face with both hands and pulled it to me and kissed him sweetly. "I'm one lucky lady, Michael. I'm really answering yes, a thousand yeses to your proposal silly, if you would only read between the lines. Okay, okay, simply put, yes, yes, yes, let's do it!"

"That's my girl," he said sexily, as he pulled me tight against his lithe, muscled body. He wanted to make certain I was feeling his love and happiness too.

CHAPTER XLIV

We agreed not to call anyone. Why get them excited about something in which they couldn't participate? And how could I possibly break good news to Juliet. I knew deep down, she'd be very happy for me, and maybe I was mistaken, maybe it'd even help, but I was afraid to take the chance. We'd keep it to ourselves for now, wait and call after it was done. The next day we rushed like crazy taking care of all the necessary little details, and located a friend of Michael's father who was a judge. That was an unexpected pleasure. He brought along an assistant and we were married, quickly. We didn't even have music except for the rhythmic beating of my and Michael's hearts. We headed up to spend the night in a beautiful lodge and our favorite petting spot, and would leave from there to return to his base camp.

The two little words, "I do," were magical. They instantly stripped away all sexual restraints and I discovered a siren had been buried deep inside, waiting to be liberated.

It was a gloriously, gorgeous day, which lent itself to playfulness, and Michael lived up to its expectations. We rolled the windows down, as we drove to the mountains. There wasn't a cloud to be seen in the azure blue sky. The warm wind blowing across our faces was exhilarating and we nuzzled and loved, tempting fate and defying gravity at every curve, in our haste to reach our destination. Our sexual excitement was almost visible and the closer we got to our room, the harder my heart pounded. I hadn't thought of anything but Michael loving me, accompanied by the fear, excitement and anxiety that was natural for one's first sexual encounter. And those feelings, intensified because of the anticipation, were enjoyed to the maximum, confirming I was correct in my resolve to remain chaste until my wedding night. Everything we had done up to this point had prepared us, paved the way for the consummation, and I don't know how living all these months as sexual partners could possibly have made it better.

Michael, being the romantic, carried me across the threshold to our beautiful honeymoon suite. I know it was beautiful, because they assured me at the front desk it was. I couldn't describe one thing about it, other than it was perfect. We hadn't eaten since breakfast and I certainly wasn't hungry at the moment. Butterflies had taken up residence in my stomach at any rate, and until they were gone, there would be no room for anything else. Michael approached me slowly and tenderly. "Well, sweetheart, here we are, finally. Are you scared? Nervous? You tell me what you want from me. I want this to be the most wonderful experience of your life." His words caressed me as he ran his fingers along my jaw line. Then, leeringly, he added, "until the next time, of course. You know everything gets better with practice, and I just know we're going to have to practice years and years to get it perfect." He lowered his head, kissing each eyelid, softly. "Oh Michael, wait, I…I…want to change. I bought this beautiful…I'll be right back."

"Sweetheart, I've waited this long, I can wait a few minutes longer. I ain't going no…where!" he responded in a sing-song manner. He pulled the covers completely down to the bottom of the bed, leaving the top sheet, folding it down a little. I heard him humming and plumping the pillows as I entered the bathroom. Moments later, I reentered the room slowly and feeling a lot self-conscious, but the look of love and admiration in Michael's eyes, his arms outstretched, filled me with confidence. "Rainey," he choked the words out lustfully and I closed the distance between us quickly. I was ready to experience all the love he had to give me.

I like to say that my life officially began that day, and it did, but a brand new life began that very day also. For just a short, wonderful nine months later, our little Savannah Grace was born. My life was full and I couldn't imagine what it was like without them.

That year, as is certain in life, was certainly filled with discomforts and small inconveniences, but I was living my dream and the only damper was Juliet's unhappiness. She found out, after all the extra surgery and repairs to her reproductive system, she'd never have children. The news was more devastating to her than any of us could every have imagined. We had discussed so often, over the years, of having children, many children, except Kiki, who wanted only two, so she could still find time to party. And just as cowardly as ever, I couldn't bring myself to call Juliet and give her the news of my pregnancy, but left it up to Mel; she wasn't thrilled about doing it either, but understood it would be easier for her than me.

Melanie and James had made their trek to the courthouse, but couldn't find the time for a honeymoon. Her passion for medicine has never waned, and she is determined to be one of the best pediatricians around.

Kiki and Gere have been together for over a year and a big wedding is in the works. Finally, one of us will have succeeded in fulfilling our girlish dreams. The plans have turned us all into a bunch of giggling teenagers, even Juliet joined in on one phone call, congratulating Kiki and said she was looking forward to attending.

Then, on a somber note, Lora, Kiki and I shared a conference call one evening with Kiki revealing to us she had confided details of her abortion to Gere. "I wasn't planning on even mentioning it, you know? I mean, to me, it was done and forgotten about, but…it was the damndest thing," she continued, "when we started talking about having kids, it was as though a sudden dark cloud descended down on me. I started having terrible nightmares…nothing to do with dead babies or anything like that, but just crappy, scary stuff, you know, the kind that make you sit straight up in bed at night. I finally told Gere 'cause it was tormenting me, and even worse than that, I started feeling so guilty, I started craving a drink. Me! Feeling guilty! Can you believe it? I didn't know it bothered me, but as Gere said, I had had the abortion under such desperate circumstances, not wanting my parents to know, but really, deep down, I would never have considered it if I'd been married. Can you imagine? Hot damn, I found out I have some morals, after all. And like he said, it was the same as with Rolley, it was there all the time, and in this case, talking about having kids, forced it to the surface. Thank God for Gere: Sherry'd probably be looking for me right now in some bar, drunk as a skunk." That would have been a serious setback for Kiki. Sherry attended Kiki's first AA meeting with her several months back and she'd been clean since. Sherry was still her guardian angel, but only served light duty now that Gere was in the driver's seat.

Sherry's mother finally took a call from her. Although Sherry described it as brief and cool, her optimism nevertheless was given a boost. Sherry was determined to never giving up, and we all believed, in time, that her love would break down her parent's resolve.

I called Lora one evening and we decided it was time for a reunion. Maybe one last time before life got us entirely entangled with children and their lives. I called Rob in Florida and asked if his offer of the beach house still stood, and he was thrilled to let us take advantage of it. Michael's mother and father were thrilled at the prospect of visiting their son and, at the same time, have the pleasure of looking after Savanah.

We arranged to meet in three weeks. It was mid August and it would be hot, but we'd have the eternal breeze from the beach. Besides, we were going to spend most of our time huddled together in an air-conditioned house talking and catching up anyway, and venture to walk the beach only at night. Mel was on school break, before she began her last year in September, so the timing was great. We communicated a lot with Ellen to help coordinate the trip for Juliet. This was another opportunity to reestablish a connection, shower her with love, and give her all the moral support we could give.

Landing in Tampa brought back a rush of strange feelings, good and bad. It was good to be reuniting, but Florida, really, held nothing but bad memories for us. Thankfully, we'd be on the opposite coast, but I was still glad we'd be there to greet Juliet when she arrived. It wasn't long before everyone began to trickle in, and it was hugs and kisses all around. Sherry had again taken the reins and had the rental car waiting. All we needed now was our luggage and Juliet. We checked our watches against the airport clock and checked her schedule from Maine. It was on time, and she should be here. We thought she must have gone to the bathroom, and we took the opportunity to locate a lounge close by in full view of her luggage area. We bought cold drinks and gabbed and giggled until we realized the time. Another twenty minutes had passed and now little niggling feelings were finding there way into our thoughts. Kiki headed for the nearest payphone, already fumbling through her purse for Ellen's number. Ellen answered right away, and confirmed that Juliet left the house fully packed. Of course, the call was witness to the obvious fact that Juliet was not with us, and Ellen broke down immediately. Kiki asked if she personally drove her to the airport. Ellen said that Juliet insisted that she go herself; it was going to be her first step back on the road to a full emotional recovery. She called a cab and Ellen kissed her goodbye. She distinctly heard Juliet give the cabbie her destination. She explained to Kiki and Sherry, who was listening as best she could, Juliet's mood swings from bad to worse, since the heartbreaking news of her inability to have children, and Ellen was not only concerned but watchful. Juliet assured her she would not do anything stupid. But now, Ellen realized, she shouldn't have believed someone so unstable.

We immediately called Rob, apprised him of the situation and decided to get a hotel room right there, near the airport, until we learned of Juliet's whereabouts, or, at least, until tomorrow. That's as far ahead as we could think right now. Once settled in our room, we changed and attempted to relax a little. Kiki was biting her nails, which was a habit she traded for smoking. Sherry and Melanie paced, constantly bumping into each other, and Lora and I talked nonstop. We were going to start a phone campaign, but the next call to Ellen cancelled that plan. She had already contacted all of the family, and no one had heard from her. As a last and final resort, she called the police. Now it was time to do nothing but sit and wait. We each called our respective spouses and Kiki called Gere, updating and alerting them to our change of plans. And what a change of plans they were. The excitement and happiness I felt upon my arrival here was second only to my marriage to Michael and the birth of my first child, only to be dashed within the hour to a terror, as I'd never experienced before, gripping at my insides. The evening dragged on. We ordered room service and picked at our food. The television was turned on and no one watched. We were going to go to the lounge hoping to be distracted, but were afraid of missing a call so we sat, attempting to enjoy ourselves, and each other. But a part of our body was missing and maybe hurting, there could be no laughter, not now.

We talked until, one by one, we dozed. Mel made one last call to Ellen around eleven thirty…nothing. She was going crazy there alone, and called a friend to come spend the night. She assured us she would call the second she heard something. We snuggled down into our beds, turned off the light, and talked, taking as much comfort from each other as possible. I wasn't the first to go to sleep but neither was I the last. I got up to go to the bathroom around three thirty and all was quiet.

The screaming of the phone, a mere fifteen minutes later, startled us half out of our wits, and we jumped to answer it. Sherry reached it first. A chill swept through me. It was Ellen. She was near hysterics, asking if we could come right away. Juliet had been found…she'd never made it to the airport. The cab driver delivered her instead to an airport hotel where she checked in, with the sole purpose of checking out. The police found her dressed for sleep, lying peacefully under the covers, surrounded by a sprinkling of sleeping pills.

A note was found on the bedside table which read: "All my loved ones, don't cry for me, I've found peace at last. Juliet."

We'd never spoken of this possibility to each other or even to ourselves, with the fear that it might, somehow, cause its manifestation, and even as prepared in our heart of hearts as we each were to hear these unbelievable words, the shock sent us reeling into waves of grief unlike anything we'd ever experienced. The remorse, the regrets, and the guilt stabbed deep into our souls; the part we played to bring her to that horrendous decision. It would take years to recover, if it was possible to ever do so. Kiki, thankfully, had been in therapy for post trauma, and would be a God-send to each of us through the upcoming months.

As I look around at my wonderful, beautiful friends standing beside me, mourning for Juliet, I wonder why, why she made the choices she made. Why do any of us make the choices we make? Why can some of us survive those choices and others not? I don't know the answer now nor do I ever expect to. The best I can do for Juliet is not let it affect me, or my life, but to live it to the fullest, fill my house with children and with love, that would bring her joy.

Printed in the United States
22141LVS00004B/38